the relative harmony of Julie O'Hagan

ANNETTE SILLS

PRAISE

"Annette Sills has captured beautifully the suburban life experienced by people who are trying to make sense of a material, sometimes self-obsessed, world. The serious issues which affect every family are told with exceptional craftsmanship – and it made me laugh too. Perfect."

Eamonn O'Neal, *The Manchester Evening News*

"An excellently observed and totally modern portrayal of family concerns which range from the mundane to the truly terrible. A highly impressive début novel."

**Madeline Heneghan,
Writing on the Wall Literary Festival, Liverpool**

"Distinctive voice, delightful humour and very engaging."

Rethink Press New Novels 2014 Competition

"This sharply observed critique of the rise of café culture in the rainy city tackles the ordinary pressures faced by modern families with wit and warmth."

Antonia Charlesworth, *The Big Issue in the North*

"Warm, peppered with funny moments and characters you can root for.'"

Laura Wilkinson, author *Public Battles, Private Wars*

"What a fantastic novel this was. I enjoyed every single word of it and it got its hooks into me really early on. How come a lot more people are not reading this book? They should be!"

Maxine Groves, Goodreads

R∃THINK PRESS

First published in Great Britain 2014 by Rethink Press
(www.rethinkpress.com)

Cover image © Ozgur Donmaz (www.ozgurdonmaz.com)

.

For my parents,
James and Philomena Corley (nee McGrath)

.

ACKNOWLEDGMENTS

Heartfelt thanks go to:

Claire Winstanley, Jo Deakin, Sheila Bugler and Bernadette Thornton Curran for their feedback and encouragement with my first draft.

Laura Wilkinson from Cornerstones Literary Agency for her wonderful editing skills.

All the lovely people from Chorlton Library.

Lucy and the team at Rethink Press for their hard work.

My lovely Nick, Jimmy and Ciara for their continuing love and support.

My father, James V Corley, for passing on his love of books to me at an early age.

CHAPTER 1

Julie

My name is Julie. Julie O'Hagan. Julie's not a name people call their daughters any more, especially around here. Recently, I've been wondering what it might be like to be Julianne, Juliet, or, simply, Jules. I called my daughter Bridget after Mum. Not Thea or Coco or Lola or Lottie. Not Brigitte as in Bardot. Bridget as in Jones, and the midget. Dad cried when I told him, and Billy said she'd get over it in time.

Clackety-clack, clackety-clack. Here's my lovely girl now, running the stick she's just picked up along the railings of Priory Road Primary. I stop and stare into the empty playground, curling my hands round the iron bars which are cool to the touch in the mid-day sun. Terrible things happened to me there on my last day. Terrible things. July 17th 1981 it was. But it was nothing compared to what happened when I got home. Nothing at all.

I sigh and bat a wasp away from my face, wishing I could make the memory disappear as easily, then I call Bridget over. We're meeting some of the other mums for coffee. I heard Samantha Pointer whisper ing something about admissions to Broadoak at a playgroup yesterday, so for once I'm joining them.

Bridget is smashing her stick against the railings and shouting out Kung Fu style when Rachel Cleaver hurries by. She looks splendid in faded Levis, a turquoise vest top and matching toe nails. Rachel has been organically reared and has long limbs, high cheekbones and a silky blonde bob. Her kids have locally produced apple-red cheeks and chemical-free white blonde curls.

"A bit fractious, is she?" She gives Bridget a disapproving look. "Tobias can get like that when he's overdosed on sugar too."

She flips past me in her Birkenstocks with her compact buggy, Tabatha smiling inside, Tobias running happily behind. I drag Bridget away and head towards the High Street.

Bridget swings open the door of Delicious and Nutritious and stands with her legs slightly apart, one hand fiddling with her earring stud, the other on her hip. A bearded coffee drinker looks up nervously from his copy of The Guardian. She meets his eye with a long hard stare then marches to the counter and points to a lonely double chocolate muffin sitting away from the carrot slices and wheat-free selection in a kind of cake apartheid. The dreadlocked girl hands the plate over and we head for the back room where the other mums have gathered.

Bridget and I have been here once before. A low burgundy corner sofa covered in embroidered cushions takes up one half of the room and cheap aluminium, garden-style furniture is squashed into the other. I had a lovely time reading the flyers and the ads on the notice board and texting Billy to ask if he fancied advanced yoga in the home, a wheat-free freewheeling lodger or a carbon footprint consultancy.

I stop outside the door, take a few deep breaths and enter. I return Rachel's mouth-only smile and pull up a chair next to her. Bridget joins the children on the floor who are colouring in and nibbling on apples and wholemeal bagels. The mums keep a close watch on The Muffin in case it gets into the wrong hands. But there's no danger of that. Bridget does *not* share her sugar stash with anyone.

"D-day on Saturday," I say, ripping open my can of Coke. "Postman usually gets to us around ten."

Saturday April 7th 2007 is a date printed in indelible ink on my mind.

Amy Richards arches her professionally-plucked eyebrows in feigned surprise.

"Really?" she asks, "Is it this Saturday the letters come?"

Amy is a sweet-natured sparrow of a woman from the Home Counties who wears pearls and pastel coloured cashmere cardigans. Her criminal lawyer husband was recently transferred to his firm's Manchester office and Amy thinks she's moved to the Bronx. She dashes across the road at any sighting of an oncoming male in a hood and is considering a private school in Altrincham if identical twins Taylor and Tallulah fail to get a place in Broadoak.

Rachel sips her decaf latte thoughtfully. "Apparently there are a lot less places available this year," she says.

A Mexican wave of heads leans in her direction. "Really?" asks Samantha.

"Large number of siblings, I think."

Samantha's face falls with the speed of a broken lift. She's not like the other Chorlton mums. She wears racy white jeans and four inch heels, lets Brooklyn eat Haribos and doesn't possess a bike.

Rachel throws her head back. "I mean, I'll be fine about Tobias going to Priory Road if he doesn't get a place at Broadoak. It's an improving school and the last Ofsted was two years ago. I mean, I just love the fact that it's so multicultural."

"Oh yes, Priory Road will be great too! Sooo multicultural." Amy is practically bouncing in her seat as she glances over at Aisha Hamad who is squirming in hers.

I hold a few babies on my knee and fend off enquiries about when I'm having my next one. I half listen to talk of mid-term breaks in Andalucía, the new restaurant on Beech Road and how great the latest Rachel Cusk novel is. Billy is very scathing about Chorlton mums like these. Over-educated and under-utilised is how he describes them. I quite like them, in the way I like Indian takeaways. They're fine once in a while but I couldn't eat them every single day. I chat for a while longer then decide to leave.

I prise my daughter away from Tallulah whose pink suede shoe Bridget is colouring in with a black felt tip pen. She is working with the energy and concentration of a shoe shine boy and has only the toe to finish. I mumble my apologies to Amy and lead my daughter outside.

As we walk along the high street we pass yet another new bar that's opening up on the corner of Manchester Road. It's about the tenth this year. Simply Sartre says the shiny new sign. These days I barely recognise the ordinary Manchester suburb where I was raised.

Sometime in the early nineties, someone, somewhere decided that Chorlton was suddenly *the* place to live. The rumour flew around the city with the speed of a George Best dribble and house prices shot up within months. Just the same houses, no extension or anything, plus the rumour, equals forty grand more. Then the Broccoli Brigade arrived, media and education types in beanie hats and goatee beards carrying canvas bags screaming, "Eat your Greens." Some even had southern accents. The traditional pubs closed down, wine bars with names like Lounge Lizard and The Left Bank opened on every corner and Poundland was replaced by a non-profit-making fruit and veg co-op, Essential Organics, where a brown loaf costs two pound fifty six and they sell six different flavours of hummus. Tables and chairs have appeared on the pavements everywhere. Café culture they call it. Then the Broccolis had kids and the parks filled up with well-behaved toddlers sharing their raisins and taking up all the places in Broadoak Primary, the best school in Chorlton.

Billy and I struggled to buy our modest terrace before the prices became ridiculous. Tucked away in a back street near Chorlton Green, where all the trendiest shops and bars are, it's a compact three-up two-down with a tiny back yard that leads out to an alleyway full of cats and bins. Well-fed cats and nice clean bins, mind you.

Our house has doubled in price now. It's worth more money than Dad earned in his lifetime. That's not right really, is it? I mean, it's not like we've actually earned it or anything. Lots of families who grew up here can't afford to stay and have had to move out to Old Trafford or Whalley Range or 'Chorlton

Borders' as the estate agents in Sherlock Homes call it. But then they also call the terraces in our road 'secluded cottages on the doorstep of the most bohemian enclave in the city'.

We moved near enough to Broadoak so our kids could go there. I had it mapped out before they were born. Well, kid. We've only managed the one so far. The tests say everything is fine, but it gets you down sometimes, all that shagging and no baby.

Broadoak and Priory Road are the only options for Bridget. Though we're in the catchment area for St. Joseph's, the local catholic primary, Billy won't have her anywhere near it, so we're left with the other two. I shudder at the thought of Priory Road. The memory of its spiked iron railings and gothic towers makes my insides staple together in fear. Rachel and Amy and the others never admit to themselves how terrified they are that their kids might be sent there.

I do. All the time, because I spent the darkest days of my life in those corridors and playground cells. But I never tell the other mums or Billy or anyone because I never talk about it to anyone. Ever.

The sun has disappeared and an April shower of fine rain forces shoppers to run for the precinct and shelter in doorways. I put my umbrella up, my arm around Bridget's shoulder, and I sing to her,

"Now that it's raining more than ever Know that we still have each other.

You can stand under my umbrella ella ella."

We pass a café where the al fresco customers are gathering their things and dashing inside.

Café culture in the Rainy City? My arse!

* * *

Saturday arrives. It's a glorious spring day. Bridget and I are dancing around our front room to one of my favourites from my clubbing days, Prodigy's 'Smack My Bitch Up'. I turn the volume down as Billy's having a lie in. He came home in a right state at two in the morning and woke up all the neighbours.

The sun is streaming through our front window on to our new pale blue and chocolate floral Next wallpaper. Bridget and I leap around with abandon in front of the interest-free, distressed leather sofa, laughing and singing along in our matching pink velour track suits. I grin at the sight of my daughter's wild copper curls flying around her face and the freckles hopping off her nose.

I'm bursting with love for my little girl and thinking, "Life can't get much better than this."

Then the letterbox slams.

"Go out into the yard and practise your penalties love," I say, conscious of the quiver in my voice as she runs outside.

I go into the hall and there it is, lying on the mat, the white envelope with the Manchester City Council stamp on it containing my daughter's future. My heartbeat echoes the thud-thud of the ball smashing against the wall outside. Trembling, I pick it up.

CHAPTER 2

Billy

Jesus wept. The smash of the ball slamming against the back yard wall reverberates in my throbbing temples. Beads of sweat crawl like stoned ants down my forehead. I reach out blindly for the glass of water on the bedside table and gulp it down. Some of it misses my mouth and falls in small pools on my pillow. I groan, slide the glass back, then plunge my face into the cool wet cotton. I am never ever drinking again.

The letter is due today. Thank God it'll be all over soon. She's talked of nothing but Broadoak Primary for months on end. It's driving her demented and me along with her.

Oh, I liked the school well enough on the tour we had. What's not to like about a shiny new, three million pound extension backing on to lush green fields and a healthy intake of middle class children? It couldn't be more different from the schools in my day, thank Christ. There is colour everywhere, pint sized tables and chairs for group work and every inch of wall bursts with paintings, collage and sculptures. No grey stone walls, no regimented rows of desks or pictures of JFK and the Pope, no threat of a leather strap hanging somewhere.

At one point we stopped outside a classroom of older children and I lingered after the others in the group moved on. A blonde boy caught my eye. He was sitting at one of the tables at the front. He looked like he'd finished his work and was leaning back on the hind legs of his chair with a bored expression on his face. Then he turned to the window and stared out, smoking his pencil like a cigarette. He started chatting to the boy next to him, and the young bearded teacher looked up from his desk where he was writing and walked over to him.

I was that boy. Restless, bright and bored. He probably got a telling off. I got a hell of a lot more.

* * *

Oh, my head. Or should I say heads? All ten of them throbbing in unison. When will I ever learn? The events of last night are coming back to me. It's as if I'm on a ghost train. Things are leaping out of the darkness and filling me with terror. Then, just when I think I'm safe, something else jumps out. If I could move my hands I'd put them over my eyes. Then comes the shame, its glare beating down on me like a Middle Eastern sun. As a collapsed Irish Catholic I know all about shame, of course. Shame leads to confession. So here goes:

Forgive me Father for I have sinned. It is a very, very, long time since my last confession and last night I committed the following sins:

1. Gluttony. I drank eight pints, five whisky chasers and took a small amount of recreational drugs.
2. Blasphemy. I woke the neighbours on both sides of our small terrace with a two a.m. rendition of The Stone Roses' 'I am The Resurrection'. As I struggled to get my key into next door's front door, Julie appeared and pulled me inside. Bob, seventy and in his vest, looked down from his bedroom window. "Don't know about the resurrection, Bob," she shouted up at him, "it'll be more like the crucifixion when I get him inside."
3. Lust. I'll come to that bit later.

It was all meant to be so civilised. Just a few pints in the Horse and Jockey with Steve and Donal. Jal came out at the last minute and nursed his usual orange juice until closing time. These days the two of us normally meet up in the park with the kids, at the pub quiz or at the match. My drinking and occasional drug-taking bore him sometimes, as his sobriety does me, but we have too much history to let it destroy our friendship.

"Good to see you out," I said as were leaving. "It's almost like the old days."

"Not quite," he said, shrugging off my drunken hug and looking wistful as the rest of us headed off towards to the Irish club.

"Cead Mile Failte." The sign above the Irish Association Club entrance promises a hundred thousand welcomes. The place has had a recent makeover. Framed Irish football jerseys, black and white photographs of deceased club members and Popes line the freshly painted walls of the lounge bar along with corkboards full of photos of painted faces in over-sized leprechaun hats. You can see your face in the varnished floorboards, and copies of The Irish Post and leaflets for last month's Manchester Irish festival lie scattered on new pine tables.

It's mainly private hire for weddings and funerals there these days. Irish gigs are few and far between. The older generation come here for the odd pint but their kids drink in the wine bars down the road.

Clubs like these are losing money and closing down all over the city as the Celtic Tiger keeps its young at home. I've never felt the need to frequent these places myself. They're too much like dusty museums, full of ghosts and songs about the past and yearning for an Ireland of priests and bogs and simple living that died a long time ago, an Ireland I'm more than happy to forget.

Last night's gig was more my style. It's run by Tom O'Brien, a gregarious type I knew on the rave scene in the nineties. Like myself, he found it hard to swap his partying shoes for the comfortable slippers of middle age, so he came up with a monthly night of nostalgia where Chorlton's thirty- and forty-something parents unlock their responsible selves, throw away the key for the night and let rip on the dance floor to The Smiths, New Order and a selection of 80s and 90s tunes. The sight would make their kids hang their heads with shame. And last night I was no exception. It didn't take much, a few Stone Roses and Happy Mondays tracks, a bit of MDMA and Steve, Donal and I were dad-dancing like we were back in the Hacienda days.

It's all coming back to me now. Steve and I were standing at the bar in a sauna of bodies at the end of the night. We'd lost Donal earlier to a blousy brunette. Then Steve abandoned me for the dance floor and the Clash's 'Should I stay or should I go'. A minute or so later I felt a tug on my arm. I turned and my heart sank. I had to pinch myself. It was probably the drugs but for a moment I really thought I had travelled back in time to those Madchester years.

She stood far too close for my liking and she was glassy-eyed drunk, her lips curled in a knowing smile that she probably thought daring or playful.

"Hello Billy."

She's almost as stunning now as she was then. She was wearing something short and black and shimmering, the hair fashionably bobbed, the face well preserved and unlined, the body fuller but athletic, all no doubt the result of regular yoga, an easy life and inherited wealth.

I first met Rachel Cleaver, Rachel Elliot that was, at a club in town when we were in our early twenties. It came as no surprise to me that she settled in Chorlton and heads up the Broccoli Brigade. She couldn't have ended up anywhere else. Neither of us has mentioned what happened between us when we've bumped into each other in Chorlton and I've told Julie nothing. But the tension between us is always there, brewing under the surface and threatening to rear its ugly head, especially now that our children could be attending the same school. So last night, brimming with Dutch courage, I decided to say something.

She bleated on and on about how the schools in Chorlton are all so bloody marvellous and there's no need to worry one teeny weeny bit if Tobias doesn't get in Broadoak, he'll be fine at Priory

Road and Bridget will be fine and we'll all be fine. Well, I wasn't fine. I'd come out to get away from hearing about schools. The more she talked the more I felt like someone hard of hearing listening to a badly tuned radio.

I asked her to move to a quieter spot and we moved over towards the exit, stopping just inside the doorway. She leaned back against the wall, tilted her head and stared at me in that feline way she has. I cleared my throat and leant down near the side of her ear, disturbed for a moment by the curve of her long alabaster neck.

"Look Rachel," I said, "I don't want you to ever mention what happened between us to Julie, and if Bridget gets into Broadoak, to anyone else at the school either. Do you understand?"

The moment the words were out of my mouth I realised what an aggressive prick I sounded. It had come out as a threat, not the polite request or desperate plea I'd intended.

"Look, I didn't mean… "

A flicker of something, pain, hatred, I'm not sure exactly what, crossed her face. She pushed past me and I grabbed her arm.

"I'm sorry for what I did," I said, "but that was the past. I was a different man altogether back then."

Then she disappeared back into the crowd.

* * *

Hey, sunshine! Who said you could creep through my blinds uninvited and throw your morning rays all over the duvet? Get lost. I'm not in the mood. I'm wrestling with the idea of going for a piss and I'm in desperate need of medical attention but shouting down to Julie for painkillers would involve energy, conversation and, God forbid, movement, all of which are beyond me right now. So I'll stay where I am.

I can hear her pacing up and down the hallway like a woman possessed then she suddenly screeches my name like a fire alarm. God almighty! I jolt fully awake and sit up on the edge of the

11

bed, my head in my hands, crushed by the filthy black cloud of my hangover. My stomach is churning, fat with dread and anticipation. The time has come. I pull on a t-shirt and jeans and make my way unsteadily downstairs via the toilet to learn Bridget's fate.

CHAPTER 3

Julie

I slump back onto the couch.

"Brigitte... offered place... Priory Road."

I feel dizzy and my breathing quickens. Then I feel Billy's comforting arms around me. I sit up and read the letter again, tears blurring my vision.

"Oh God, why us? Why Bridget?"

I cling to Billy and sob on his shoulder, strings of snot attaching themselves to his t-shirt like stalagmites.

"How could they? Priory Road was my fourth choice after Woodlands and the Islamic School for Girls."

We sit in shock and silence for a while then my mobile buzzes and dances around the glass coffee table. I pick it up and glance at the screen.

"It's Rachel Cleaver," I whisper, even though there's no one else in the room. Rachel never contacts me. What does she care if Bridget gets into Broadoak?

Billy stands up.

"I'll go and see to Bridget," he says, kissing the top of my head and hurrying outside.

Rachel is practically panting down the line and I wonder if she's having celebratory sex with her very small husband as we speak.

"Hi, Jules. Has the postman been then? Are you in?"

"We got Priory Road," I squeak.

I put my hand over my mouth to stop a wail escaping. A long pause follows, then a change of tone and an Oscar deserving,

"Oh, Jules. Sweetie, I'm sooo sorry. But you know, Priory Road is such an improving school."

I jab my middle digit repeatedly in the air.

"I gather Tobias got in then?"

"Yeah. Oh God, poor you. It's the sibling thing. Aisha didn't make it either. She lives 524 metres away to your 515."

"Sorry?"

"Oh, you know." She suddenly sounds uncomfortable and the end of her sentence rises hesitantly.

"Distance from the school as the crow flies?"

"No I didn't know. What about Amy?" "In."

"Tara?"

"In."

"Sarah?"

"Scraped it at 457 metres."

I whack the arm of the couch. The unfairness of it all! These fuckers have lived in Chorlton for all of five minutes and their kids have got places in the best school. Dad's family have been here for three generations and Bridget is heading for the educational equivalent of Broadmoor.

Rachel clears her throat. "Brooklyn Pointer's in too." My whole body stiffens.

"What? I thought the Pointers lived in Whalley Range?"

"Mmm. Not sure. Odd isn't it? Think Samantha's parents live near Amy in Vicars Road. Anyway, sweetie, I'd better rush. Tobias has got ukulele practice. Chin up now."

"Bye Rachel."

I put the phone down and sit with my head in my hands, imagining the journey to Priory Road every morning, walking across that playground with Bridget, revisiting what happened there every single day. Then Bridget bounds into the room followed by Billy. Her cheeks are pink and she's trailing dirt everywhere.

"It's hot out there, Mum," she says. "Put the telly on."

Then I burst into tears all over again.

14

✤ ✤ ✤

That evening after tea Billy returns from the Co-op with a box of Blossom Hill dry white and a box of Quality Street. Bridget falls asleep on a bed of orange and purple wrappers during *Come Dine with Me* and Billy carries her up to bed. I'm crying again when he comes downstairs. He slides me on to his knee, takes my face in his hands and says,

"Well, if you really, really want her to go to St Joseph's... "

I shake my head.

"It's too late to apply. They're massively over-subscribed. Besides, I don't think Bridget's the religious type, do you?"

He hugs me and holds me tight.

Later on Dad comes round to commiserate. Jal also drops by on the way home from his run. He is a vision of health. His face is glistening with sweat and he radiates endorphin rush. I have difficulty recalling the pill-popping, beer-swilling hedonist I used to know.

The four of us sit in the living room with long faces: Jal and Dad are on the couch and I perch on the edge of Billy's armchair. Jal does his best to reassure us about Priory Road.

"Hameeda reckons the last Ofsted was good, the teaching especially," he says, sipping the Earl Grey we keep especially for him.

It's alright for you. Your twins skip happily round the corner to Broadoak every morning from your five hundred grand detached in Chorltonville.

Dad rages about how religion should be taken out of faith schools.

"Then," he yells, "there'd be more good schools open to everybody, not just the phony, bible-bashing bastards who are licking priests' and vicars' arseholes to get their kids in these days."

"I'll drink to that," says Billy, leaning towards him and clinking glasses.

15

Jal clears his throat.

"Well actually, I think there's a lot to be said for faith schools. If there was an Islamic state funded primary around the corner, I'd send my two."

"Bleeding hell, Jal," says Dad spluttering on his drink, "Islamic state funded primaries? Do they actually exist? What does the *Daily Mail* have to say about that? Though come to think of it, why not? It's not like we're a Christian country. If they can fund Catholics and Protestants, then why not Muslims?"

He brushes the wine from his trousers and tuts. "What the hell am I saying? The tax payer shouldn't be funding any faith schools. Your average British citizen isn't religious at all."

Jal sits back and folds his legs.

"That's debatable, Tony. Surveys show that a lot of people in the UK do actually believe in one god or other."

"I'm not convinced."

Jal ignores him and continues, "Kids who go to faith schools get more of a moral dimension to their education. There tend to be fewer behavioral issues and so they get better results."

"Nothing whatsoever to do with God or Allah in your case," says Billy shaking his head vehemently. "It's to do with admissions, mate. Faith schools have the power to admit anyone they like so they choose middle class kids who tend to be better behaved kids."

Jal goes on, his face even more flushed than when he came in, "And you're telling me Broadoak don't admit middle class kids? Isn't that why you wanted Bridget to go there? So she's not mixing with the scum in Priory Road? I mean that's hardly a fair admissions system either, is it? If you can afford the expensive houses near to Broadoak, then you get in."

"And we can't, Jal," I mumble. "But thanks for the reminder."

He looks at me, genuinely crestfallen and I feel bad. He leans over and squeezes my arm.

"Oh I didn't mean... I'm sorry Julie. I'm such a twat."

"I know you didn't. pet," I reply patting his hand, " I'm a bit tetchy, that's all. It's such a huge blow."

After a few drinks things lighten up. Billy puts on Pink Floyd's 'Another Brick in the Wall' and we all sing along to the chorus. Jal leaves early for a meeting at the mosque, then Billy, Dad and I get roaring drunk and end up dancing around the room to The Pogues until one in the morning.

At one point, Dad puts a drunken arm around me. "Don't worry pet," he says, "you went to Priory Road and look what a little smasher you turned out to be. Your mam would be so proud of you."

"I miss her, Dad," I sniff. "Even now after all these years."

"Me too, love," he replies. "Me too."

I wanted to tell him what was going on back then, I really did. But she was in the hospital, the tumour eating away at her, and he was a broken man. I couldn't do it to him though. I couldn't bring home any more grief.

* * *

I call Broadoak on Monday and they tell me Bridget is second on the waiting list behind Zaidan Hamad. I am lifted by the news and I ring Rachel who tells me that everyone who has been offered a place is definitely going to accept. Deflated, I crawl under a duvet on the couch with Bridget and watch *Power Rangers*. Rachel's probably right. We've got no chance.

The next week I avoid all play groups and stop wearing make-up when I go to the shops. The other mums are not sure how to react when they meet us in the street. They place a hand on my shoulder or ruffle Bridget's hair (which she does *not* like) and mumble, "I'm so sorry," or "I can't imagine how you must be feeling." Samantha Pointer, on the other hand, gives me a shifty "Hi" when I bump into her outside Essential Organics and then takes Brooklyn swiftly by the hand and hurries away, her heels click-clicking down the street.

I mull over Rachel's comments about Samatha's parents living close to the school in Vicars Road and I lie awake into the early hours consumed by the idea that Samantha has used her parents' address to rob Bridget of a place at Broadoak. How the hell could Brooklyn be in otherwise? Siblings? None. Special needs? None.

Two days later the situation reaches crisis point when I get a text from Rachel telling me that Tara Pring has decided to go private and put Poppy in The Barking School for Young Ladies in Altrincham. This frees up a place in Broadoak for Zaidan Hamad. I ring the school who confirm that Bridget is top of the waiting list. Now the only obstacle in her path to nine GCSEs and a place at a good university is Brooklyn Pointer.

The following Tuesday is Jingle Jongles play group. I drive over to Dad's house on the Pittsburgh estate, known locally as The Pitts. As Bridget and I walk up the path of the red brick council house where I grew up, I make a mental note to tell Dad to mow the lawn and weed the flower beds. I must get on to Billy about painting the outside too. Mum would be appalled to see how he's letting things go. She was so house proud. She persuaded Dad to buy the house under the Right to Buy scheme in the Thatcher years. It was against his principles as he's a bit of a commie at heart, but he did it for her.

I haven't told Dad or Billy where I'm going today. Billy says I should let go and accept that Bridget's going to Priory Road but I can't, not yet, not until I know that Brooklyn Pointer has a legitimate place in that school. I kiss Bridget goodbye then leave.

"What's with the baseball cap and sunglasses?" Dad asks, "I thought you were going to the dentist?" "And where's your own car?" he shouts after me, as I run back down the path.

"In for repairs," I shout back as I'm getting into Billy's white transit. I told him the brakes were dodgy on my Astra and asked him if he could get a lift into work today.

I drive back to Chorlton, overcome by a wave of nausea as I pass Priory Road. I've felt sick on more than one occasion since that letter arrived. I'm in luck. Samantha Pointer's Mercedes CLK is parked just inside St. Clement's Church Hall car park where

Jingle Jongles is held, so I stop across the road. I sit and wait, my stomach a whirlpool of anxiety and adrenalin. At one point I ask myself if I'm behaving like a lunatic, but when I think about Priory Road I feel justified. I look in the rear view mirror and check if my hair is tucked well into my cap. Flame-coloured curls can be a dead giveaway in an undercover operation like this.

Suddenly, they all pour out into the car park: Amy, Rachel, Tara and Samantha, smiling and laughing in the knowledge that the futures of their children are secure. Samantha totters towards her car, the skinny jeans pink today, the hair newly bleached. She's very pretty in a doll-like way but her skin has a distressed leather look due to sun bed abuse. She opens the door for Brooklyn and waves to the others who are probably heading off to Delicious and Nutritious for lashings of yummy mummyness.

There are rumours floating around Chorlton about Samantha. They say her husband is a drug dealer who is part of a Salford crew. I don't know about that. I've only ever seen him once. He was wearing a suit; there wasn't a trace of gold near his neck or fingers, but come to think of it the Mercedes does have tinted windows. As Samantha is getting into the front seat I take a quick snap with my phone, then put it to my ear and whisper, "Suspect on the move," in an East Coast drawl while I'm pulling out.

I drive carefully, aware of the South Manchester Reporter headline hovering at the back of my mind.

MUM SLAIN IN CAR TERROR OVER SCHOOL PLACE.

But the chase goes smoothly. I follow her through the late morning traffic on the high street then up Wilbraham Road and on to Edgerton Road North. I almost lose her when a car pulls out in front of me as she makes a quick left into Brantingham Road. I hang back, passing the endless rows of identical bay-fronted semis until she turns right into a small development that I never knew existed.

I stop at the end of a cul-de-sac and watch her park up outside the double garage of a palatial new build. Spotless white pillars prop up an enormous porch, the mosaic tiled drive looks like it was finished yesterday and the black front door has got more brass on it than Samantha herself. I look around at the other equally luxurious houses. If the Pointers can afford to live here, they can certainly afford to live near Broadoak.

Samantha and Brooklyn head up the drive of number 9 Daresbury Row. Then, with an unbelievable stroke of luck, the postman follows them and hands Samantha a parcel just as she is putting her key in the lock. I reach for my phone and snap her as she's signing for it.

Gotcha! Caught red-handed with the help of Parcel Force.

CHAPTER 4

Billy

Tony eases himself into my armchair, his bony elbows denting the leather, his long legs stretching forever under the coffee table. He is all edges, like a huge bicycle frame, apart from the roundness of his smooth bald head.

"Did you put a bet on this morning?" I ask.

"Fiver on Elan to score."

I laugh. "Optimistic."

He sniffs. "Delusional I'd say."

Julie and Bridget are shopping at the Trafford Centre and we're waiting for the derby to kick off. I sit on the sofa with a can and throw him the Frank Sidebottom opener for the bottle of real ale in his hand. A battered leather satchel lies at his feet and Labour Party leaflets spill out on to the floor. He's been delivering all morning and his face is sun-blushed but he is refusing to take off his City bobble hat and scarf.

I wouldn't give up my armchair for many but I'd never refuse Tony. I love the man. I love his irreverence towards religion, his Old Labour principles and, though I'd never admit it, his lifelong devotion to a football team that haven't won a trophy since 1976.

"Is she still worked up about the school thing?" he asks, pulling the edge of his hat off his eyes.

I plump a cushion, put it behind my head and stretch out.

"She's up to something."

"What do you mean?"

"She's suddenly as happy as Larry again and she keeps giving me these Mona Lisa smiles when I ask her why."

21

"I can't understand why she's so hell bent on Bridget not going to Priory Road anyway. It was never that bad."

"I get the impression she never liked it there." Tony screws his eyes up like he's trying to remember.

"Really? She never said anything. She was such a quiet little thing." He grins, "Not like now."

He takes a swig from his bottle then glances down at my United shirt with disdain. Roy Keane No 9. He was gutted when Bridget asked for one too.

"I remember a lot of people supporting Liverpool when we used to visit Julie's mam's family in Galway."

"United too. I was the only one in our house though. My sisters were all Liverpool. Da wasn't interested in soccer. He was a Gaelic football man, a Mayo supporter."

I crack open my can and drink.

"He took me to matches when I was a boy." I say turning towards the window.

Tony continues, "Tough, the Gaelic game. I went to a few local matches. Makes soccer look like croquet."

He then launches into an analysis of how the two games differ but my mind is elsewhere.

I am nine or ten years old and I am at the stadium with Da, his hand in mine, my stomach lurching with excitement. We're walking into the ground surrounded by a sea of green and red and the noise is deafening. As we jostle to find seats I can smell the mustiness of his tweed jacket as he holds me close. When we sit down he turns to me with a smile and ruffles my hair.

"Just in time, son," he says, as the throw-in starts and the crowd surges and roars around us.

I feel a sudden heaviness, like a weight is pressing down on me. I get up and leave the room clutching my can, surprised at the intensity of my grief. I go into the back yard.

The sky is grey white, a few clouds shifting and darkening. I take the emergency supply of Silk Cut that I keep in the bird feeder along with a lighter, then I lean back against the wall and light up. I think about Da again.

He is standing in our living room in his work overalls in front of the grey slate fireplace the night before he died, one arm draped over the mantel, my Leaving Cert results slip in his other hand. Normally a serene and placid man, he is pink-cheeked and agitated. I sit facing him on the sofa, hunched, legs apart and head down, hormonal and seventeen, a wild bullock ready to charge.

"Don't end up like me, son, driving trucks at all hours just to make ends meet. Get yourself an education. Please now, I'm begging you. Father Gibbons says you have so much promise." He waves the piece of paper in the air. "He reckons you might even get a grant for college if you carry on getting grades like these."

He steps towards me but I say nothing.

"We wouldn't have to pay a penny if that's what you're worried about."

I put my head in my hands, my voice rising. "How many fucking times? I've told you again and again, Da. I'm going to England."

"Shovelling shit for the Brits? Some life you'll have."

"Well, at least it'll be my life. Now will you fucking well leave me alone?"

I bolt for the door.

"Don't throw it all away, son." he says quietly. They were the last words he ever said to me.

The Saturday afternoon drone of traffic is fading and the streets are quiet, a large part of the city at home or in pubs waiting for the kick-off. I watch Spider, next door's cat, sprinting along the wall with the grace of a trapeze artist. She curls up on the shed roof and stares in my direction. How I envy her simple, untroubled life.

When I go back inside, Tony is emptying crisps into a bowl. As I sit down, he hands me another beer and pushes the bowl towards me without meeting my eye.

"Get those down you, lad," he says gently. I pick up the remote then we both turn to the TV and listen to what Gary Lineker has to say.

23

CHAPTER 5

Julie

Exactly two weeks after the first instalment of Operation Broadoak, Bridget and I are in the kitchen making an apple pie and singing along to her favourite Smiths' song, 'Please, Please, Please, Let Me Get What I Want'.

Manchester City Council are in possession of Brooklyn Pointer's real address along with incriminating photographic evidence so it shouldn't be long now before the letter arrives confirming Bridget's place. She's just been trying on her new uniform that we got from Marks & Spencer in the Trafford Centre yesterday. No supermarket trash for Broadoak! I've been thinking a lot about Brooklyn Pointer. I feel for the boy, especially if he ends up in Priory Road, but if the Pointers don't want to send him there then they can easily afford to go private. We can't.

I show Bridget how to flake the butter into the flour, gently like Mum used to show me. We used to spend whole afternoons baking together: Victoria sponges, chocolate chip cookies and brownies. Dad reckoned her soda bread was second to none. I sigh as I cream butter and sugar around the bowl. If she was still around, she'd be mad keen for Bridget to go to St. Joseph's.

When Bridget was first born I wanted to get her baptised so she could go there It has the best exam results in the area and you don't even have to live near to get in. You simply have to hand in a baptismal certificate or an Irish passport with your application, then sit in the front pew in mass for a few Sundays, singing loudly so the priest knows you're there.

Mum was Irish and Catholic, Dad English and Protestant, a

24

match not made in either heaven in the late sixties when they met. Fed up with the religious bigotry fired at them from both sets of in-laws, they sent me to the nearest non-denominational school. Enter Priory Road. Dad consequently became a fervent atheist who blames all the world's problems on religion, including the lengthy absence of trophies at Maine Road. Much to his dismay, Mum later returned to her faith with a vengeance and she wanted to take us out of Priory Road and put us in St. Joseph's, but Dad flatly refused.

Oh, how I envied my friends there, with their lovely communion dresses and selection of saints! There was one they could contact when they lost stuff and another who was good with animals. When Bridget came along I'd daydream about her kneeling at the altar rails in white, Mum's pearly rosary beads entwined around hands clasped in prayer, her grandma's face smiling down from above.

But Billy, Irish, Catholic and educated by Christian brothers in Galway, was having none of it.

"They are not having her; they are *not* having my little girl," was all he said the few times I brought up the subject. As well as being stop-and-stare-handsome and clever, Billy is very principled. But he is also prone to mood swings and losing it big time, so I didn't press the matter. There was finality in the way he said it and I could see the gates of heaven closing slowly before my eyes. So tragically, Bridget, like her mother, was denied her day in white and hotline to the saints, and I gave up the idea of St Joseph's long ago.

I hear the slam of the letter box. My heart skips a beat. Here we go again. I wash my hands, go into hall, open the letter and read.

"With regards to the application in question, the investigation did not reveal a fraudulent submission."

And the final knife wound?

"Good luck at your choice of school."

"What fucking choice?" I yell, lashing out and smashing my fist through the frosted glass panel.

Bridget comes running in covered in flour and finds me curled up, weeping amongst the bloodied shards.

* * *

"Ginger bitch. Fucking swot. Have a lick of that."
The stench of the turd as they push my face further into the toilet bowl.
"Go on, teacher's pet. Eat shit pies while Mummy dies."
Squeals of schoolgirl laughter as they yank my head backwards; my hair coming away in their hands. "Oohh, ginger bits. Disgusting! Ha ha. Bet she's got ginger pubes too."
They strip off my shirt and smear me with shit then they drag me into the packed corridor and push me through the gym door onto the top of the steps that overlook the playground. I stumble and fall onto my knees like a hostage released into daylight. As I put my hand up to shield my face from the sun I feel another almighty blow to my back and whoosh, off I go, rolling and bouncing down the steps, the heat searing through me, the flesh on my back and legs grating and flaking against the baking hot concrete. Heads turn, playground laughter ceases and the last day euphoria freezes into silence. I look up to see Claire Breheny's mum with her hand on the back of Claire's graffitied shirt, urging her away towards the gate. Susan Burchill is staring down at me with her hand clasped across her mouth, Adam Ant stripes on her cheeks and her tie knotted around her head. Then Miss Barton is hurtling towards me in white court shoes and a lilac Lady Di dress. She kneels down, slips off her jacket and covers my exposed upper body.
I'm screaming as I wake, "They're not having her.
They're *not* having my little girl!"
Billy reaches for me.
"Jesus, this has to stop, Julie. You have to let it go.
You're getting as bad as me."
He holds me for a while until he falls back to sleep. Like me,

Billy has nightmares. He screams out in terror, staring wildly like a hunted hare. Then he wakes, whimpering like a child and I put my arms around his broad shoulders and kiss the dark bristles on the top of his head until he calms down. Neither of us ever talks about our dreams.

I toss around, unable to get back to sleep. I am consumed by thoughts of the Pointers, their rumoured drug money, their massive house, and how they have robbed Bridget of a decent education. I have failed her. Failed to protect her from unspeakable, savage acts that will damage her for life.

I cannot bear it. Millions of rioting horned devils have taken up residence in my brain. I try to retaliate with reasonable thoughts, but I lose the battle. I feel myself disconnecting, moving outside of myself, like I used to at Priory Road when they tormented me. I am floating. Watching myself. Not feeling anything.

I pull on a sweatshirt, leggings and trainers, then go downstairs and take my car keys from the hook in the kitchen.

The wind and rain batter against the windscreen as I drive along the empty, silent streets towards Whalley Range. Soon, I am turning into Daresbury Row and parking up outside number nine. The estate is dreaming, the Pointers' house is in darkness, the Mercedes tucked in the garage.

I lean over the steering wheel, sobbing, playground screams and laughter searing around the bell tower of my head.

"Eat shit pies while Mummy dies." "Ginger bitch. Disgusting ginger bitch."

I wipe my eyes and look up at the bedroom windows to where the Pointers lie in snug, unbroken sleep. Then I lean forward and take a closer look. Strange. The upstairs curtains are wide open. Downstairs too. I strain to see more but the silver shield of rain on the windows prevents me, so I pull my hood up, get out of the van and dash up the drive to the porch, keeping to the shadows of the trees.

Bottles of milk are piled on the doorstep, leaflets and letters are stuffed in the letter box and as I press my face against the wet glass of the living room window I see a chaos of DVDs and toys scattered around Samantha's beige carpets. I run round to the garage and look in the side window. Empty. Through the French doors I can see that the show home dining room is littered with cardboard boxes, the walls are bare and there's not a family photo in sight. My heart leaps with hope. Samantha and her family have gone and something tells me they went in a desperate hurry.

But what I want to know is, are they now living less than 515 metres from Broadoak Primary?

CHAPTER 6

Billy

The front door slams and Julie bursts into the kitchen weighed down by carrier bags of shopping.

"We're in! We're in! We're bloody well in," she cries.

I am sitting at the table with Tony. The pair of us are about to head out to the pub quiz at the Horse and Jockey and he's still wearing his creased beige raincoat that Julie calls his flasher mac.

She throws the bags on the work top and groceries spill out everywhere. Pink cheeked and breathless, she yanks off her denim jacket, takes a copy of tonight's *Manchester Evening News* out of one of the bags and waves it in the air. Then she thrusts it at me, her hand shaking, and I open it out on the table.

On the front page is a large photograph of an ordinary looking man, possibly in his thirties. He is slim and clean shaven with receding hair and he is wearing a grey pin-striped suit and carrying a brief case. He could be any office worker on his way home if it wasn't for the headline:

THE MOST WANTED MAN IN THE NORTH WEST

I read on.

"Following a series of synchronised raids across the city on Thursday night, Greater Manchester police are on the hunt for the man said to have masterminded a drug and guns haul worth £5m on the streets. Derek Pointer, from the Whalley Range area, is rumoured to have fled abroad with his family after a tip off about the raids. He is said to have had no previous convictions.

Julie stands in front of the sink looking expectantly back and forth at Tony and myself who look blankly at each other.

29

"Don't you see?" She waves her arms around like a born-again preacher. "It's Derek Pointer, Samantha's husband and Brooklyn's dad. They've all fled the country so he won't be going to Broadoak. And we're next on the waiting list!"

"Mummy."

We all turn our heads to the doorway where Bridget is standing in her pyjamas rubbing her eyes. Julie dashes over to her, grabs her by the hands and twirls her round.

"We're in at 515 metres, Bridget, we're in," she cries.

I jump up and hug and kiss them both, three, maybe four times.

"Fantastic news." I avoid Julie's gaze, burying my face in her shoulder. Tony pulls a bewildered Bridget onto his knee.

"Bloody marvellous. Oh, I am delighted for this little one. For all of you. Oh my, what a week. This calls for a double celebration."

He bounces Bridget up and down and starts to sing, "Blue Moon. You started singing our tune. You won't be singing too long. Because we beat you two one."

"You're dead right there, Dad," grins Julie. "City win the derby and Bridget gets into Broadoak. Could it get any better?"

She turns to me and kisses my cheek.

"Only if United were to win the League, of course." She hums to herself as she puts away the groceries.

"Right then," she says. "Forget the pub quiz. I'll ring Azad Manzil's for a take-away and Billy, you get down to the offy."

Tony and I exchange a resigned glance. He starts to take off his flasher mac and Julie looks at me expectantly.

"Well go on then," she says. "What are you waiting for?"

Bridget is fizzing with excitement by bedtime and has trouble settling. When I go to the toilet I can hear Julie telling her one of her made-up stories about a girl called Shirley who's allowed to take her pet monkey with her to Broadoak, the best school in all the land. When she's finally asleep I dish out the Indian, the three of us tuck in and attack the Cava.

A few minutes later, Julie says she has a confession to make.

Then she tells us how she stalked Samantha Pointer, followed her to her real address in Whalley Range and reported her to the council.

"Didn't I tell you she was up to something?" I say to Tony, who is staring at his daughter open-jawed as he rips off a slice of keema naan.

"Crikey," he replies, dipping it into his korma sauce, "you were absolutely determined she was going nowhere near Priory Road, then?"

A flicker of annoyance crosses her face and she looks down at her plate.

"Broadoak's a much better school, Dad, that's all," she says quietly. I slide my chicken tikka off the skewer with my teeth. It has just the right chewy texture and is perfectly spiced.

Soon we're speculating about the Pointer family. Tony says they're probably on the Costa del Crime or in Brazil with Ronnie Biggs

Julie giggles and pushes her curry around her plate. "Yeah. And Samantha serves cocktails by the pool every day at six to the criminal glitterati."

Tony sighs and shakes his head. "What a story," he says. "You really couldn't make it up."

Julie puts her fork down and rubs her stomach.

"I hope Brooklyn's happy in his new school, wherever it is."

She looks pale and tired as she tops up our glasses, ignoring her own, which she's barely touched. I put my hand on her arm and raise my glass.

"To my courageous wife who soldiered on in the face of adversity. To her victory in the Battle for Broadoak."

"To the Battle for Broadoak," says Tony and we all clink glasses.

After we've eaten, I throw out the empty cartons and put the dishes in the sink then I go into the living room where Julie is lying on the sofa and Tony has installed himself into my armchair. I put Phil Collins' 'Against all Odds' on the iPod and as we're singing along Julie mumbles something about not feeling well feel then rushes out of the room. Shortly afterwards Tony and I are wincing at the sound of her being sick in the bathroom.

"It'll be the excitement of the day," he says. "She's very emotional, our Julie."

"But then again," I sigh, "Phil Collins has had that effect on me at times too."

Tony and I polish off a third bottle of Cava, followed by a number of whiskies, then I call him a cab. He's singing 'Blue Moon' at the top of his voice as I help him inside, and the cabbie joins in.

"Cheeky bastards," I mumble as the car moves off, then I stagger inside.

After I've locked up, I go up to our bedroom, sit on the edge of our bed and look down at my sleeping wife. She's snoring gently, her mouth slightly apart. Her lovely copper curls are spread across the white pillow and her skin is almost translucent in the dim light. Although she doesn't think it, my wife is very beautiful. She reminds me of a rag doll my sister had when we were kids. She has a cute button nose sprinkled with light freckles, and large honest grey blue eyes that I couldn't live without. I kiss her forehead and whisper that I love her. Then I think about her euphoria tonight and about Broadoak and Bridget. Of course I'm delighted my girl is going to a good school, but I'm also starting to panic. How can I not? If Rachel talks and Julie finds out what happened between us she will be devastated, not just about what she will discover about me but also because she's poured her heart and soul into getting a place at that school and is desperate for it all to go well. I start to undress, a tight knot forming in my chest.

CHAPTER 7

Julie

Six months later

I insisted he was called after his Dad. Billy gazed at him with pride as we huddled over his cot discussing names and shielding it from Bridget's punches.

Billy said William was too regal and I thought Billy or Bill too confusing. He'd only end up as Little Billy or Little Bill which brought to mind feathered head dresses and totem poles. We both agreed Billy Junior was a bit Waltons and Willy, for obvious reasons, was not to be considered. So we decided on Will. Sturdy, fashionable and unpretentious. Will Anthony O'Hagan, Dad getting a mention in the middle as well.

He's asleep here, next to me, in his Moses basket, after his four week check up with the health worker. I lean over and look at my beautiful boy. I did two pregnancy tests the day after we read about Derek Pointer's life of crime and learned that Bridget had a place in Broadoak. It was the end of April and I was nearly four months gone by then. My periods have always been irregular, so I didn't even notice their absence. That was one of the reasons we'd had so many problems conceiving in the first place. I was never really sure when I was ovulating. I'd been feeling knackered and nauseous off and on for ages but I just thought it was another symptom of the school debacle. Then, when I could only manage half a glass of Cava and a mouthful of curry on the night of the victory celebrations, I knew something was seriously amiss.

I sat on the edge of the bath and wept when the blue lines

appeared on those two white sticks. After nearly two years of trying we thought we'd never have a sibling for Bridget. I somehow managed to wait until she was in bed before breaking the news to Billy. I wrapped the tests in silver foil and handed them to him on a tray with a can of Red Stripe and a packet of his favourite red hot spicy Monster Munch as he was settling down to watch *Newsnight*. He was well happy. He jumped up, punched the air with his fist then kissed me on the mouth and Jeremy Paxman on the TV screen. I cried a few weeks later at the five month scan when we found out we were having a boy. Bridget cried too. She was inconsolable when we told her she wasn't getting the sister she wanted. But I felt blessed. Bridget had a place in Broadoak and we were expecting a son.

Dad picked Bridget up after school today and he's taken her into Chorlton. I hope they're warm enough out there. It's a bitterly cold October evening and there's a thin layer of frost on the ground. I was nervous about having her around the baby when Hayley health worker was here. To say she's not taken to her baby brother too well is something of an understatement.

After Hayley left, I contemplated cleaning the kitchen and tackling the pile of ironing upstairs, but I turned up the heating and decided to lie on the couch with Noel Edmunds and an episode of *Deal or No Deal* and gaze at my baby instead. He looks just like his dad. He's enormous, long, with thick heavy limbs and tufts of dark hair, but that's enough about Noel. He weighed ten pounds two when he was born, but he's twelve one now. Hayley said she rarely sees them this size.

"You should try feeding him," I said as I watched her prod and poke him like a prize marrow.

As predicted, she gave me the usual breast feeding propaganda spiel. A fully paid up member of The Nipple Nazi League, she was hardly going to say, "Put him on a bottle then," when I told her how hard I was finding the whole thing. I bottle fed Bridget, which didn't go down too well at the baby groups with the Broccoli Brigade mums. Every time the Cow and Gate came out they looked at me like I was burning smack on a spoon. I'm making a huge effort with Will but I've yet to discover the earth mother in me. The interrupted sleep is the worst. I need my kip. How Thatcher ran the country on four hours I'll never know. I need a good eight to function normally. No wonder she was such a cranky fuck.

The minute Hayley left, Will started yelling for fuel and I fed him for twenty minutes either side. He pulled and yanked like we were in a tug of war, then we both passed out. I woke up in a cold sweat half an hour later. I dreamt I was breastfeeding and I could feel a strange chafing sensation around my nipples and when I looked down Noel Edmund's face was smiling up at me, beard and everything.

I hear Dad's key in the lock followed by mumblings from Bridget. I call out and they come into the living room. Bridget has an unholy look on her face. She throws her coat, scarf, gloves, hat and school bag on the floor next to the Moses basket, waking Will. When he starts crying she puts her face into the basket, yells at him to shut the fuck up and pinches his leg. I am about to swing for her when Dad whips her away from the blood red proximity of my rage. I shake my head and put Will to my breast as Dad hurries upstairs with her.

He returns ten minutes later and knocks on the half opened door.

"It's OK. I'm done, Dad," I shout.

"She's calmed down," he says as he enters, averting his eyes as I button up my top. He sits in the armchair and I place Will in his lap. He smiles down at his grandson, lines spreading over his face like ripples on water.

Dad has an interesting rather than handsome face. It's on the thin side with angular cheekbones and a nose that's a bit too long. He was a hippy in his youth and I've got a stack of black and white photos of him taken on demonstrations behind Labour Party and CND banners. In his wedding photo he has strawberry blonde, shoulder-length hair and towers over Mum in a purple velvet suit and a lilac shirt with ruffles. I reckon he took a shed load of drugs in his day that he's not telling me about. Today he's wearing odd socks, one grey, one black, and I wonder if he genuinely didn't notice when he was getting dressed or if he doesn't care anymore.

He thinks I don't know about his new lady friend, Rita Sherburn, but I do. I spotted her when I went to pick up Bridget from his house the other day after a visit to the clinic with Will. I'd got the day wrong and I arrived back earlier than expected. As I was driving towards the house, I saw her hurrying down the path. Who could have missed the canary yellow tracksuit, the red stilettos and the white blonde bouffant? Bridget told me about her in the car on the way home. She said a scary woman with birds nest hair had been round and kissed him on the lips.

I watch him stroking Will's cheek, his fingers thin and mottled against the plump baby flesh.

Oh, Dad. You're intelligent, funny and dignified. I know you get lonely and need company. But Rita Sherburn?

"She ran off in the precinct," he says. "She was gone for a good few minutes. Gave me a right scare." My heartbeat quickens. Five months on and the stories about Madeleine McCann are still everywhere. I can't help myself. I devour every single lurid one of them.

"Oh I am sorry, Dad," I sigh. "She's been in trouble again at school as well."

He rolls his eyes.

"I do worry about her. What if she gets expelled?" She's still not completely safe from Priory Road yet. Not by any stretch of the imagination.

"Give over, love," he says making clicking noises at Will. "They don't expel five year olds."

I get up and tidy the room for the umpteenth time, throwing toys into the box in the corner and lining the baby paraphernalia along the rickety Ikea shelving. I'm desperate to move. Everywhere is so cluttered and cramped now that Will's here.

Billy laughed when I told him, and pointed out that there's a recession out there. Things aren't going too well with his business. Anyway, we could never afford anything bigger in this area, and if we move further out there's no guarantee Will would get a place at Broadoak. Not that I'm obsessed or anything.

When I've finished I head for the kitchen, put the kettle on and stare out of the window at the purple-tinged sky. Rita Sherburn won't last. None of them do. Dad's had a string of girlfriends since Mum died but he wasn't serious about any of them.

"No woman will ever take your mam's place in my heart," he once said to me. "I loved the bones of her, simple as that."

I blush when I recall how horrible to his girlfriends I was when I was younger. There was one called Carol who worked in Greggs in the precinct. She was lovely, a little plump and in her forties with no kids of her own. She was keen to mother me but I was fourteen, hormonally lethal and did *not* want to be mothered. I used to lock myself in my room when she came round and call her all the fat names under the sun, but she put up with it because she was in love with Dad. She was devastated when he ended it and she asked him if he wouldn't mind buying his pies elsewhere for a while.

I head back into the living room, pausing in the hall to listen to Bridget playing *X Factor* with her toys. Will has fallen asleep and Dad has put him back in his basket.

I hand him his tea then slump into the armchair and fold my arms across my aching boobs.

"Bridget told me about Rita Sherburn," I say. He reddens.

"It's a bit of fun, that's all."

"She's hardly your type though, is she?"

"What do you mean?"

"You can do better than that. You have to admit she is a bit, well… on the common side."

"Rita's a very nice woman if you must know." He throws me a sharp glance as he puts his mug on the coffee table, "And like I said, it's just a bit of fun."

"I'm not saying you shouldn't have fun, Dad. But her? She looks like Lily Savage and she's part of the most notorious family on the estate. She's as rough as they come."

"She is not."

"She's a loud-mouthed gold-digger. Everyone knows that."

He starts to grind his teeth a habit he has when he's angry. Then he sits bolt upright and slaps his palm on the arm of his chair.

"Now watch your mouth, young lady," he growls. "There's no need for talk like that. You're speaking about someone you don't even know."

"I know enough about that family to know that I don't ever want to speak to her. I know more about them than you'll ever know, Dad." I jab my forefinger at him. "They're scum, pure scum, every one of them, including her."

A shadow crosses his face and I know I've gone too far.

"I'm not putting up with this," he says, then he gets up and leaves the room and a minute or so later I hear the front door slam.

I am sitting with my head in my hands when Bridget enters the room shortly afterwards. How could I have been so mean? It's official: I really am as vile as Thatcher on four hours sleep.

It's all so fucked up. Rita Sherburn was a dinner lady at Priory Road. I told her when Mandy and Donna did stuff to me, but she shrugged it off and turned a blind eye, just like all the other dinner ladies and teachers did, so I stopped telling after a while. I became resigned to my leper-like status. The taunts, the exclusion, the stealing and the casual brutality had become part of my daily routine like brushing my teeth and packing my school bag. Rita Sherburn could be a really nice woman and the love of Dad's life but all I know is that being within twenty yards of any member of the Sherburn clan sends cold shivers of terror through me. I hurry across the road at the sight of one of them on the estate, I walk out of shops and hide behind displays in supermarket aisles to avoid them. And all because of something that happened when I was eleven years old. It's irrational and complete madness as none of them have a clue who I am, but I have absolutely no control over it any of it.

Bridget runs over to me and puts her arms around my neck.

"I heard you fighting about Granddad's girlfriend. Don't you like her, Mummy? Is she a naughty lady?"

I lift her on to my knee.

"Oh, sweetheart, I don't really know if she's naughty or not. But a long time ago two girls did naughty things to Mummy at school and Rita is their auntie." I watch her eyes widen like saucers, her mouth drop open and I pull her towards me and cocoon her in a tight hug.

CHAPTER 8

Billy

The pub is emptying. The other teams are pulling on coats and scarves, and a drunk fifty-something in an army jacket is arguing the toss with the quiz-master over a football question. Tinsel and garlands snake around the low wooden beams and holly sprigs adorn the Victorian fireplace where a log fire burns and a vintage Santa flies over the mantelpiece. Once one of the roughest pubs in Chorlton, the Horse and Jockey has now acquired the air of a country drinking establishment in the Home Counties, with prices to match.

Jal returns with our prize money. Tony is about to leave and he pockets his share, slips on his double-breasted camel Sopranos coat and taps me on the shoulder.

"You deserve it all really," he says. "You were on top form tonight, lad." He glances over at the table of students behind us and lowers his voice. "You trounced everyone in here, that lot over there included."

Jal nods in agreement. "Such an impressive knowledge of Egyptian Pharaohs for one so young."

The bell goes for last orders and he looks at me and raises his eyebrows.

"Just half of shandy," I say.

He pulls a face of mock horror.

"I'm on strict orders not to get hammered. We're out tomorrow night."

Jal says goodbye to Tony then disappears to the bar. Tony pulls his Russian fur hat over his ears and I pick up his City scarf up from the floor and hand it to him. He hasn't been his usual mischievous self tonight. He looks pale and drawn. Something's not right.

I get up to go outside for a smoke but one of my favourite tunes comes on so I stop. It's James and they're telling me to Sit Down, so I do. I hum along to the song that was once my mantra.

"I'll sing myself to sleep, a song from the darkest hour, Secrets I can't keep inside of the day."

The memories come flooding back. 1989, ecstasy, the Hacienda and my first night in Manchester.

It was a biting cold February morning when I left behind the small village just north of Galway where I was raised. Suffocated by reminders everywhere I looked, I left my country, my family, and my past with the desperation of someone fleeing a raging fire. As I stood on the deck of the ferry leaving Dun Laoghaire Bay, I watched the foam of the waves curl and roll behind me and I could finally feel myself breathing again.

I landed at my Aunt Teresa's house in Bury in the evening carrying a fat ghetto blaster, a vast collection of Undertones, Pogues and Smiths CDs that weighed heavily in my back pack, a few pairs of jeans and jumpers, and very little else. Teresa was my mother's older sister, recently widowed when her husband John Joe was killed in an accident on a building site. She lived with her only son, Declan.

"Declan's at the university. He took the opportunity when he got it," Mam had said to me the night before I left, as she handed me a piece of paper with the address on. My sister Clodagh looked up from where she was loading the washing machine.

"Leave it, Mammy," she said. "God only knows when we'll see him again."

I walked out of the room. She couldn't fucking let it go, not even on my last night.

Declan answered the door of a large run down Edwardian terrace overlooking a busy main road. Frost was misting over the stained glass of the windows and I wondered how I was going to sleep with the rush of traffic on the doorstep.

"Alright?" he said in the broadest Mancunian accent I'd ever heard. He stepped back to let me into the dimly-lit hallway and pulled on an olive green parka over an oversized smiley T-shirt and low slung flared jeans that showed half his pants. He glanced down at my Levis, Saw Doctors sweatshirt and duffle and I shrank inside.

"Mam's down in the English Martyrs. She was expecting you earlier." He helped me as I struggled to get my back pack off. "Want to come clubbing in town?"

"Grand." A current of excitement shot through me. I'd heard rumblings about the Madchester thing back home. They were calling it The Second Summer of Love and I couldn't believe my luck. Within minutes of arriving here I was about to get a taste of it.

I abandoned my luggage in the hall and we caught the bus into town. I looked down from the top deck through the icy windows at the drab streets below. There were boarded up shops everywhere, people sleeping on the streets and walls daubed with anti-Thatcher graffiti. Earlier, on the way in from Piccadilly Station, I'd glimpsed the highrise ghettoes of Moss Side and Salford, some of the most deprived areas of the country, the papers said. It was all such a long way from the melancholy beauty and expanse of green at home. Declan and I chatted about United; I said I was looking for building work. He said he was in his final year of his business degree.

"You heard of A Guy Called Gerald?" he asked, as we neared the city centre.

"Is he a cousin of ours?" I replied.

He scrutinised my face then threw back his head and laughed.

"You're serious, aren't you?" He's a DJ, you twat. He's massive."

I shrank inside again. Once more and I'd disappear altogether. I'd just about heard of the Stone Roses and The Happy Mondays but that was about it. We jumped off the bus at Deansgate. The dismal grey streets of earlier were now a kaleidoscopic rush of colour and noise. Rivers of gorgeous girls in lycra and baggy jeans and tie-dyed tops spilled out of buses and cabs, and headed for the pubs and bars. Some of them joined the snake of kids in sheepskins and parkas heading towards a huge red-bricked warehouse building on Whitworth Street. We queued outside for over an hour in the biting cold and Declan slipped me some speed.

"Do you come here every weekend, then?" I looked up at the looming warehouse.

"Most weekends, but there's The Boardwalk, Man Alive and Devilles as well. I'll have to take you to Affleck's Palace to get you some decent clobber before we go anywhere, though."

"I get the message, mate," I grinned. I was getting the lingo already.

I devoured his every word like a hungry puppy, and when we finally got into the Haçienda I got high on acid and speed and danced like a whirling dervish until four a.m. Declan introduced me to his friends, one of them a skinny Asian guy called Jalal Akbar. I'd hardly met any Asians before. I'd only been out of Ireland once, to London, where I'd seen a good few but not spoken to them. Jal and I didn't do much talking that night, though. He gave me my first E and I was immediately smitten. For the next decade or so, ecstasy and I became inseparable. It did for me what any good lover should. It made me feel at one with the world and dismissed the dark thoughts I had about myself, anxieties that slithered deep inside me like black eels on the sea bed.

That night I leapt into the Madchester party with the abandonment of a child leaping into a swimming pool on a hot day with arms outstretched and legs akimbo. I partied like a savage on and off for nearly ten years, until it all started to get out of control.

A grungy-looking couple are entwined next to Jal at the bar. She is sallow-skinned and beautiful, he is thin-faced and attentive, tugging at her scarf and kissing her neck hungrily. They are still at it a few minutes later when Jal returns and places his orange juice and my shandy on the table along with a packet of upper class, overpriced crisps.

"Get a room," he says, glancing back in their direction.

"They're young and in love," I reply. "Sure, weren't we all like that once?"

His face gets a haunted look and I know he's thinking about Claire. I pick up the crisp packet. Hand-baked with sea salt, it says on the front. I open it and, changing the subject, I ask him when Hameeda's due.

"End of March. Got the five month scan next week."

"Bet you can't wait. Sleepless nights, grumpy wife. No sex."

He grins.

"How is the wee lad doing?"

"Grand." I flush with warmth at the thought of my boy. "Though there's nothing wee about him. He's fucking huge. Tony's taken to calling him Rambo."

I reach for a handful of crisps.

"Bet the boys are excited about the birth, eh?"

Jal has polite, well-behaved, six year old twin boys at Broadoak, Danyal and Amir. Both have tutors and follow a strict homework regime. Apparently Danyal is already something of a maths prodigy. Part of me thinks Jal and Hameeda are obsessive about their offspring's education, but part of me understands because of Da. It pains me to know he died thinking I was a disappointment to him, but he never knew the truth about my real reasons for leaving school.

Jal has his own dental practice in Stretford, a Range Rover and a detached house in one of the most sought after roads in Chorlton. He deserves his success more than anyone I know. He was born to Punjabi-speaking, Pakistan-born parents and raised in Rusholme, a deprived area of Manchester famous for its Curry Mile, a Vegas-like strip of Indian restaurants near the city centre. He and his four siblings are all graduates and professionals: two brothers are doctors, one sister is an architect and the other a

44

lawyer. When we first met he was a third year dentistry student at the university, working on decorating jobs alongside me to support himself through college and help out his family. Now and again I envy the big house, the season ticket at Old Trafford more, but mostly I respect my friend's achievements. They were hard won and come without any airs and graces, with a sense of humour and justice intact.

I down my last drop of shandy, flatten out the empty crisp bag and look up at Jal.

"Guess where we're going tomorrow night."

He shrugs his shoulders. "The Ivy?"

"Close. Rachel Cleaver's gaff."

He pulls his chair towards the table. "You are fucking well not."

"I fucking well am."

"Why?"

I flick a beer mat on the edge of the table.

"Julie insists. She says we need to make friends with the other parents in Bridget's year because Bridget's not getting invited to any parties. Something along those lines. Apparently Rachel's a big shot in the PTA and knows everyone.

I can see from his face that he's chewing over the situation, working out what the odds are for a catastrophe to strike, just as I have lain awake in a cold sweat for some time imagining the same thing.

"I've tried, but I just can't get out of it."

"So Julie still doesn't know about you and Rachel?"

I shake my head.

"Not even that you were together?"

"No."

He pulls a pained face. "Ouch."

"I know, I know. I should have told her as soon as they first got to know each other at those fecking playgroups. But they don't get on and I thought it wouldn't matter as they'd never be friends."

45

"I saw her the other day at the school. She's still a stunner. But I don't get it. Why would she want to invite you for dinner after what went on between you?"

"Mind games probably. She always was a bit of a sadistic bitch."

He gives me a sharp look.

"That's hardly a fair comment in the circumstances, is it?"

I look away, stung, then I push down on my knuckles and crack them.

"I'm crapping myself in case she tells Julie. I don't doubt she's told a few of the other mums at the school already. That's what women do, isn't it? They tell each other everything. I hate doing the school run in case I bump into her and her gang of self-righteous yummy mummy cronies."

Jal rubs his cheek with his palm and frowns, "Why not just come clean and tell Julie?"

"What? Tell her what I did? Are you fecking mad?"

He leans forward, his face softening.

"We've all done things in our youth that we regret. Rachel was obsessed with you. She wasn't the only one. I remember how women used to throw themselves at you. I was mad jealous."

I meet his eye.

"To be honest I was always jealous of what you and Claire had." I choose my words carefully. Talking about her is like treading around broken glass "You were locked together like pieces of a puzzle." I pause. "Do you ever hear from her?"

He shakes his head and looks away.

He and Claire were inseparable for fifteen years. She was from Birmingham and a fashion student at the university when I first met her. Kooky and petite, she changed the colour and style of her naturally blonde hair so often it was like she had an eccentric collection of hats. She shared Jal's sense of humour and the pair of them partied recklessly, but his family knew nothing about her. Jal went home to Rusholme after our nights out and observed Muslim ritual in the same way I might have partied, shagged around, then been dragged to mass on Sunday by my mother if I'd not left Ireland.

He looks at his watch and takes his wax jacket from the back of his chair.

"Better make a move."

"Don't you miss any of the old life?" I ask, reaching for my leather.

"What? The two-day hangovers, the coming down and the empty wallet? Nope."

"There is that. But I was thinking more, well, your freedom."

He frowns and yawns and puts his hands over his mouth.

"We've been here before, mate. Islam isn't a prison. It's my home."

Jal once described his conversion to me as a quiet earthquake, but I never fully understood it at all. After 9/11, Afghanistan, Iraq and the backlash against the Muslim community here, he changed almost overnight. He left Claire, gave up drinking and drugs (I have yet to decide which was the greater crime) and embraced Islam. Within a year he was married to Hameeda, the nineteen year old daughter of a wealthy restaurant-owning family from Rusholme, a nice enough girl but not the soul mate Claire had been. I can't help thinking how many more personal tragedies that September day in New York created in corners all over the world. Jal and Claire were meant to be together for life. Everyone who knew them could see that.

Outside the pub we go our separate ways. I pass the tastefully decorated tree on Chorlton Green and the Edwardian villas in the background that lend the scene an old fashioned Christmas card look. I think of the flashing light extravaganzas and inflatable monstrosities bouncing on the roofs all over Tony's estate. Chorlton really is a suburb of two halves. The revellers are spilling out of the bars and restaurants in Beech Road. They're flushed with festive good humour, but my own reserve is rapidly draining out of me. I am heavy with dread at the thought of tomorrow and an evening in Rachel Cleaver's company.

CHAPTER 9

Julie

I put my hand in his.

"It won't be that bad," I say. "We'll get bladdered."

Billy glances up at the darkening sky. He looks rugged in his black leather, cream chinos and loose shirt that matches the cornflower blue of his eyes. He used to have a fine head of black-blue wavy curls, but his hair started to fall out a few years ago so he shaves his head now. I like it. I think gives him a criminally sexy air.

I hated the way women used to stare at us in the street when we first started dating. They looked slightly puzzled, like they were wondering what Jim Morrison was doing with the little one from the Krankies. Billy's an eagle of a man, six feet two with a huge wing span while I'm five two and more of the garden bird variety. Believe me, it's not easy being married to a sex god when you're a pint-sized ginger chubster. But he genuinely seems to find me attractive and he doesn't mind my fleshy bits either. Earlier, when I was trying to squeeze my postpartum flesh into a pair of size fourteen not so skinny black jeans and a new red glittery top, I asked him if he liked the Christmas robin look.

"You look gorgeous," he said, grabbing me round the waist and nuzzling my boobs.

Dad's babysitting for us tonight. I rang him up after our tiff last week and apologised for slagging Rita Sherburn off. I've even agreed to meet her, though I can't say I'm too thrilled at the prospect.

It's mine and Billy's first night out since Will was born. I stopped breastfeeding last week in time for a few festive drinks. I managed three and a half months, which I think is pretty good going. We celebrated with a couple of bottles of red from our Christmas crate and a take away from the new Asian restaurant, Yaki Soba (or Yaki Not So Sober, as it's now known). I overdid it, of course, and woke up fully clothed the next morning next to the baby bath, its Winnie the Pooh motifs splattered with vomit. Billy glanced over at the scene of devastation and mumbled something about a perfect image of motherhood.

A fierce wind whips around our feet and buffets us from side to side as we walk along Chorlton High Street. Leaves whirl around the pavement and a road cone rolls into our path. I pull up the hood of my Puffa jacket and try to keep my newly straightened hair under wraps.

Billy's going to trip over that face it if it gets any longer. He's not at all happy about this evening. United are on *Match of the Day* and he's not too keen on Broadoak mums.

If I'm honest, I was surprised myself when Rachel Organic Cleaver, earth mother of Tobias and Tabatha and supportive wife of animal rights campaigner and cabbage expert Rufus, invited us over for dinner. I see Rachel and baby Tabatha at various baby groups during the week and Tobias is in Bridget's class at Broadoak, but I've always had the impression she views me as shit on her shoe. However, she knows everyone in Broadoak and I've been feeling a bit of a pariah at the school gates recently. The other mums are all pleasant enough, but I'm not feeling the vibe of true friendship with any of them yet. It's partly to do with Bridget's behaviour. She's been lashing out at the other kids at playtime and is pretty unpopular at the moment. She rarely gets invited for play dates and I search her school bag every day for party invitations but there's never anything there. It breaks my heart, it really does. But my isolation could be self-induced. I've never found making friends easy. I've always been on the mistrustful side. Such is the legacy of being bullied. Some of those Broadoak mums can be pretty intimidating too. They're high flyers, lawyers, business-women and lecturers, and I'm a former a pen-pusher for the council and stay at home mum. Yesterday in the playground I was listening to a group of them complaining about the low level of reading books Bridget's class were taking home. They were so articulate and confident in their opinions. I felt like a cleaner listening in on a meeting in the U.N. Anyway, I'm hoping tonight could be the start of something more positive, a stepping stone to a new social circle.

The bottles of wine we bought earlier at Oddbins clink in the carrier by Billy's side. I thought I'd give the Chablis a go as they mention it a lot on *Come Dine with Me*. Rachel and Rufus probably go to those wine tastings where you spit out and everything, but Billy and I know naff all about wine except that it gets you drunk.

As we approach Corkland Road, the heavens suddenly open and it starts to lash down. I grab Billy's hand and we make a run for number eleven. As we approach, Amy Richards' husband Rory is coming through the gate carrying a child's scooter. He's tall and athletic with long sandy hair that flops over a boyish face and he has a cheeky grin. When I've seen him at school he wears trendy suede shoes and cool mod style suits and looks a bit of a Jack the Lad. He's so different to Amy, who's so prim and proper. Their twins Taylor and Tallulah are very pally with Tobias. Rory gives us a quick wave.

"Have a great evening," he shouts out before throwing the scooter into the boot and diving into the driver's seat of a gleaming black BMW four by four.

Rachel lives in a huge, three-storey Victorian semi.

I went round for coffee once after meeting her and some other mums in the park. It really is a house to die for, with vast rooms, high ceilings and original features. But it's also a filthy, stinking pit. It reeks of damp, boiled vegetables and the great unwashed. Overflowing boxes of Animal Rights leaflets clutter the rooms, dying plants shed their leaves onto the dusty wooden floors, and papers, books, toys and forgotten dirty nappies are piled high on tatty sofas and broken chairs. Rufus is a sculptor and his collection of "erotic" works of art are on display everywhere. Erect cocks and bullet-like tits expose themselves above the fireplace in the living room, and there's a big gaping fanny on a shelf in the bathroom next to the toilet rolls.

He opens the door.

"Rach is just putting Tabatha to bed," he whispers, a forefinger on his lips. Billy and I follow him through the long hallway past a real Christmas tree dripping with homemade decorations, and walls adorned with children's scribble. Rufus is about five inches shorter than Rachel and is dressed in a shabby, oversized grey jumper and jeans. He has a greying pony tail, protruding chin, wire wool beard, and there's something of the garden gnome about him. He works part time in Essential Organics, the vegetarian co-op so he evidently feels at home in lots of greenery.

Billy and I shake and shiver like two wet dogs as we sit down on benches on opposite sides of the large pine kitchen table. I hand Rufus the wine and I feel relieved when he glances at the label approvingly and thanks us. As he searches for the cork screw among the mountain of unwashed pots and pans I put my hand on the cold radiator remembering how Rachel told me they rarely have the heating on to conserve energy. I am about to mouth the words "Fucking freezing" to Billy when Rufus turns around with two very small glasses of Chablis.

I look at the family calendar on the far corner wall and imagine the entries scribbled there.

Monday – Rufus meeting with gnomes from number thirty three.

Tuesday – Rachel leafleting for the Campaign for the Abolition of Sugar.

Saturday – Charity night. Dinner with Jules and Billy, proletarian parents of psychotic Bridget.

Billy wipes his wet face with the sleeve of his shirt and gulps down his wine. I can see him scrutinising Rufus and I break the mounting silence.

"I can tell from your accent you're not from round here, Rufus."

"No. I'm a Londoner but I've been in Manchester for years," he replies. The accent is a strange mixture of Mockney and Received Pronunciation.

He pours himself a glass of Chablis and remains standing in front of the worktop.

"Do you still have family down south?" He strokes his beard mysteriously.

"In a manner of speaking." Obviously not keen on following up my fascinating line of questioning, he walks over to the CD player, turns up Coldplay's 'Yellow' and starts to hum along. Then he takes a handful of tomatoes out of the fridge and starts chopping at the worktop. Billy rolls his eyes, makes a noose in the air and pretends to hang himself. He's not a Chris Martin fan and is still tugging on the noose when Rachel appears behind him.

I sigh. She looks effortlessly beautiful in an emerald, low cut wool dress that reveals not the slightest hint of back or muffin fat. Her blonde bob is sleek and shiny and, unusually for her, she is made up with ruby lips and a glitter on her eyelids that brings out the green of her eyes.

"Great to see you both," she says, coming over and giving me a bit of double kiss action. Then she leans over to Billy and does the same, revealing a pertly formed cleavage and a whiff of something French and expensive. I am suddenly conscious of the rolls of fat bulging out of the top of my skinny jeans and I raise my hand to my ginger mop. As I thought, it's gone to frizz in the rain.

Rufus hands Rachel a glass of white and I hold up my empty one, refusing to move it until he fills it to the brim.

"Chin chin," says Rachel huskily, then she slides onto the bench close to Billy. Not normally a blushing man, the colour rises up in him like the breaking dawn. I hear the thud of my heart as it drops on the floor. So that's it. That's why he was so adamant about not coming. He bloody well fancies her. I shrink inside and feel like disappearing through the French windows into the night.

The conversation turns to Broadoak. Rachel does most of the talking and the rest of us agree it's a good school.

"So do you think you'll get chair of the P.T.A., then?" I ask sharply.

She flicks her hair away from her eyes and throws her head back.

"Probably not. Vicky Lowe will. She was Treasurer last year."

Vicky Lowe can't wait to leave the P.T.A. Nobody wants to run it apart from Rachel. They can't be arsed.

Rufus interrupts his chopping, puts his hands on Rachel's shoulders and starts to give her a light massage.

"Of course she'll get it," he says, looking at Billy, then me. "But we hardly see her these days as it is. If it's not the hula hooping classes, it's the book group or the Gospel Choir."

She shrugs his hands off and helps herself to more wine.

"You don't do too badly yourself with your Liberation Front and Socialist Worker gatherings."

I catch Billy's eye. He is trying hard not to laugh. I kick him under the table. He's drunk. He had a couple of whiskies before we came out and he's been filling up his glass despite Rufus' disapproving looks. Rufus goes back to his chopping, Billy starts to tell a few anecdotes about his childhood in Ireland and Rachel hangs on his every word.

"Mummy, I don't feel well."

Tobias suddenly appears in the doorway, a halo of light from the hallway illuminating his blonde curls. His jumper is stained, his pyjamas dull and grey. His cheeks are flushed and he rubs his eyes, then glances over at me and Billy.

"Hello," he says, smiling weakly.

Billy turns round and offers Tobias his hand. He shuffles over and shakes it.

"Nice to meet you, Tobias."

Billy then puts his hand on Tobias' forehead and looks at Rachel. "Think the wee man might have a temperature."

Looking like he's about to cry, the boy runs over to his dad and throws his arms around his waist. Rufus presses his hand on his back and forehead.

"I've got some Calpol sachets here if you need them," I say, reaching down for my bag.

Rufus waves a hand dismissively in the air.

"No. No thanks. We never touch the stuff." He looks over at Rachel who is staring at Billy.

"Rachel?" he snaps. She turns round quickly.

"We can always do the water and eau de cologne thing again if he wakes in the night," she says, "though he'll probably sleep it off."

Rufus hands Tobias a tumbler of water and he gulps it down.

"Back to bed now, darling," he says, kissing the top of his head.

In an award winning act of maternal concern, Rachel holds out her arms for hugs and says goodnight, then the minute he's out of the door she turns her attentions back to my husband.

The evening drags on like a dentist's visit without an anaesthetic. I'm famished. I'd better eat something quickly to soak up the wine or Winnie the Pooh will be getting it in the face again in the baby bath later. I'm as sober as a judge despite drinking copious amounts, but Rachel is pretty hammered after three glasses. Without the kids around I realise I have very little to say to her, but she's too busy slavering all over Billy like a hungry whore to notice me. What kind of behavior is that from the future Head of the PTA? Billy's looking red in the face and very uncomfortable. When Rufus sets the table I pick up a knife and grip it tightly, turning it slowly in my hand.

Dinner is a plain salad for starter, a few joyless brown dollops of lentil stew for main, followed by an offering from the fruit bowl. I feel like crying. Then it gets worse. The conversation turns to politics. Rufus tells us he tore up his Labour Party membership after the Iraq war and joined the SWP.

"At least they're not afraid to use the word 'socialist'," he says, then he rolls his eyes when Rachel says she might vote Lib Dem in the next election because she finds Nick Clegg rather dishy.

After a visit to the upstairs loo, I hear Rufus chatting to Tobias in his room. I go downstairs and cross the hallway. I'm about to enter the kitchen when I hear Rachel's raised voice. I hide behind the half open door and peer in. I can't hear what she's saying and it's difficult to see everything because of the angle of the door but I can see that she is sitting very close to Billy and is talking animatedly. Though his face is tilted away from her and his expression is glum, I sense a familiarity between them, an uncomfortable one but a familiarity nevertheless. When I hear Rufus' footsteps at the top of the stairs I push the door open and enter. Billy and Rachel immediately move apart then Rachel gets up and says she needs the bathroom. She hurries past me out of the room, leaving Billy staring down at the floor.

Shortly afterwards I get a text from Dad saying Will is awake and won't settle. Trying not to show my delight too much, I mutter my apologies and say we should go. Rufus swiftly corks the remainder of the wine and says he has to be up at six the next day for delivery of Polish cabbage at the Co-op.

The four of us say muted goodbyes on the doorstep.

"Our turn next," I shout as Billy and I hurry down the drive and out into the street.

The rain is firing down on us from all angles and the wind is howling as we walk to the end of Corkland Avenue in silence. As we're turning into the High Street, I stop, secure my hood tightly and give Billy my iciest stare.

"So what was all that about?"

"What?"

"She was all over you like the fucking plague."

Fury ignites in the blue of his eyes.

"Nothing to do with me."

"Yeah, right."

"Look, I never wanted to go in the first place," he hisses,

kicking out at a plastic water bottle that has blown into his path," but I did it because *you* forced me to, because *you* want to be in with the in crowd at that fucking school."

He walks off and I hurry after him, grab his arm and hold it firmly. I look him directly in the eye and keep my voice as steady as I can.

"Tell me the truth, Billy. Have you ever met Rachel before? Before Bridget started at Broadoak, I mean?"

"No, I haven't," he snaps, pushing my hand away, "and I don't particularly want to meet her or her smug little gobshite of a husband again, thank you very much."

I'm not convinced. But I am convinced that he wasn't enjoying her attentions back there. He couldn't wait to leave.

On the corner of Manchester Road he puts his arm around my shoulders.

"Sorry," he says, kissing my soaking wet face.

We walk on arm in arm and he seems lost in thought. The rain has eased a little. I check my phone again. No more texts from Dad. Will must have gone back to sleep.

"I remember one of the mums telling me that Rufus' family are loaded," I say. "Something to do with a butcher's business. That's how come they can afford that massive house, when she doesn't work and he sells spuds for a living."

"Yeah?" he replies, still distracted.

Then it suddenly came to me and I stopped in my tracks.

"Of course, that's it. Cleaver's Butchers. *The* Cleaver's Butchers, the high street chain. They were massive in the seventies and eighties. You won't have heard of them, though."

I recall the name on a red and white awning in Chorlton Precinct years ago and wonder why I'd never made the connection before.

When we get in I go straight upstairs and check on the kids. Will's cheeks look slightly red but he's fast asleep, Bridget too, and I can hear Dad's snores coming from the spare room. As I'm coming downstairs I look around and sigh. It's like coming back to a doll's house after the spaciousness of number eleven Corkland.

I make a brew and Billy turns on *Newsnight* Then I turn on the computer in the corner of the room and google the words 'Rufus Cleaver'. A few seconds later a younger Rufus with cropped hair is staring back at me from the screen. He has multiple earrings and is wearing cycling gear. Underneath the photo is a newspaper article dated 24th April 1999.

"Butcher's Heir Masterminded Street Riots"

The only son and heir of the Cleaver's Butchers empire, reportedly worth £30 million, was taken into custody last night in connection with the riots that took place during the anti-capitalist march in Central London last week. Rufus Archibald Cleaver, 28, was arrested on suspicion of coordinating the march after police found hundreds of leaflets and a number of e-mails on his computer at his £300,000 Camden flat. Cleaver, unemployed, who reputedly lives off a £50,000 a year income from a £3 million trust fund, has been detained overnight for questioning.

"Oh my God," I exclaim. "Billy, come and have a look at this."

He stands over my shoulder and reads. "Archibald," I giggle.

Billy sits back down. "Looks like that big house and those veggie principles are paid for with the blood of slaughtered animals, then," he sniffs.

* * *

Later, when Billy and I are lying in bed in a post-coital glow, he's gets a bit emotional, telling me over and over how much he loves me. He gets like that when we have sex, and now and again he cries. I sometimes wonder if something's wrong but mostly I think it's a lovely trait in a big strapping man.

We end up talking about Rufus and his secret life of crime, imagining him tearing around Chelsea with a handkerchief emblazoned with the family crest tied around his face, throwing Molotov cocktails at the boys in blue and making his escape on a very small bike with stabilizers.

Soon we're rolling around the bed laughing. We haven't laughed like that since.

In fact we've rarely laughed at all.

CHAPTER 10

Billy

I can hear her in the bathroom, the flush, the rush of the tap, the gargle and spit, the pre-bed ritual. I lean back on the pillows and close my eyes. I want her badly and I start to get hard at the thought of her. But then Rachel's face appears instead, her angry words of earlier slicing into me. She's destined to haunt me. She just won't go away. A lump rises in my throat. "Fuck!" I beat my clenched fist into the mattress. "Fuck, Fuck, Fuck!"

* * *

"Call me soon."

She scrawled her number across the front of my hand, her eyes never leaving mine. Then she touched my lips with her forefinger and slid it slowly down my neck and torso. Minutes later I watched the perfect curves of Rachel Elliot's lycra-clad arse disappear into the back of a taxi. It was the early hours, sometime in November 1993 outside Devilles nightclub in town.

Every man in there had his eye on her that night as she swayed on the dance floor to the Stone Roses, arms raised, water bottle in hand. Sinewy and graceful, with waist-length, honey-coloured hair and slanting green eyes, she was a model in the making. We locked eyes more than once during the evening but I kept my distance, determined to play hard to get, and it paid off in the end when she approached me outside.

My cousin Declan, standing with me watching the taxi drive off, slung his arm around my shoulder.

"Lucky bastard," he said, his mouth turned downwards in a mock glum expression. "Bet they don't have totty like that down south."

It was his last night in Manchester. He was moving to London the next day to start an accountancy job after trying unsuccessfully for two years to find work here. I'd moved out of Aunt Teresa's house in Bury six months previously and was living in a house share in Fallowfield, the student area. I was getting cash in hand doing decorating and labouring jobs across the city.

Declan became maudlin as we walked up Market Street towards the bus station.

"I love this city and I don't want to go," he groaned, digging his hands into the pockets of his parka. "Why are all the fucking jobs down south, cuz?"

The wedge haircut had been replaced by a short back and sides, but to me he still seemed an unlikely-looking accountant. We approached the ship-like structure of the Arndale Centre. Three years later, on one of his weekend visits home, Declan and I would visit the same spot and look in awe at the devastation left by the I.R.A. bomb and a city centre in tatters.

He suddenly grabbed me in a headlock.

"Promise me you'll slow down with all the drugs and shit when I've gone," he said with his face close to mine. "You're a mad fucker and I worry about you."

"Sure I'm fine," I said, turning away. I was going to miss him.

I was anything but fine. Most of 1993 is like the black hole where my two wisdom teeth used to be. I prod around with my tongue and try to remember what it's like having them, but the memory's just not there. I'd taken to small time dealing in the months previously and I was suffering from a large dose of denial about my addictions. I was dipping into my stash and was hammered or high on coke, tabs and amphetamines at least five days out of seven. I was out of control, ruled by a savage appetite for drugs and drink.

I was also shagging half of the female student population of Manchester.

For some reason I never fully understood, women always seemed to like me far more than I ever liked myself. I wasn't bad looking, I suppose, or maybe it was the accent they liked, the siren's song that drew them towards the rocks, towards the disaster zone that was Billy O'Hagan. A few years earlier it would have sent them running for the bomb squad, but in the nineties English girls loved it. It was the posh girls who liked me most, the Home Counties Hannahs and the Cheshire Emilys, the lefties, the politics and sociology students, the ones, like Rachel, who liked a good cause. I lost count of the number of women I slept with. I rarely got involved for more than a night as intimacy was an anathema to me. I never slept with anyone when I was sober, and sex often felt mechanical, like I was somewhere else watching it happen. But I was hooked. I'd shut the door on one girl, feeling full of self-loathing, then the next night I'd get high and do it again. I took risks too. I did it in public places, with married women and now and again with prostitutes. I was damn lucky not to have caught anything. Looking back, sex was just another drug to me, a temporary high to obliterate the badness swimming around inside me.

On our first date, Rachel and I went to a spit and sawdust student pub in Fallowfield. We staggered back to my house, got stoned and fucked all night long, a pattern we followed for the next three months. She became my longest relationship to date. She was uninhibited in bed and I became physically addicted to her. I stopped turning up for work and got fired from the job I was on. We'd spend most afternoons in the pub then go back to bed. She paid for everything, courtesy of Daddy, the owner of a chain of health and leisure clubs in the North West. At first I genuinely liked her. She spoke up for herself, a quality I admire in a woman. She was in the final year of an M.A. in anthropology and I was impressed, my only educational qualification being an honorary degree from the University of Life. But I very soon got bored. What I initially took for intelligence turned out to be received opinion and I wearied of her clichés and platitudes and forced compassion for every cause going. She'd read the first and last page of a novel and make out she'd read the whole thing. She was the rich girl Jarvis Cocker sang about in 'Common People', the one who played at being ordinary but called on Daddy the minute things got tough.

We started to argue. I ended it many times but she kept turning up at my place, often with drugs. Unable to say no I'd let her in and we'd end up in bed and fight again. Then one morning after a particularly heavy cocktail of coke and drink I woke up and she had gone.

It was the Christmas holidays, the house was empty and there was snow on the ground. As the day wore on I started to panic about what had happened the night before. I remembered a blinder of an argument but nothing else. Nothing at all.

Late in the afternoon I dragged myself off the couch to answer the doorbell. Dread swilled around the pit of my stomach as I reached for the door latch. She looked small and brittle against the blanket of snow and had a huge grey scarf wrapped around her head, like Meryl Streep in *The French Lieutenant's Woman*. She took it off and I stepped back in shock.

"You don't remember, Billy, do you?" she said in a small hoarse voice as tears dripped over the huge red swelling under her right eye. Her face was a smash of yellow and brown, her neck a mass of purple bruises and raw scratches. When she raised her right arm to wipe her eyes I could see it was in plaster. It took a moment to sink in then I slammed the door shut.

I slumped against the wall and dropped to the floor, waves of shame and self-hatred crashing over me. I'd fallen to a new level of depravity altogether.

I could hear her pleading out in the cold.

"Please, Billy, open the door. We need to talk. Billy, please."

I thumped my fist against my forehead. I was crying.

"I'm so sorry, Rachel. So sorry. Now go away. Can't you see I'm bad news, I'm fucked up? Go away, Rachel, and don't ever come back."

The rage that had been locked inside me for years had escaped and I was terrified of the monster I was becoming. To this day I don't know why Rachel didn't go to the police. I should have been locked up. In the weeks that followed, the darkness descended over me for the first time. A thunder cloud curled itself around me, disconnecting me from the world. I couldn't get out of bed, I lost my appetite, my mojo, and any desire to look for work. I know exactly why Churchill called his depression his black dog. Mine's a glossy black Labrador with red staring eyes who never leaves my side. It's a Joy Division track left on repeat; it's drowning in the black of night.

That was my first real episode and by far the worst. I've never spoken about it to anyone, not a doctor, not to Jal or anyone else, though I did eventually tell Jal what happened with Rachel. If I talk about it I will have to unearth my past and some things are better off left buried. I'm not part of Jeremy Kyle and Oprah's confessional culture. I'm working class, Irish and male. Men like me don't find it easy to talk. Rachel went to live in India not long afterwards and I never saw her again until I bumped into her with Julie in Chorlton earlier this year. Julie had been talking about a Rachel at the playgroups for some time, but I never realised it was the same one. From the look on her face when we met she had no idea I was married to Julie either. But she must have been waiting and planning since then to tell me what she told me tonight. Julie was right, she was all over me the whole evening, and she was doing it to punish me, to make me feel as uncomfortable as possible.

The minute we were alone in the kitchen she turned to me.

"I invited you here because there's something you need to know, Billy. I've been trying to tell you for a while but you avoid me at the school and you cross the road when I see you in the street."

"What is it I need to know, Rachel?" I sighed, rolling my eyes. "If it's about what happened, I've already… "

"Shut up. Shut the fuck up and listen for once," she hissed. "I wondered whether to ever tell you or not. I really didn't want to bring it all up again as it was a painful time for me. After it happened I went to India and dealt with it in my own way and I thought I'd put it all to rest. But that night in the Irish club. The way you spoke to me. You deserve to know what you did." Her eyes bore into me like burning coals. "I was pregnant that night you beat me up. I didn't know it at the time but I was eight weeks gone. The following week I miscarried. I don't know if it would have happened anyway, but I thought you should know."

I looked away and recalled the scene on the doorstep, the smashed up face and the snow. She sat back and spoke very quietly and very slowly.

"If you ever dare speak to me like that again I swear I'll tell Julie everything. You better believe it. And I'll also make sure that every fucking parent in that school knows exactly the type of man you are."

I struggled to say anything. Then Julie came into the room.

* * *

I catch sight of myself in the dressing table mirror and struggle to understand the face I see there. I was a lawless savage back then and I hate myself for what I did to Rachel and those countless other women. But I've changed. I know I have. I refuse to be tethered by my past. I'm a decent, hardworking husband and father now and I deserve a second chance.

The wind is raging outside and the branches of the tree are battering against the bedroom window when Julie comes into the room. She walks past the foot of the bed and puts a jar of cream on the dressing table. I can see she is naked under the black silk kimono. She turns to me then comes over and stands close to the side of the bed. I sit up and we lock eyes then I tug the loosely tied belt around her waist. The kimono falls open and she slides the silk off her shoulders. As I pull her down beside me I can smell perfumed lavender on her creamy skin.

"I love you," I say, cupping a hand around her soft breast and looking into her face. "You know you really are the best high I've ever had."

CHAPTER 11

Julie

The week following her sensational dinner party, Rachel disappears from the baby groups and the school run. This is a not a bad thing as I've been mentally plotting her demise, which involves a tragic accident with one of Rufus' penis sculptures. Billy reckons MI5 have uncovered Rufus' latest plans to derail the establishment in a file hidden in his vegetable patch and the whole family have been transported to Guantanamo Bay where they're being fitted for orange jumpsuits right now.

I actually haven't given too much thought to Rachel as I've been too busy elbowing my way through the Christmas crowds in the Trafford Centre, stocking up on cheap tat that will end up in someone's bin and trying to keep the lid on Bridget's excitement. School breaks up this Friday, it's going to be Will's first Christmas and I'm determined it's going to be a good one.

* * *

On Wednesday in the playground I catch up with Amy Richards, and ask about Rachel. I like Amy. She's well posh, with an accent straight out of a BBC nineteen fifties film, but she's got a good heart and she always wears different shades of pink lipstick which cheer me up. She's lovely to Bridget, whereas some of the other mums stare at my daughter like she's Damian from *The Omen*.

"You haven't seen anything of Rachel recently, have you?" I ask, leaning over the buggy and tucking the blanket over Will's feet.

She fiddles with her double row of pearls.

"No, sorry Julie, not for a while." She reddens, then hurries towards the door as the kids come pouring out.

I hear the rumours the next day after Advanced Baby Yoga in St Barnabas' Church Hall. I'm heading into the toilets with Will in my arms when I hear the booming Dublin accent of Eileen O'Toole, a St. Joseph's mum. She and Josie Ryan are engrossed in conversation and bouncing their screaming babies up and down.

"Jenny Raddings said at least nine kids are in hospital," shouts Eileen.

Josie makes the sign of the cross.

"Jesus, Mary and Joseph, Eileen. I wonder if they'll shut the school down. It can have terrible consequences you know. It can make you blind and deaf and... "

Both of them look startled to see me. Josie's jaw drops.

"Sorry, Julie," says Eileen looking down at her watch,."Lord, is that the time?"

They make a quick exit, steering their babies carefully around myself and Will.

By the time I get back into the hall they've both disappeared, but two of the other mums are talking about the headline news, the MEASLES OUTBREAK IN BROADOAK PRIMARY. I am desperate for information but it's time for the school run and everyone is shoving their babies into their buggies and sprinting out of the door like they're in the pushchair Olympics. I arrive at Broadoak ten minutes late. The children are still in class and the parents, grandparents, child minders and a couple of teachers are all gathered in the playground. It's a cold day with a chill wind and Mrs Pinker, the Head, a tall, stick-like woman in her fifties with a blonde basin haircut, is standing on a chair in front of the Year Two classrooms in a tailored purple coat. Her hair is whirling around her face and she's rubbing her hands together to keep them warm. I sidle up to Amy with the buggy. She glances down at Will and smiles nervously.

Mrs Pinker clears her throat and asks for silence. It's a bit like assembly, except nobody is fidgeting or picking their nose. She speaks solemnly and carefully,

"Four pupils in Reception and one child in Year One have been infected. None of them are in a serous condition, though all are in hospital for precautionary measures. I can't tell you very much else at the moment but the children have been given an information sheet to take home in their book bags." She wobbles on the chair then steadies herself. "I'll keep you informed of any further developments when we return from the holidays. Thank you, and please bear with me."

As she steps down, parents swarm all over her like paparazzi. I think about Rachel's disappearance and Tobias' illness at the dinner party, then I turn to Amy.

"Tobias and Tabatha have got it, haven't they?" She looks at the ground and nods.

"Why weren't they vaccinated? Was it the autism thing?"

"Well, ya, partly. But also I think it's something to do with them being homeopathic practitioners."

"Who else has got it?"

"Dexter Smith, Joshua Pertwee in Reception and Joshua's sister Ella in Year One."

"So the Pertwees weren't vaccinated?"

"They were in the middle of a course of single MMR. jabs and were infected in a period between jabs when they weren't protected. Dexter Smith wasn't vaccinated."

"You've known all this for a while, haven't you, Amy?" She winces. "Why didn't you tell me this when I asked you about Rachel the other day?"

"Look I'm sorry, Julie, I really am. She swore me to secrecy."

I bite my lip.

"I bet she fucking did."

Then it suddenly dawns on me and I am filled with terror. I've only been thinking about the possibility of Bridget being infected. But she should be fine as she's had all her jabs. Will hasn't, though. He's only four months old, his first MMR immunisation is eight months away and he and I have spent at least three mornings a week recently in close proximity to Rachel and Tabatha Cleaver.

It all happens so quickly. That evening Will becomes listless. At bedtime the coughing and the high temperature start, and Billy and I look for the telltale grey white spots in his mouth. We keep him in our bed and I lie awake for most of the night watching him, agitated by his every move.

As soon as we've dropped Bridget off at school in the morning we rush to Dr. Chang's emergency GP surgery. A blotchy red rash has appeared behind Will's ears and neck and she diagnoses him immediately. She says that most children fight the infection in a week or so, but because of Will's age and the slight possibility of complications she wants to have him monitored in hospital for a few days as a precaution. Complications. I know all about those. I was up at dawn googling them. Inflammation of the brain, pneumonia, bronchitis, eye and ear infections, hepatitis, followed by death. Billy was at pains to point out how rarely these things happen, but it was no use. In my head we were already lowering Will's tiny white coffin into the ground and I was heading for a stint in the psychiatric ward at St Mary's.

Billy grips the arm of his chair and asked how a child could get measles in this day and age. Dr. Chang explains that the uptake for the MMR is a lot lower than average in Chorlton, which had resulted in the outbreak of the disease. She says it's happening in pockets all over the country. As we're putting Will's coat on, Billy turns to Dr. Chang.

"I thought all that stuff about the MMR causing autism had been discredited," he says.

"It has," she replied with a long sigh, "but at the end of the day it's a parent's choice. We in the medical profession can't force anyone to vaccinate their children."

Two hours later we arrive at Wythenshawe Hospital. It is located in the largest council estate in Europe and has a reputation as Manchester's Bronx. A new, sprawling red brick complex, the hospital shines like Florence Nightingale's lamp in the war zone.

We park up and I take Will's car seat out. He is agitated and coughing sporadically, his breathing laboured. His face is flushed and the ugly red welts have now spread all over his body. I glance up towards the main entrance, over the grass verge at the waiting ambulances and I feel a sudden lurch in my stomach. A weight falls over me, like someone has suddenly placed a suit of armour over my shoulders. In my anxiety about Will I had completely forgotten. I've never been back here since the day she died.

Dad is locking the door of our battered blue Ford Cortina. Despite the desperate heat, he's wearing a brown cord jacket with a small CND badge on the lapel. Strands of salt and pepper hair are sticking to his forehead and his face is etched with pain as he takes my hand and we hurry over the grass verge into the hospital. It's a perfect summer's evening. The sky is alive with burnt oranges and pinks and I am confused and churning inside as it dawns on me what I might have done.

I am crying as I hand the car seat to Billy who puts his arm around me and reassures me that everything will be fine. We follow the signs to the Starlight Paediatric Ward in silence.

We're given our own isolation room with Thomas the Tank Engine and Peppa Pig on the wall, and its own bathroom.

Will's temperature remains high for the next three days. His voracious appetite dwindles and he wakes throughout the night. The doctors say all we can do is watch and wait and monitor him around the clock.

I sleep fitfully on the camp bed provided. Dad stays over at ours to help out with Bridget while Billy is at work.

I lie awake at night listening to the wail of ambulance sirens and the click clack of the nurses' footsteps in the corridor. I stare through the bars of Will's cot, touching his forehead compulsively, wanting to rub the blotches from his beautiful skin, worrying whether he'll be scarred for life. When he's asleep I wander down the corridor and chat to the nurses on night duty. I tell them about Mum and how she was a nurse here on the stroke ward. The style has changed but the uniform is same royal blue colour. She was wearing it the morning she collapsed in our kitchen. It was June 2nd 1981. She was clearing up the breakfast things and holding a blue willow bowl that slipped out of her left hand. I was sitting at the table with our cat Lily on my knee and, as the plate smashed to the floor, Lily leapt off my knees and scratched my thigh before leaping on top of Mum who'd fallen to the floor. It was a bright morning outside, Dad had just left for work and I was doing my best to be late to avoid Mandy and her gang who had taken to hanging around the row of shops I passed on my way to school. Mum fell into a coma that day and died in this hospital six weeks later. She was thirty-nine. Dad and I travelled to Galway in late August and scattered her ashes in the field at the back of the house where she was raised. It was a breezy day with grey skies and her family were gathered around us. Dad could barely stand, buckled under the weight of his grief. I was still in shock and high on adrenaline and hadn't yet processed the fact that she was gone. I was also consumed by guilt about what I'd done and the shame of it enveloped me like a low hanging black cloud.

I close my eyes and try to remember her, her lavender smell, the powdery tip of her nose and the lilt of her voice as she read to me at bedtime. Mum and I were close. She was my world when she died. I was a miracle baby and a cosseted only child. Mum had always wanted a large family but she suffered a series of miscarriages before and after me. For an Irish woman of her generation to have only one child was a rarity, a social stigma almost, and I know it weighed on her. I hated being an only child. Not used to the knocks and bruises a life with siblings naturally brings, I was over sensitive to comments at school or playing out on the estate. I was needy and submissive, I let other kids take my toys and I did everything they said so they'd be my friend. Looking back, I can see I was easy prey for Mandy and her gang.

I was a bully's dream: a loner, with no older siblings to call on for help; a sensitive cry baby. They sought me out with the ease of a hawk swooping down on a field mouse.

Billy arrives with chocolates and a soft toy for Will from Amy, and I receive a few consoling texts from some of the other mums at school, but I hear nothing from Rachel. Billy says he has heard that Tobias and Tabatha Cleaver are now at home after spending ten days in the BUPA hospital in Altrincham. They have both fully recovered, as have Joshua Pertwee, his sister and Dexter Smith. Billy's face darkens at the mention of the Cleavers. His mood of forced jollity has evaporated, replaced now by the silent broodiness I have come to accept as part of his makeup. Billy is funny and clever and all the rest, but I am gradually coming to terms with the fact that he suffers from depression.

"BUPA, eh?" he says, staring vacantly out of the window. "No doubt the trust fund will be paying for that."

By Sunday, Will is well on the mend. His temperature is stable and he's eating small amounts of baby rice. It's all looking very positive, but then I notice a slight inflammation around his right eye. I immediately ring the nurses' bell and Ruby, the big-boned Nigerian sister, arrives. Will's face lights up when he sees her. She sings to him on her visits and she has a smile the width of the Salford Millennium Bridge. She shines her torch into his right eye humming Whitney's 'I will always love you'.

"I bet people in Nigeria vaccinate their kids, don't they?" asks Billy as she moves the light to the other eye.

"Mister, in my country people fight to have their children vaccinated."

"You know what they do here, Ruby? They spend an afternoon on the internet then decide they know better than the World Health Organisation."

She sighs.

"I am sure in their own way they are thinking to do what is best for their children."

"Yeah? But what about other peoples' children?"

Are they thinking about them?" She steps backwards.

"Slight inflammation in his right eye. I'll get the doctor to take a look on his round."

That evening when Dr. Stratham examines Will on his ward visit, he tells us he has a mild case of conjunctivitis but it's nothing to worry about. He reassures us it will go of its own accord within a week. He asks the nurse to give us some eye patches and says we can go home tomorrow, which is Christmas Eve.

The skies are cloudless and blue when Billy and Bridget come to bring us home. Will has eaten well and his mood has improved. As we're leaving the car park, a rare bolt of sunlight appears and I turn to the car window and feel the warmth on my face after being cooped up inside for so long. I am thinking how happy I am to be going home when I see Dad and Rita Sherburn walking towards the entrance of the Outpatients Department.

"There's Dad," I cry, watching Rita's leather-clad backside disappear into the door.

I turn to Billy.

"Where are they going?" I ask. "He knows we're coming out this morning."

"They'll be visiting someone. You know how many sick friends they have at that age."

"Funny, he never said."

When we get home there is a card on the mat from Rachel. It's got Tobias' art work on the front cover and inside it says:

"Hope Will is better. Such a dreadful business, all of it.

Thankfully we're over the worst now. Hugs,

Rachel and Rufus and kids xxx"

Billy tears it up and throws it in the kitchen bin.

I get to work, tidying and cleaning the house in preparation for tomorrow. Billy has wrapped all the presents and done the food shopping. Later in the afternoon, as I'm polishing the glass coffee table to within an inch of its life, Billy puts down the *Horrid Henry* book he's reading to Bridget and suggests we all go into Chorlton to pick up the turkey from Frost's the butchers.

73

His mood has lifted since we left the hospital and he's making a huge effort to get into the festive spirit.

It's dusk by the time we get the kids ready, wrap ourselves up and get into Chorlton. It's a still evening with a layer of frost on the ground and the branches of the trees are skeletal against the dark purple sky. I wish I'd put on more layers as I feel the cold biting the tips of my toes through my thin trainers.

Chorlton is welcoming under the blaze of Christmas lights. Families are leaving the precinct with Iceland and Boots bags, teenagers are laughing and chatting in groups outside the bars and restaurants and there's a police surveillance van outside Woolworths in case any trouble kicks off. *The Big Issue* seller outside Johnston's the Cleaners is doing good trade and Billy gives Bridget a few coins to put in the basket of a group of middle-aged carol singers outside Oxfam. Then, as we turn right and head towards Barclays Bank, I spot them. They are about ten feet in front of us in the middle of the small group huddled around a table covered with an Animal Rights banner that says "Stop the Cruelty – Have a Conscience this Christmas".

I see Rufus' fingerless gloves clutching the petition, his ridiculous bobble hat and Rachel's pious expression as she chats to a passer-by. As we approach they both stop and glance over at the buggy, at Will and his crooked eye patch. Rufus steps towards Rachel, whispers something to her, then turns his back on us and starts to walk away.

I glimpse the raw rage in Billy's face before it happens, before he leaps towards the table, turning it upside down with one hand, before he pushes the others out of his way to get to Rufus. Someone cries out and coffee, pens, papers and leaflets of tortured dogs and caged cats fly into the air. Rufus turns around and Billy grabs him and lifts him effortlessly off his feet by the lapels of his jacket, a roaring bear with a weasel wriggling in his grip.

"Don't you walk away from me, you self-righteous little cunt," Billy yells into his face and nods towards the banner. "Have a conscience! *Have a fucking conscience?* Where was your conscience when you decided not to vaccinate your kids knowing they could infect others, eh? Where was your fucking conscience then?"

He nods at the buggy, at Will and his eye patch, then looks over at Rachel who is cowering by the cash point.

"Look at him, the pair of you. Go on. Look at your handiwork."

Billy throws Rufus to the ground like a piece of rotten fruit and he cries out in pain. Rachel and a dreadlocked man rush over to him. Billy then picks up the upturned table and smashes it to the ground, kicking it repeatedly. He's cursing and yelling at the top of his voice and has completely lost it. It's like an army of demons has been unleashed inside him. I scream at him to stop and turn Bridget's head away. Then I see a flash of yellow vests and I watch in disbelief as three policemen struggle to get him in handcuffs. As they are dragging him into the waiting van he is still yelling like a lunatic at the top of his voice.

"You know what you are, Rufus Cleaver, heir to the slaughterhouse millions? You're a butcher. A fucking butcher."

CHAPTER 12

Billy

I take my seat next to a small elderly man in a tweed cap smelling of cheap aftershave and coughing sporadically. An olive-skinned beauty with violet eyes sits cross-legged next to the receptionist's desk texting and smiling to herself. She really is a fine thing, a ray of light in my morning. When her name comes up to go in, I watch the curves of her arse sashay down the corridor. Maybe she'd run off to Mexico and lie with me on a white sandy beach for a while. That'd be a far, far better cure for my depression than the pills I'm about to be prescribed.

It was only a couple of weeks ago that I was sitting here with Julie, waiting for Dr. Chang to diagnose Will. Two long tortuous weeks. I still can't believe the bastards put me in a cell on Christmas Eve. And for what? For teaching that smug fucker a lesson after what he did to my child?

I lie awake most of the night staring at the four walls of my cell, Shane McGowan's lyrics from 'Fairytale' playing over and over in my head.

"It was Christmas Eve babe, in the drunk tank."

I'd done it again. I'd completely lost it. I'd ruined the Christmas, but this time I'd done it without a drop taken.

They released me at eleven on Christmas morning after interviewing me in the early hours. As I was signing for my things, a spotty-faced kid behind the desk told me I'd have to come back in a month to see if I was going to be charged with a public order offence. He made a point of telling me how lucky I was that the Cleavers weren't pressing charges.

"On account of you having previous," he said with a stern look as he handed me my belongings. The patronising cunt couldn't have been more than twenty years old.

Julie refused to come anywhere near the station and waited for me in the nearby car park. She was stony-faced and silent all the way home, ignoring my repeated apologies. Christmas dinner was subdued to say the least. She barely said a word, Tony was very withdrawn and he left soon afterwards to meet Rita. I followed him out into the street. He was a little unsteady on his feet on the icy pavement but he refused to let me get him a cab. Before I could explain myself, he put a hand on my shoulder.

"Look," he said, "what Cleaver did was wrong, walking away like that, but you've got to get a grip on that temper, lad. You can't go around thumping folk like that."

I went inside feeling like I'd been told off by a teacher I really liked and respected.

In the evening when the kids were in bed, I fetched the expensive bottle of Cava I'd bought from the fridge, switched off *Only Fools and Horses*, and held out a glass to Julie who was sitting on the sofa. She waved her hand in refusal and I could see she was crying.

"You missed the kids opening their presents," she sniffed.

I put her glass back on the coffee table, took a few gulps from mine and sat down beside her.

"Don't you think I know that? Don't you think I thought of the three of you every minute I was in there?"

She inched away from me.

"Then why didn't you think of us when you were battering Rufus?"

"I did *not* batter Rufus. I threw him on the ground, that was all."

"You behaved like a fucking madman. And in front of the kids. God, I was so ashamed."

I stared down at the pear-shaped coffee stain on the rug in front of me.

"Look, I just lost it. I couldn't help it. He turned his back on us after everything that happened. I couldn't let him get away with that."

She jumped up, stood in front of the fireplace and jabbed her forefinger at me.

"Don't you think I wanted to punch his fucking lights out just as much as you? But not all of us resort to violence, Billy." She stamped her foot. "So much for making friends at Broadoak. Bridget's behaviour is bad enough but now they'll all know exactly where she gets it from, won't they?"

"Is that what upsets you most? What the Chorlton chattering classes will think of you?"

She folded her arms.

"Well I'm the one who has to face them every fucking day at the school gates."

I sat back.

"Look, how many more times. I'm sorry, OK?"

She moved over to the arm chair and sat down with her legs folded, stroking her fingers absently along the leather of the arm..

"You're depressed, Billy," she said, her voice now softened, "That's why you lash out. Rage turned inward is depression. Your moods are getting worse and it's starting to affect me and the kids."

The brutal honesty of her words hit me like a smack across the face. She was crying again.

"Don't we make you happy?" she said quietly. "Aren't we enough?"

I went over, knelt beside her and took her hands in mine.

"Of course you're enough. You and the kids are my world. It's just that sometimes I get down and at other times the red mist descends and I can't control it."

"It's to do with your dad, isn't it? His death, I mean."

I take my hands away. She's never said anything like this before.

"What makes you say that?"

"The way you never talk about him."

I turn away, afraid of any further probing. "Possibly. I don't know."

"But you weren't to blame for his death, Billy. You were only a boy. You were sixteen when he died."

My sister Clodagh's words came hurtling back to me from that day: "Sure, run, why don't you? Weren't you the one who killed him?"

Julie grips my shoulder.

"Please get some help. Counselling or antidepressants at least. It's not just about Rufus Cleaver. It's about us, your family. You keep disappearing into these black moods where we can't reach you. Please, do it for us, for me and the kids."

I looked at her red swollen eyes and the anxiety there, thinking how much more she deserved, then I buried my face in the nook of her neck. "Yes, OK. I'll do it," I said.

I look up at the posters asking me how many units of alcohol I drink, if I'm a victim of domestic violence, if my pregnancy is unwanted. I think with shame about Rachel, about the child she lost and how she must have suffered. That young cop was right. I was lucky Rachel and Rufus didn't press charges. I might even have faced a custodial sentence. It would have been her perfect revenge, but once again, and for reasons beyond me, Rachel has let me off the hook.

I look down at my watch. I wish they'd get a move on. I don't even know why I have to see a doctor. They give antidepressants out like Smarties these days. Why don't they just have a basket on the counter at reception so we can help ourselves? My phone vibrates. I take it out of my pocket and read. Another fucking customer making excuses to avoid paying me money they owe. I'm spending all my time chasing unpaid debts these days.

I glance at the date on the screen. 4th January 2007. I put it back in my pocket, lean forward and close my eyes. Twenty years ago tomorrow.

It was a Saturday. I was at the McConnell quarry in the village, my best friend Davy's family business. I worked there at the weekends and holidays. Davy and I were both shovelling stone onto trucks in the yard. It was a brutally cold morning and the sky was overcast. The previous evening I'd absconded from my room after another fierce row with Da about me wanting to leave school and go to England. I jumped out of my bedroom window and joined Davy at a house party in the village where we stayed until 3a.m.

We were now both still half drunk, messing around and laughing about the craic we'd had the night before. Davy's father, Paddy Jo, who has known me from birth, had been giving us thunderous looks all morning. As he made his way slowly towards us from the small office hut, hands deep in his pockets, I was convinced I was for the boot. Then I saw the look in his eyes.

"Go down to your mother. She needs you."

He spoke gently, looking past me into the distance with watery eyes and touching my elbow.

"Go easy on that bike now, good lad," he said.

I entered the kitchen where Mam and my sisters were sitting at the old pine table. I'd noticed my aunt's car outside and I could hear murmuring coming from the front room. Mam gestured to me to sit down. She had one hand curled around Tara on her knee, a cigarette in the other. She stubbed it out in the shell-shaped ashtray we'd given her after a day out at Enniscrone beach. A tap was dripping somewhere as she lifted her hand to her face and told us Da was dead. I stared at the rosebud button on the cuff of her shop uniform and none of us made a sound. Then my sisters started to wail and clutch and question. I got up, my legs weak, and I headed for the door. As I ran outside, Clodagh was shouting behind me:

"Yes, you run, why don't you? Didn't you break his heart and kill him?"

My father was a gentle, bookish man whom I loved far more than my mother, a pious pragmatist. She swept his encyclopaedias and novels under the marital bed and mumbled to herself when he crept away, volume in hand, to the silence of the front room to read. He loved science, the natural world and Russian novels in particular. As youngsters we would walk with him in the lanes and fields around the village and he would name every plant, tree, flower and berry in sight. He'd gather us onto his knees in the evening, draw pictures of the solar system from memory and have us chant the names of the planets back to him. Testing us on our dreaded Irish, he'd invent competitive games and magic up sweets from his trouser pocket for winning pronunciation. We had very little money but he always came home with books, often shabby and well-thumbed, a novel or children's book of stories he'd picked up somewhere on his travels in the lorry that day. He never said where they came from and I used to fantasise about rich, beautiful women in large houses letting him help himself from their packed bookshelves in return for a delivery of bricks or cement. Looking back, he probably pilfered from the libraries in the larger towns but was careful to remove any evidence. Da drove trucks for a local construction company for a living. He was one of the many intelligent Irish men and women of his generation, who, had they been born thirty years later, might have had a college education, a white collar life and a stack of bookshelves of their own. Instead they laid pipes and bricks and wiped arses in London and New York, or, if they stayed at home like Da, they picked up what bits of work they could to keep the hunger away from the door. They had no choice. Unlike me.

I think of that last evening twenty years ago and his final words to me:

"Don't end up like me, son, driving trucks at all hours just to make ends meet. Get yourself an education. Please now... I'm begging you. Don't throw it all away. It'll be such a waste, son."

The next time I saw him he was in that same room lying in his coffin at his wake. He had a heart attack at forty-one at the wheel of his truck which then toppled over a ravine out on the Connemara Road.

The buzzer goes and I look up to my name in neon above the words, "Dr. Abercrombie". At last.

I head down the corridor and stop outside the black door, the darkness staring back at me. I think of Julie and the kids, and reach out, the handle cold in my damp, trembling hand. Then the panic returns. My heart is tearing around my chest like a dog on a greyhound track and sweat starts to trickle down my forehead. I stand there for a minute, maybe more. Then I take my hand away.

I can't do it. I'm afraid what will happen in there. If I start talking I may never be able to stop. I turn around, hurry back up the corridor and exit through the side door.

CHAPTER 13

Julie

The first day back after the holidays was the worst. I arrived late on purpose to avoid waiting around in the playground while everyone had a good gawp at the school jailbird's wife. I was hoping to rush in and out with my head hunkered down but the caretaker was late with the keys and I had to stand at the front of the gate for a good ten minutes in my bright red cloak of shame for the world and his wife to see. Looking back, I should have worn a faux fur, tight white jeans, over-sized sunglasses and adopted the "fuck you" air of a criminal's wife. Where was Samantha Pointer when I needed her?

I continued to walk around with lowered eyes for the next few days and I avoided Rachel and her yummy gang. However, I was heartened by the number of parents who approached me and asked about Will and said how terrible the whole measles episode had been. Amy was particularly supportive. I could be wrong but I'm starting to get the impression that Rachel isn't quite as popular as I'd originally thought, even if she did get Chair of the P.T.A. I'm mostly ignored again now, though, as I'm sure Mrs. Kray was when she did her East End school run.

I'm filling with dread at the thought of my appointment in ten minutes' time. Miss Williams took me to one side yesterday and asked if we could have a chat about Bridget's behaviour. That's just what I need, another member of my family in trouble with the authorities. We're not exactly popular in Broadoak Primary right now.

Will is getting restless and kicking around in his buggy. I lean in and give him a Rich Tea biscuit to suck on. Apart from a couple of marks on his cheeks he has recovered with a vengeance and his ferocious appetite is back. He's leapt off the percentile chart for his size and weight and he's in age one to two in clothes. I push the buggy to the door near Bridget's classroom. I can see her face squashed up against the window, palms outstretched, her eyes searching out mine. Dylan, the little boy three doors down, is coming over for tea today and I know she's excited about having a play date. I invited him yesterday after an incident here at the school which left me in tears.

I forgot Bridget's P.E. kit and walked down with Will to drop it off mid-morning at the school office. It was playtime and as I was leaving I hid behind the fence and looked for her in the playground. She was sitting alone in a far corner chalking on the ground and talking to herself while the other kids played tag and skipped in groups around her. I observed her for some time. At one point she got up and went over to a couple of girls in her class. It looked like she was asking if she could join in their game but they turned and ran away and left her standing there, her head bowed like a rejected puppy. I couldn't bear to watch anymore. I hated those girls with every irrational bone in my body and I wanted to take Bridget home there and then and shield her from it all. As I walked away I thought about what had happened. I knew I'd been looking in a mirror. I was that same lonely girl in Priory Road. That's why they chose me. I'd give anything in the world for my daughter not to be like that, I really would.

As I hurried away from the school I bumped into Dad and Rita Sherburn on the corner of Brookburn Road. She really was the last person I wanted to see at that moment, but I had promised Dad I'd meet her at some point and as it was a decent enough day we took Will along to Beech Road Park for a play.

Rita looked very different to the frumpy dinner lady I remembered. She looked like she was heading for a night out at

Blackpool Mecca in a red PVC pencil skirt, a leopard skin fur and a gigantic pair of stilettos you could go to sea in. She must be at least a size nine. I kept looking out for any physical or psychotic resemblance to her nieces, Mandy and Donna, but thankfully I found none. She was pleasant with Will and we chatted when Dad took him on the swings. She started to tell me about *The Phantom of the Opera*, which she'd seen with her friend Marjorie in London at the weekend. Her face became animated, the lines creasing in and out like a concertina as she talked me through the plot and the songs and the stage set. She rambled on, barely pausing for breath, partly because I wasn't saying much but also because she was nervous, which I have to confess I found endearing. She was still talking about *Phantom* when Dad came back.

"Rita's got a great voice herself," Dad said tentatively.

"I'd like to hear it at some point," I replied. Against all my better judgement I found myself warming to her. It would be hard not to. She's got a childlike quality about her and she's very funny without meaning to be half the time. I never thought I'd say it, but when she left I felt like a splash of colour had disappeared from my morning.

At three forty-five I am sitting at Miss Williams' desk and she is slipping a leaflet into my hand.

"Even the best parents need a little help sometimes, Mrs. O'Hagan," she says.

Bridget's teacher is as wide as she is tall, wears brightly coloured nylon trousers with elasticated waists, and owns a large selection of orthopaedic shoes. She also owns a pair of piercing blue eyes that can switch from grandmotherly kindness to Jack Nicholson terror in an instant. Bridget has been colouring in quietly outside the classroom throughout our meeting. I get the impression that if anyone can deal with her, Miss Williams can.

She has been very gentle with me, playing down the fire alarm incident and reassuring me that the shouting out and swearing at carpet time is improving.

I blame Billy for the swearing. Fecking this and fecking that. I told him it has to stop.

"But the Irish use of feck," he protested, "is only syntactically interchangeable with the English fuck, not in terms of meaning at all, as many people tend to think."

"Again, and in English this time."

"Feck is not the same as fuck."

"Yes it fucking is."

"No it's fecking not. In Ireland teachers and members of the clergy use it all the time."

"But Bridget doesn't go to St. Fucking Francis of Assisi in Galway, Billy. She goes to Broadoak."

Bridget's swearing wasn't Miss Williams' most serious concern, though. She was more worried about the way she lashes out at other children.

"I'm afraid we are obliged to tell the other parents if their offspring are involved in any kind of physical altercation," she said in a very serious tone, "but we do not mention any names."

No wonder she never gets invited to anything. She's probably been beating up half the class then the kids are going home and telling their parents.

"I've tried everything with her, Miss Williams," I sigh, "I really have."

It's true. I've replaced the Haribos with hummus and raisins, cut down on her TV time, been more consistent with the naughty step and stopped her weekly scratch card. But none of it seems to be working. She still stands out like a horned devil in a chorus of angels in Broadoak Primary. Miss Williams glances at her watch and stands up.

"I've heard good things about the parenting course," she says patting my arm, "and anything is worth a try."

That evening I show the leaflet to Billy and ask him what he thinks. He's hunched over the computer, absorbed, and he doesn't reply, so I read the front page aloud:

" 'A four week course led by one of Manchester's leading child psychologists. For mums, dads and guardians who need help with parenting skills, particularly behavioural issues. Whalley Range Sure Start Centre. Starts Feb 15th. Free to all.' That's next week. They've got a crèche where I can put Will."

"Great." His eyes don't move from the screen.

"So you think it's a good idea, then?" He doesn't reply. "Try not to get too enthusiastic Billy."

"I'm a bit busy right now."

He gulps from the can of lager that's his permanent companion most evenings now. When he places it on the computer table I snatch it up.

"Not too busy to drink though, eh?" He snatches the can back off me.

"Busy looking for work so I can actually feed my kids. Look, I said it's a good idea. What else do you want? A fucking medal?"

Fuming, I take the leaflet, go into the kitchen and slam the kettle on. Then I stand by the window and glance up at the night sky.

He's gone back to his grumpy ways. After promising to get antidepressants, he never went anywhere near the doctors and his moods are now swinging high and low on a daily basis. He needs help but he won't open up to me about whatever it is that's getting to him. Oh I know he's worried about the work situation too, but so am I. There's a recession out there. It hasn't turned me into Saddam Hussein, though. He ignites over the smallest thing, drinks most nights, then growls at the kids all the next day. No wonder Bridget has behavioural issues. If I was being yelled at by my dad twenty-four seven and saw my parents arguing all the time I think I'd have behavioural issues too.

Poor Bridget.

I pick up the leaflet and read through the content pages:

Distraction techniques. Using the medium of play.

The importance of boundaries. When to use Time Out.

She is not going to like it.

My thoughts turn to the play date with Dylan today. I can see the poor lad sitting at the kitchen table sobbing as I tried to console him with a compensatory ice lolly.

"She's hidden it," he sobbed. "Luke Skywalker was my special toy from Daddy but the rotter has hidden it."

Dylan is the only son of two lecturers who had him late in life. He's a lovely, polite boy but he does have a mental age of about twenty-six. He's been round to play once before with a modicum of success, but today was a catastrophe. I searched everywhere in the house and the yard for the Star Wars figure, but I couldn't find it anywhere. He cried and cried and said he wanted to go home. When his mum arrived she looked as devastated as him when I told her about the toy. I insisted we'd replace it but she shook her head. "Not possible," she sighed. "It was his dad's original from the seventies. They're like gold dust now. Never mind, it can't be helped. Just let me know if it turns up."

"She hit me too, Mummy," I heard him say as they were walking down the path. "She's a bully, Mummy, a big fat bully."

The word lodged itself like a bullet at the forefront of my thoughts and has not moved since.

I read through the leaflet for the parenting course one more time, tear off the application form and fill it in.

CHAPTER 14

Billy

My back is wracked with pain. The ground is hard beneath me but my cheek is pressed against something cold and wet. I shiver. I am numb with cold, a body of ice, unable to feel the tips of my fingers or toes. I smell earth and flora. I open my eyes at the rattle of a passing milk van. In the darkness I can make out dew glistening on leaves inches away from my face. I raise myself slowly, something clatters at my feet and I watch a beer can roll onto the path and stop beside a small boy's bike propped against a wheelie bin. To the right, more cans, wine bottles and an overflowing ash tray crowd on top of a small plastic garden table. I stand up. The garden isn't mine. Neither is the house. It's a whitewashed maisonette with houses on either side. A dim light flickers in a downstairs room.

I consider going back into the house to warm up but instead I hurry out of the back gate, through a ginnel and into the desolate street. I glance at my watch in the lamplight. Five thirty. Across the road in the distance I can see Tony's club. So I'm somewhere on the Pittsburgh Estate. I jog in that direction, rubbing my hands together vigorously to get the circulation going. I can find my way from there. Pain clamps my head and my limbs feel like they're made of metal.

I start to panic as I struggle to piece together the events of yesterday. I am thirty-nine years old, I have just woken up at dawn in a stranger's back garden and I haven't a fucking clue how I got there.

I remember a text from Julie at about midday when I was in

the van on my way home from the plastering job. Saturday morning or not, I have to take work when I can these days.

'Dad in Ladbrokes with Bridget. She's not supposed to be in there. Can you go and get her? Don't want her getting any more bad habits. Xxx'

I parked up in Oswald Road and hurried through the busy High Street to the betting shop, dodging the patrolling charity workers outside with their fluorescent armour and clipboards and fixed smiles. I wondered if any of them had ever persuaded a punter to sign up with Save the Children instead of putting a tenner on the one o'clock at Doncaster.

Queues were forming in front of the glass counters inside and a mass of heads were turned towards the race coming to an end on the giant plasma screen. I jostled my way through the crowd, surprised how many women were in there. I can't remember the last time I was in a betting shop. Gambling is about the only vice I don't engage in. I made my way towards the far corner where I could see Tony's mottled head, broad shoulders and blue windcheater. Bridget was sitting behind him on a high stool by the window scribbling on betting slips.

As I approached I could see that Tony was talking to Father Kearney, the parish priest from St. Joseph's. I hung back. I have met Kearney a number of times at various weddings and christenings. He's a youthful sixty-something from Sligo with a spring in his step, a fecund head of white hair and a wealthy set of Manchester Irish friends. Unlike Jesus Christ, Kearney is not often seen in the company of the poor, preferring instead five star hotels and a seat in a company box at Old Trafford. He has tried to engage me in talk about home on a couple of occasions, but I have no interest in his slick charms. Surprisingly, Tony isn't a fan either.

I arrived at the tail end of their conversation.

"But I'm sure the late Mrs. Pattenden would have loved to have seen this one in St. Joseph's," Kearney was saying. "Indeed, down at the church I remember her telling me many a time how she wanted her own girls in the school."

Tony dug his hands in the pocket of his jacket and stood with his legs apart.

"Well, I'm delighted to report that Bridget, like her mam, is being educated in a school where her head isn't filled with rubbish about saints and miracles and all that other fictional stuff you peddle for truth."

Kearney straightened his shoulders and both men locked eyes. It was high noon in Chorlton.

"Strange how she returned to her faith, though. 'My time in the wilderness' she called it. I remember now." An icy smile spread over his face. "The Lord works in mysterious ways, Mr. Pattenden," he said.

"My arse he does," Tony laughed, a little too loudly and too forcefully. Some of the punters glanced over and Bridget's mouth dropped open, but he didn't stop there.

"That's always the answer to everything when you lot can't prove anything," he sputtered. "You're making things up again, Father. You're making things up."

Bridget put her pen down and hopped down off the stool.

"I'm bored, Granddad."

"Of course you are, pet," said Kearney, red-faced and looking for an escape. "This is no place for a child." Then he bent forwards and placed his hand on the top of Bridget's head.

I pushed past the man in front of me, bent down and lifted her out of his reach.

"Daddy," she squealed. I gave Kearney a curt nod, grabbed Bridget's coat and told Tony I'd wait for him outside.

He came out a few minutes later as I was pulling Bridget's red gloves over her tiny fingers one by one. I shot him a stern look.

"It's very good of you to have Bridget, Tony, but what the hell were you thinking of, bringing her in there?"

"It was only a quick bet."

"She's five years old, for Christ's sake."

I took Bridget's hand and walked on for a few yards. Then I stopped and turned round, waiting for Tony to catch up, my anger melting at the sight of him shuffling along, his pale face slightly bowed. I've enquired a few times about his health but he always insists he's fine and changes the subject.

"By God, I could swing for that smug git," he fumed. "He's got some cheek. I cannot tell you how much I love winding up pious bastards like him. The way they walk around in frocks telling the rest of us how to live our lives: vicars, nuns, priests, imams, rabbis, ministers, bishops, mullahs. The lot of them should be lined up against the wall and shot, along with Alex Ferguson and Bob Monkhouse."

I dissolved into laughter. How could I stay cross with him for long?

He still looked angry as we turned into Manchester Road and I checked for fire and smoke coming from his nostrils.

"Religious bigots," he mumbled, "the bane of my life. Did I ever tell you how Bridget's family nearly stopped us from getting married?"

"You did, Tony."

More than once, in fact, and usually when drink was taken. Misty-eyed, he launched into the story of how he fell head over heels for his late wife at an Irish dance in Levenshulme in the late sixties. But she was from a fervently Catholic, nationalist family with relatives on The Falls Road at a time when the Troubles were brewing, so they weren't too happy about their daughter marrying an Englishman whose mother was a Northern Ireland Protestant to boot. A widow, Tony's mother wasn't too keen on him marrying a "papist" either, and two years of warring and silent treatment from both families followed. Tony and Bridget finally decided they'd had enough and married quietly in the registry office in Manchester Town Hall. No in-laws attended and the couple made a vow to lead a secular life from then onwards. Tony was devastated when Bridget returned to her faith a few years later after suffering a series of miscarriages. She thought God had punished her for turning away from the Church.

"But Bridget's family took to you in the end, didn't they?" I asked, pulling Bridget away from a toy shop window.

"I was about as popular as Cromwell at first," he replied. "But, yes. We got to like each other. I fell in love with the place, to be honest."

Tony insisted on getting the bus home so we left him at his stop, then Bridget and I made our way to Etchell's newsagents in the precinct. Meeting Kearney and all that talk and thoughts about Ireland had reminded me to pick up my weekly copy of *The Irish Independent*.

That evening Julie went to bed just after nine, Will having kept her up most of the previous night with his teething troubles. I finished the dishes, opened a bottle of Merlot then spread my newspaper on the kitchen table. Rain spattered gently on the windows and New Order's 'Blue Monday' blared out from one of the houses backing onto ours. I listened out for any movement from upstairs but they all remained sound asleep.

I picked up *The Independent* and turned to the obituaries at the back, something I do every week, hoping to see his name there, hoping to see him dead. But my luck wasn't in this week either. So I turned to the first page and read through the paper, when an article at the bottom of page four seized my attention. I swallowed and took a deep breath. Then I hunched over the table and read, gripping the edge of the table to stop my hands trembling. I read the article again twice, slowly, taking in dates, places and names. 1976 to 1986. Galway, Cavan and Wexford. Seeing his name in print was like drinking a slow dose of poison.

My body reacted immediately. I bolted into the backyard feeling like I wanted to vomit. The rain caressed the back of my neck as I thought about how much bile I have kept down over the years, how much badness has swilled around inside me. I took the Silk Cut and the lighter from inside the bird table, went back inside and turned the lights off. I stood over the sink and watched the newspaper burn until the last glowing embers melted.

I didn't want this. This was everything I'd dreaded. What I wanted was to see him dead.

I sat in the darkness for a while, chain-smoking and finishing the Merlot. The music from the party house had quietened down and I watched as a tunnel of light from an upstairs window threw patterns across the kitchen wall.

Memories flooded back to me, taunting me and refusing to leave me alone. I knew I had to free myself of them somehow and the only way was to search out oblivion. I left Julie a note and texted Les Coppul, an acquaintance and dealer who hangs out in the Spread Eagle, a Chorlton pub with a violent reputation and full of unsavoury and damaged types like myself. Les is a short, elfin-faced Scouser and an extremely funny man. I drank cheap double whiskies with him and his friends until closing time, then there was talk of a party, coke and ketamine. It all sounded good to me. I'd never taken ketamine but I'd heard it was the best antidepressant ever. And everyone did keep banging on at me to take those.

A faint pink and orange sky is rising over the roof-tops of the restaurants and bars on Beech Road as I near home. A lonely cyclist in full fluorescent gear pedals down the empty street and, as I pass, the early morning smell of fresh bread in the bakers that would normally lift me to high heaven makes me want to retch.

I remember the taxi ride to the party. I remember sitting in a sparsely furnished room drinking from cans and watching girls shaking their arses on MTV, but I don't remember anything about the garden. I do remember my dream though. Vividly.

I was waiting behind in class as the other boys filed slowly out of the door in silence. Davy was looking back at me with a look of compassion on his plump, eight-year-old face. I felt Brother's dark presence beside me and I heard the whistle of the belt in the air. But I felt nothing more than a tickle across my backside when it landed and when I finally stood up straight and opened my eyes

94

Brother was gone and Da was standing in front of me in his place dressed in an orange, blood-splattered cloth dress. He grabbed my hand and tried to drag me out of the classroom.

"No," I screamed, digging in my heels. "No. Stop it, Da. I want to stay."

CHAPTER 15

Julie

The Sure Start Centre in Whalley Range is a light and airy, glass-fronted building overlooking the park. Sunny yellow walls are covered with photos of a multicultural paradise of children engaged in educational play, and the staff bound along the corridors with welcoming smiles. The place yells OPTIMISM as you walk in the door, which is just as well as this part of Whalley Range is the arse end of South Manchester, a well known red light and drug-dealing area. No doubt Derek Pointer earned well around here. To my knowledge, he, Samantha and Brooklyn are still on the run. They haven't turned up anywhere in the UK and there have been no Interpol sightings of Sam's tight white jeans on the continent either.

I am early. Will settled in easily at the crèche next door. He's such an easy going child. So unlike his sister. I hope he's this good when he gets to Broadoak. Then everyone there will know Bridget's behaviour is down to nature not nurture. I help myself to tea and biscuits and look around. You'd never find parenting courses and a Sure Start Centre like this in Chorlton. The Broccoli Brigade don't need to be told how to parent. They read all the books ever written on the subject when Tarquin was a twinkle in Mummy and Daddy's eye. But barely a mile up the road, here families are on the poverty line and teenage mums and parents with dependency problems are the norm. The room starts to fill with women: some are Asian but most are white and thirtyish. No dads, just mums. Figure that one out. We smile and nod at each other and I leaf through some of the pamphlets I picked up in reception. I was looking for a course in anger management for Billy, which they don't have. But they do have something to help you support your child through the death of a pet, and swimming sessions for Muslim mothers and daughters.

Manchester's leading child psychologist enters the room ten minutes late, wearing loose-fitting khaki trousers, a grey t-shirt, and emerald green Doc Martin boots. She has henna-red, shoulder length hair, a nose ring and a thin horsey face that shines with sweat and intensity. Her name badge says Sam and, as she rifles through the pile of papers she drops on her desk, one of her marker pens rolls off onto the floor. I pick it up and hand it to her with a sycophantic smile. I was always such a teacher's pet. No wonder I was bullied.

My thoughts turn to the invitation that arrived in my Friends Reunited inbox last night.

"Chorlton High Class of '86."

Friends Reunited invites you to a reunion. 7th June 2007 at The Irish Association Club, High Lane, Chorlton.

I'd like to go but I've been weighing up the chances of Mandy and Donna being there. Donna probably will be though I'm not sure about Mandy. She only attended Chorlton High for a year before she disappeared.

As I'm taking out the name badge from my folder I hear a familiar, honeyed voice.

"Sorry I'm late Sam, hon. Had such a dreadful time getting Tabatha settled in the crèche."

I look up to see a flustered looking Rachel Cleaver giving Manchester's leading psychologist some double kiss action.

"No worries, Rach," says Sam, "we've not started yet."

Rach? Christ almighty! The woman is stalking me. She scans the room, her face falling for a brief second at the sight of me, then it returns to its usual ventriloquist smile mode. She removes her black faux fur jacket and silver scarf and opts for a seat in the far corner of the room.

Rachel and I have not spoken since the measles episode and

Billy's incarceration. It hasn't been easy as we are in each other's company at least three times a week at various playgroups, but we're now both pretty adept at pretending the other doesn't exist. What the hell is she doing here, though? She needs a parenting course like I need a fat suit. Tabatha is only a baby and Tobias is the Angel Gabriel of Broadoak Reception. He's even nice to Bridget, for God's sake. What could her kids possibly have done for her to enrol? Refused to do their nightly meditation or share their raisins? Dissed their Dad's cabbages? Nothing, I sigh, in Bridget's league at all. How can I talk openly about Bridget's problems with Rachel in the room? It also looks like she and Sam are best mates so it won't be long before she tells her what Billy did to Rufus. Maybe I should just jack it all in and walk out right now. But then I think of Bridget on her own that time in the playground. Fuck Rachel Cleaver. I take the name badge, write my name in massive letters on it and slap it above my left breast.

The class gets confessional very quickly. It's a bit like being in an A.A. meeting in one of those afternoon American True Movies on Sky, and I just about manage to suppress the urge to jump up and say, "Hi guys, I'm Julie. I'm a shit parent but I love you all."

Women take it in turns to say why they are here. Some talk about juggling work and childcare, others talk about temper tantrums and the nightmare of bedtime routines and one lady seethes from behind her hijab about her husband, calling him a useless fuck who's more trouble than all her five kids put together. When it's my turn I play the generic card and say my five year old is a bit of a handful at the moment, without going into too much detail. I can see Rachel's eyes boring into me and I look down, grip my pencil, and write "Rachel Cleaver is a big fat pig" so hard the lead breaks.

Sam is now addressing the woman sitting next to me. Her name badge says Tracey. She is white blonde with two inches of black root and smells of sweat and fags. She has the name Kyle etched in ink on the four fingers of her right hand and I like the fact that she has not let the size of her belly dictate whether she wears skinny jeans and a cropped top. Sam is particularly interested in Tracey and waits patiently for her to answer. After about a minute she speaks in a broad Mancunian accent that makes me sound like Penelope Keith.

"The thing with Kyle is… He just fucking cries all the time."

We all wait for more with baited breath but that's all she says. Sam creases her eyebrows and nods slowly.

"Thanks for sharing, Tracey," she says. "Thanks for the honesty."

I look at Tracey's sad desperation and her belly and I suddenly feel so much better about being here.

Then Rachel coughs and says, "God, it's just, oh I don't know… it's like… "

She tilts her head back and runs the tips of her fingers through her hair, the light from the window pouring onto it and giving it extra shine and lustre.

"Take your time, Rach."

A loud wailing sound erupts from the crèche next door. We all sit up quickly and a tiny Asian woman in a business suit says, "It's mine," and hurries out of the room. When it's quiet again Sam says, "Go on Rach."

We all lean in her direction, the only sound the crunching of my teeth into a Hob Nob.

"I know I'm lucky. I don't work but it's the relentlessness of parenting that's so hard: the twenty-four seven of being a full-time mother, the total lack of *me* time."

"Yes, Rachel, the relentlessness of parenting is hard," says Sam glancing over at Tracey, "and if we're feeling frazzled we find it harder to be calm parents."

Hold on a minute. Me time? According to Rufus, Rachel's out nearly every night and Tabatha is in Ecocots nursery three days while Tobias is at school. By my calculations that's at least eighteen hours of latte-swilling, panini-nibbling, gospel choir-singing Me time per week.

At the end of the lesson we are told to read the first two

chapters in our file, "How to deal with Temper Tantrums" and "The Naughty Step – Punishment or Rehabilitation?" Sam tells us to apply some of the techniques we read about at home and record our findings.

There's a chill wind in the air as I push the buggy home through the streets of Whalley Range, but I feel warmed. I have a spring in my step and I am buzzing with ideas and good intentions about how I am going to be a better parent and get Bridget's behaviour on the right track. Then she'll make a shed load of friends and won't end up being a bully or getting bullied like me.

*　*　*

"Oh God, no," I mutter under my breath. "Not the Disney shop."

It's Saturday afternoon in the Trafford Centre and Bridget and I are shopping for school shoes. There are over two hundred shops and though we've only just got here it feels like we've done a ten mile trek. Billy loathes it here and refuses to come. He says the place is full of soulless people worshipping at the late night temple of consumerism and it should be blown off the face of the earth. I replied that I didn't want to hear any more talk from Irishmen about blowing up shopping centres in Manchester, thank you very much.

Bridget charges through the doors of the Disney shop and heads straight for the Bratz dolls. She grabs one of the biggest. It's almost her height, has lashings of black eye liner, a short leather mini skirt, three inch heels and an electric guitar. She holds it up.

"Please, Mum."

I fill with dread at the thought of what's coming next. It's like standing on a beach watching a tidal wave rising towards me. I close my eyes, take a deep breath and remember what it says in my parenting file.

(Be resolute not to give in to their demands in difficult situations like shopping trips.)

100

I take a deep breath.

"No, Bridget, no toys today. We're here to buy shoes."

I take the doll from her and start to walk away but she runs up behind me with Rock Chick's baby sister in her hand.

"Just a little one then. Please, Mum."

"No," I say firmly and return it to the shelf.

"What about this then?"

She picks up a small, white furry dog identical to the other two hundred she has on the top of her bedroom cupboard. I prise it from her fingers.

"No toys today, Bridget. We're here to buy shoes."

"A key ring then. Go on, Mum. It's teeny weeny."

"I said *no*."

As I'm dragging her out of the shop behind me, I feel an almighty kick at the back of my right shin.

"You are the *worst* mummy in the *world*. I *hate* you."

(When the tantrum starts, find a quiet place, hold the child on your knee facing away from you, make no eye contact and do not speak.)

I look around. I am surrounded by tens of thousands of shoppers but I spot an empty space on the bench in front of the fountain. I manage to drag her over there and position her on my knee.

"I *hate* you. I only love Daddy. You're a fat cow!" She screeches and lands a kick at the arm of the hooded teenager eating his burger on the next seat. He turns towards us, looks Bridget up and down slowly, then moves away.

(Take deep breaths, remain as calm as possible until the tantrum has subsided.)

The insults and the wailing continue for another five minutes. A group of Chinese tourists in front of the Disney shop are looking over at us. Passing shoppers stare, mothers with young children look away in sympathy and old men shake their heads in disbelief.

(When the tantrum is over, praise the first positive thing the child does.)

I am still shaking with rage as I loosen her from my grip. We stand up.

"Bridget, you're being a very good girl now, so we're going to buy some shoes."

"That's what you think, Fatty," she says and she runs back to the fountain, climbs up onto the edge and leaps in. I run after her and manage to grab her by the coat before she wades in out of my reach.

"You little fucker," I yell, "You ungrateful little brat."

She turns to me with a smirk on her face and I just can't stop myself. I hit her. I feel the smart of my hand on her bare leg and she screams out in pain.

My world stops. I am immediately overcome with remorse, trembling and on the verge of tears as I pull her out of the fountain. She is sobbing and I cradle her on my knee, oblivious of who's watching now. I tell her I'm sorry, then as I'm walking away carrying her in my arms I feel a tap on my shoulder and I look around to see the luminous orange jacket of a security guard.

"I'm afraid you're going to have to restrain yourself, madam," he says. "There's been a complaint about you hitting your daughter. I'd rather not take it to the authorities, but I think it's best if you leave."

CHAPTER 16

Billy

"Higher, Daddy!"

I push the swing. Bridget stretches her legs out and reaches for the bare branches of the beech tree in front.

"I did it," she squeals. "I touched them."

It's rained for most of February and today is the first dry day for a fortnight. It's biting cold, but Longford Park is full of parents and kids desperate for some fresh air. A girl of about eleven whizzes by on roller skates, her waist-length, ebony hair blowing behind her. She knocks against the handlebars of Will's buggy then stops and apologises. I lean in and check, but he's still fast asleep. My eye catches the slender figure of a runner in dayglo as she sails past on the path next to the playground. She's a Broadoak mum, one of Rachel's cronies: blonde, with a great body that's usually tucked into a business suit whenever I've seen her at the school. She waves over at me then picks up speed.

Jal, Danyal and Amir are making their way from the football pitch towards us, heading and kicking the ball as they go. They've been playing for over half an hour now. Jal's as fit as his boys and has had no problem keeping up with them. I managed ten minutes myself, puffing and panting like an old crock then standing in goal and scrutinising the rolls of flesh that have recently appeared around my middle. With his marathon running, his sobriety and his god, Jal is a picture of physical and mental health. I'm thinking of ending our friendship. He is just too perfect for words.

Bridget hops off the swing then together we push the buggy

over to an empty bench. When the boys arrive she follows them to the roundabout. Jal eases himself onto the bench and takes a bottle of water from his rucksack. He gulps it down, wiping his face with the sleeve of his pale blue Fred Perry hoodie, then leans forward with his elbows on his knees.

"Explain to me again why you have to go back to the police station on Monday," he says, still panting and holding the bottle out to me.

"To see if I'm going to be charged with something called a public order offence." I take a sip from the bottle and hand it back to him.

"Even though the Cleavers dropped all the charges?" he asks.

"Yes. Breach of the peace type thing. Disorderly conduct in a public place."

I look over at Bridget. The boys are pushing the roundabout and she is whizzing round fearlessly with screams of delight.

"They made a big thing in the station about how lucky I was that the Cleavers didn't press charges." I clear my throat. "On account of me having previous."

"Previous?" Jal sits up and frowns, then his eyes widen, "Surely they didn't bring that up? That was years ago."

It was early 1997 and we'd just come out of the Hacienda in the wee hours. We were as high as kites. The club was in a bad way by then, management had lost control, dealers were at war and gangs were on the make inside causing trouble. The euphoria and the happy, trippy feel of the place had soured, security were brutal and the police were no better. We stumbled onto a scene of mayhem on Whitworth Street. A young lad, no more than sixteen, was lying face down on the pavement, the back of his head a smash of blood, red black trickles spreading down the back of his shiny white track suit top. He was barely conscious, groaning and lifting his head from the ground like a wounded animal that had just been run over. Police officers were trying to surround him while at the same time trying to control a group of about twenty hysterical clubbers. They were yelling and charging at the leather-clad bouncers who stood sullen-faced by the door. The police were trying to make way for the ambulance to get through. It was pandemonium and Jal and I got caught up in the baying crowd as we tried to cross the road. I lost him and when I pushed my way back to find him he was being dragged along the pavement by the hood of his parka by a burly, ginger-haired officer.

"You stupid paki," he was shouting, "Get out of my way you stupid fucking paki."

The O'Hagan red mist descended and I went for him. I remember the stunned look on his face after I landed him a right hook and I remember the way he staggered backwards and fell against the wall. I yelled at Jal to run, which he did. I wasn't so lucky.

I was convinced I was heading for a spell inside that night as I waited in my cell, but to my amazement I was let off with a caution. Apparently there were witnesses queuing up to testify about what they had seen and heard. It wasn't long after the Stephen Lawrence episode. The stench of the trial and the Met's questionable behaviour was still in the air and the police didn't want the publicity of another racially sensitive case on their hands.

Jal puts the bottle of water back in his bag then looks up at me.

"Want me to come with you to the station?"

"No, you're grand. It's just a five-minute job. Reckon I'll get a fine at worst."

He nods slowly.

"Give me a shout if you need help with that."

I nod and zip up my jumper against the cold breeze. "I mean it."

"I know you do."

We both look away. Jal and I don't do emotion. "Rachel Cleaver is on the parenting course that Julie's doing," I say, changing the subject.

"What the fuck? She's stalking you."

I never told Jal what Rachel told me about the miscarriage that evening. I am already ashamed enough about what happened.

"Don't I know it? Rachel's pally with the teacher on the course and Julie reckons she's told her what I did to Rufus. She goes on and on about it like a fucking broken record, how we're the shame of Broadoak. I can't seem to do anything right by her these days. She's on my case the whole time."

Two women standing nearby turn around and I lower my voice. You have to be careful in Chorlton. Everyone knows each other.

"She's looking around for jobs but there's not much out there. She wants to be at home with the kids but what else can I do? The mortgage has almost doubled. I wish to God we'd got a fixed rate."

"So work's pretty slow, then?"

"I've got a few jobs on," I lie, "for now anyway." I've got nothing lined up and I'm owed thousands. He takes two apples out of his bag and offers me one. I shake my head. He bites into his and looks at me.

"If you ever need… you know… any help that way." For about a second I hate him, the big house, the fat salary, the money in the bank. I hate him for making me feel such a failure.

"We're fine," I reply, momentarily distracted by the orange trainers of a bearded man in a beany hat lifting a toddler into the baby swing. He looks about fifty and I wonder if he's the father or a very young and trendy granddad.

I sit up.

"Actually, we're not fine," I say. "Tony has cancer."

Jal stops chewing.

"No!" His jaw drops. "Fuck. What type? How bad?"

"The early stages of bowel cancer. There's hope, but bowel can be aggressive."

"Oh, man." He rubs his forehead, "He doesn't look that well, now I come to think of it."

"He's been having tests for a while."

"How's Julie taking it?"

"He hasn't told her. He only told me yesterday. He's preparing himself." Jal pulls a pained face.

"That'll hit her hard. They're so close."

Will wakes up and starts to whine. I unstrap him, lift him out of the buggy and, anticipating a post nap wail, plug in his dummy. Jal squeezes the flesh on Will's thigh.

"Looks like you're having a bit of a shit time all round, mate."

"It's not great, alright. Tony's tumour is still in the early stages though. And sure, we could always win the lottery."

I tickle Will and he starts to laugh. Jal smiles. "You could always sell him by the pound. He's massive."

"He's a fine fella, isn't he?"

We chat about United's chances in the Premiership and after a while he takes his phone out of his bag and glances at it.

"Better be getting back. The folks are coming for tea. They're off to Pakistan for a week and want to see the kids before they go."

Dusk is falling by the time we are walking back through the flower gardens. There's a lilac blossom tree there. It is small and wide and beautiful when in full bloom. The kids love to climb it. Daniyal and Amir charge at it now and make their way up its bare branches like nimble chimps. Bridget makes a valiant attempt but gets stuck; Jal hauls her up then climbs up himself next to her, beating his chest and making Tarzan noises. I take a picture with my phone of their silhouettes against the fading sunset.

On our way out we turn into the path that leads to the car park. Ahead of us are two boys, one about twelve, the other maybe fifteen or sixteen. They are both wearing black puffa jackets and sitting on chopper bikes. They are facing a young couple sitting on a bench who look like typical Chorlton teenagers. He has a wedge of hair falling down over his eyes and Elvis Costello glasses and she is wearing a short coat, with strawberry-blonde curls cascading from under a pink woollen hat. They sit frozen, the front wheels of the bikes inching threateningly towards their feet. As we approach, the bikers turn around and Jal and I exchange a look.

"Stay back," he says ushering all three kids behind the buggy. "Stay with Billy."

Before I can object he is striding on ahead. He stops in front of the bench and turns to the kids sitting on there.

"Alright, Dylan? Alright, Jane?"

They nod stiffly then he looks directly into the faces of the bikers.

"Alright, lads?" he says with the same equanimity. Nobody speaks. The older boy turns his Mohican head towards me then he turns back to the teenagers and rams his front wheel over Elvis Costello's Timberland boot and rides off. His sidekick follows, yelling something indecipherable into the evening air.

The couple get up off the bench, mutter something to Jal then hurry past us looking visibly shaken.

"Poor kids. Friends of yours?" I ask, glancing back at them as Jal walks towards us.

"Never met them before," he says with a grin. He puts a hand on Daniyal's shoulders.

"Come on, guys," he says. "Let's get a move on. Grandpa and Nana are at home. They're dying to see you."

CHAPTER 17

Julie

I write "Lesson" on the top of the page in green, then "Two" in purple, with my new multi-coloured pen. My ear is cocked, listening out for Will. There were tears earlier when we parted in the crèche but I'm alright now. Lord knows how I'll cope with the separation anxiety when I go back to work.

I lean over and extricate my third Jaffa cake from the pile of biscuits on the table in the middle of the room. Rachel is giving me an anti-sugar look so I take another. Her karma is amiss today. She's got dark red crescents under her eyes, her hair is lacking the Timote shine and her forehead is creased into a permanent frown. Somebody or something has knocked her off her pedestal of serenity and, though I'm not sure he can reach up that high, I have a feeling that somebody is Rufus. I heard his name mentioned in not very complimentary tones more than once when I was walking behind Sam and Rachel on the way in. It doesn't surprise me one bit that all is not well at number eleven Corkland. As an anti-capitalist, free-thinking member of the Broccoli Brigade she's bound to deny it, but it's obvious she only married him for his trust fund. It's also obvious that she's on the look-out for other men too, a certain Billy O'Hagan for one, if I'm not mistaken. I don't believe him when he says he's never met her and he can't stand her. I constantly think back to that time I saw them together in the kitchen at her dinner party. They were too familiar with each other. At the moment I don't care, though. If he carries on with his moody ways much longer she can bloody well have him. I've still not forgiven him for disappearing the other Saturday night and arriving home stoned at five in the morning when I was up all night with Will and his sore teeth.

The lesson gets under way and Sam asks if we've been trying out any of the new calming techniques from our file. She leans forward, sticking her neck out like the scrawniest of chickens. "How about you, Tracey?" she asks.

Tracey is the sweetest vision of motherhood today in cut off jeans, Doc Martin boots and a vest top that reveals a heart tattoo plunged with a dagger at the top of her left breast. Her eyes are bloodshot, she's chewing gum and there's a strong smell of alcohol emanating from her. I'm refusing to pass judgement on the alcohol. Who hasn't smelled like a night club carpet at the school gates the day after a heavy session? I met her boy Kyle in the crèche earlier. He's a slight child with a cherub's head of blonde curls and startling honey-coloured eyes. He's a few weeks older than Will and half his size, but that's hardly unusual. We're going to have to invest in a wider buggy for Will, or a wheelchair, if he gets any bigger.

Tracey switches her gum to the other side of her mouth and says nothing. After about a minute's silence Sam gives up and asks someone else.

Some of the mums talk about the different Time Out techniques they've tried during the week and their varying successes. A sharp intake of breath fills the room when one woman says her four year old's behaviour improved after she locked her in a darkened room for ten minutes instead of putting her on the naughty step. Rachel launches into tedious detail about Tabatha's response to controlled crying at bedtime and when it's my turn I say I've had mixed results with Bridget but I don't go into detail. It's true I've seen some improvement in her behaviour when I've shouted less and reasoned more, though she was a bit suspicious at first and mumbled something about me watching too much *Supernanny*.

Sam moves towards the whiteboard, marker pen poised. A patch of sweat lingers under the armpit of her cap-sleeved t-shirt where long, dark tufts of hair are creeping out. I wince. It's like the Black Forest under there.

"OK," she says, elongating the two letters like she means business. "Today we're going to discuss one of the most important issues any parent has to deal with. Any suggestions as to what that might be?"

Hands shoot up.

"Juggling work and child care?" "Pester power?"

"The healthy food debate?" "Crack whores on your doorstep?"

It's Tracey's first contribution in class to date and everyone turns and stares at her. She is rolling her eyes and slouching back on her chair, thumbs in her jeans pockets, eyes glazed. An awkward silence follows, interrupted by my snorts of laughter. Maybe it's the nervous tension in the room or the horrified look on one of the older ladies' faces, but I get an attack of the giggles which lasts at least five minutes. Sam humours me with a few smiles at first but as time goes on I can see she's impatient to start the class. Someone suggests putting me on the naughty step, and even though I don't find it remotely funny I roar with laughter again. I am still drying my eyes as Sam starts to speak.

"OK. Thanks, Julie. Well, the issue we're looking at today is this." She turns and in blood-red letters in the middle of the whiteboard writes the word "SMACKING", then underlines it three times.

I'm not laughing now.

I sink back into my chair, into a pit of deep shame. As the debate rages around me I hear the thwack of my hand as it landed on the back of Bridget's leg in the Trafford Centre and the look of shock and pain in her eyes. Sam writes a number of sentences on the board:

"Children who are smacked will only smack other children. Violence breeds violence."

"Smacking is often a release of parental anger. It has nothing to do with the child."

"Other punishments such as the removal of toys or TV time are more effective."

"Why should we be allowed to hit a child and not another adult?"

She then informs us she has been campaigning for years to have smacking made illegal, but a recent proposal was blocked by the government.

"Bastards," hisses Rachel.

There's a knock on the door and a short fleshy woman in purple puts her head around and beckons to Sam who then apologises and leaves the room. An uncomfortable silence follows and Rachel says, "Violence breeds violence. That's just so true." She puts her right arm over the back of her chair and sweeps one leg over the other, Kenny Everett style, and continues, "But I think it's especially important for fathers to be non-violent role models for our children too."

Then, with the vitriol I could never imagine an Earth Mother to possess, she looks me directly in the eyes and says, "Don't you agree, Julie?"

My jaw and my pencil drop. I am stunned. Did she really just say that? In front of everyone? I try to speak but nothing comes out, which is a first for me. I look down, heat rising from my toes to my neck. She's not getting away with this. The resentment that has been building up towards her has reached boiling point and the lid finally blows off my kettle. I get up slowly and make my way towards her. I stand directly in front of her, my hand trembling as I thrust my forefinger close to her face, spittle flying out of my mouth like a lawn sprinkler.

"How dare you?" I say quietly. "My Billy is ten times more of a man than your short-arsed fuckwit of a husband will ever be. He did what he did because you put our son's health in danger."

She sits up and waves her right hand in the air dismissively, like I'm an irritating fly she's batting away.

"Why don't you face it, Julie? It doesn't take much for him to lose it, does it? Get your head out of the sand. Can't you see?"

"Enough," I snap, bending down and putting my face close to hers. "Just you listen to me, Cleaver. If you ever speak like that again about Billy, I'll... I'll punch your fucking lights out."

A chair clatters in the deathly silence and someone moves behind me.

"Yeah, too right. Lamp her one."

I turn around to see Tracey staggering around the room like Liam Gallagher on a bad day, her chair on the floor behind her. She's as drunk as a skunk, waving one hand in the air and opening and shutting the other in beak-like movements.

"Talk the talk. Walk the walk. Dishtraction this and boundaries that. Well fuck the lot of you. Just fuck you, you bunch of tossers."

Then she turns and heads for the door where Sam is standing. She watches on anxiously as Tracey catches her foot on the table leg and trips, sending hot coffee and shattered Hob Nobs flying across the room.

* * *

That evening as the *Corrie* credits roll, I fill my glass from the half full bottle of Blossom Hill Rosé on the coffee table. Billy holds out his. He's sitting in his armchair and barely looks up from his novel as I pour. Endless Love it's called. He'll be lucky.

I turn the TV off, ask him to put his book down, then blurt out what happened today. He already knows about the smacking incident in the Trafford Centre as Bridget told him before I had chance to. I wondered how he'd react. Once, in the early days of our relationship, he told me about the beatings he got from the Christian Brothers at school in Ireland and he's always been vehemently against anyone lifting a finger to their kids. But he didn't get mad at me or anything. He said Bridget would test the patience of any saint and he'd been close to slapping her himself a couple of times.

He looks into the distance and says nothing when I tell him

what Rachel said but there's a glint of something in his eyes, flintiness, fear or panic, I can't pin it down. When I've finished telling him everything he puts his glass down and comes over and sits beside me, stretching his arm across the back of the sofa.

"So you won't be giving me any more gyp for losing my temper with members of the Cleaver family, then?" he says, softly.

I rub my temples.

"Oh, Billy, I'll be doing the walk of shame at that school again," I say. "Rachel will tell everyone I threatened her and Bridget will never be invited anywhere on a play date, ever. I've let her down. It was going so well and I've let her down."

I lower my head and start to sniff.

"If her behaviour gets worse she'll get expelled."

"Hold on, girl. Nobody's expelling anybody. She's a feisty little girl, that's all."

He cocoons me in his arms and it feels good. It's like we've been separated by glass these past few months, watching and circling each other but not connecting.

"The reason she will not turn out badly is because she has a wonderful mother," he says, "and you have not let anyone down. You were being loyal to your family, that's all. And Christ knows, I haven't deserved your loyalty recently, the way I've been behaving."

He kisses my forehead, "You know I love you and the kids more than anything, don't you?"

I nod and curl my face into the curve of his neck, thinking how it belongs there. We remain still like that for a while, then my thoughts turn to Tracey.

"I wonder what will happen to Kyle," I say.

He reaches over to the table for my wine glass, "His mother obviously has addiction problems," he says, taking a gulp. "Maybe she'll get another chance or he may go into care. Who knows?"

"Social Services must have forced her to do that course. She so did not want to be there."

"And who can blame her?" He puts the glass to my lips, "Being made to talk about her problems, real problems, in front of a group of middle class mums who sound like they didn't need to be there at all."

"She was well and truly plastered," I sigh.

We chat some more about how to deal with Bridget's behaviour and decide to get some more parenting books out of the library and look into online courses. I cannot go back into that class and face Rachel Cleaver.

"It's funny, really, if you think about it," I sigh.

"What is?" he says, unbuttoning my shirt.

"Threatening to punch someone's lights out in a lesson about not smacking your kids."

We look at each other and dissolve into laughter and Billy holds me tight.

"You're a mad fucker by times," he mumbles, searching for my mouth. We kiss tenderly for some time. He unbuttons further, his fingers exploring the top of my bra, searching for my nipples. I lie back and shift under him as he manoeuvres himself on top of me. My arms circle his neck and I'm pulling him closer towards me, when his phone rings on the coffee table.

"Leave it," I whisper, gripping my legs around him. He lifts his head and looks over at the phone.

"Naveed," he says, frowning, "third call in the last hour. I haven't heard from him in months."

He kisses the nape of my neck then slides off the sofa.

"Back in a minute, I promise."

When he leaves the room I start to undress. I am taking off my shirt when I hear a muffled cry from the hallway. I sit up and call out Billy's name.

He comes back into the room, slumps into the armchair and bends forward, staring down at the floor, the phone dangling in his hands. His face is grey white in the glow of the table lamp and he makes a low moaning sound.

"Jesus, no... no... no."

I sit up and cover my breasts with my hands. I can feel my heart thumping.

"It's Dad, isn't it?" I ask, weakly.

He shakes his head, his eyes never leaving the floor.

"No," he says in a barely audible whisper. "It's Jal." He looks up at me. "Jal's dead."

For one brief terrible moment I am overcome with relief.

CHAPTER 18

Billy

Claire turns off the ignition off and I look past her at the neat terrace further down on the other side of the narrow Rusholme Street. An orange glimmer of dusk hovers over the roof tops and a group of elderly men in white caps and light coloured loose clothing lingers on the pavement outside. The long road joins on to the main strip of Curry Mile where pink and green strip-lighting flickers in the windows of the cafés and restaurants and groups are gathering ready for the busy Saturday evening trade. I fumble for the door handle and yank it open.

"Business as usual up there," I say with my best grim irony. "Life goes on, eh?"

Claire says nothing and leans her head against the car window, the grey blue of her eyes bright again with tears. I place my hand on the shoulder of her emerald wool jacket where strands of her fine blonde hair have escaped from a loose pony tail.

"I won't be long," I say, softly. "You sure you'll be OK?"

She nods and places her hand fleetingly over mine. I get out and cross the road, the mint of my chewing gum mingling with the taste of the vodka shots I had earlier with Donal and Steve after the burial. A cool breeze fans my face as I walk towards the house. I am still in shock, removed from the events of the last fortnight, like I'm under water in a busy swimming pool, hearing only muffled sounds and seeing blurred shapes moving around me.

I greet the men outside on the pavement. The front door is ajar and the smell of feet and sweet curried food hit me as I enter the hallway. I slide off my shoes, add them to the pile behind the door, then notice a huge hole in the big toe of my right sock. I bend down and bunch the wool around it as an elderly man comes out of the kitchen where I can hear women's voices and the babble of children. He is carrying a dish of samosas and when I ask him for Mr. Akdar, he nods towards the door on the right and I follow him in.

The tiny living room is heaving with men of all ages dressed in shalwar kameez, a few whom I recognised from the cemetery earlier. Some are chatting above the hum of prayer and others are drinking tea and eating from the large platters of naan breads, dahls and rice dishes on the low table in the middle of the room. I recognise Jal's father immediately and move towards the floral-covered armchair where he is sitting, averting my eyes from the rows of family photographs on the wall, feeling like an intruder, a slightly drunk Paddy with a hole in his sock who does not belong. But when I look into the faces of the other men, I feel a connection. They too have the look of someone just pierced by a bullet, that paralysing look of disbelief when someone has been taken before their time, a look I recall only too well from my own father's funeral.

Our living room was full of men that evening too. I remember it was late and my mother was moving among them picking up empty glasses, bottles and ashtrays, her face pinched and pale, severe in her black high necked blouse. She had not stopped the whole day. "It's her way of coping," they whispered. Da's older brother Joe was twisted drunk and dozing off on the sofa next to me. He and Da were close and he'd wailed like a small child at the graveside. I was leafing through a pile of sympathy cards on my knee when Joe woke up suddenly.

"You're the man of the house now," he slurred, slumping on top of me. I pushed him away, knowing it was only a matter of time before I left for England.

Mr. Akdar, a white haired, bearded version of Jal, was sitting with his head slightly bowed in concentration. I could not

118

contemplate what he was going through. Normally when a Muslim dies, it's the custom for the family of the deceased to bathe and enshroud the body within hours of death. But the Akdars had to wait two weeks for the post mortem and as Jal's death was so violent his body had to be fixed up and prepared at the morgue before he was given to them for the washing. Who knows what state he was in when they finally got him.

I shake Mr. Akdar's hand and mumble something pathetic about how Jal was a wonderful friend and father. My words sound empty. They are like a broken set of tools I am carrying around, useful for nothing. He has lost a child. How can any words ever be of comfort to him?

As his deep set dark eyes linger on me, it's as if I'm talking to Jal again and for a brief moment I am happy.

"My son spoke fondly of you," he says, his use of the past tense bringing me crashing down to earth. Then he lays his head back on the armchair and closes his eyes and I know he has gone. He is somewhere else now, and I thank him and return to the hallway.

I contemplate asking one of the men by the stairs if it's possible to pay my respects to Hameeda and Mrs. Akdar. There were no women at the burial earlier and I have no idea what the custom is here at the house. I look down at my sock. At the risk of behaving like an arse, I decide not to and I am moving towards the pile of shoes when I feel a tug on my right leg. I look down to see Daniyal with both arms wrapped around my thigh.

I lift him up.

"Hello, wee man," I whisper, straightening the lopsided cap on his head.

"A bad man killed my daddy, Uncle Billy," he says with the excitement and breathlessness of someone giving news for the first time. I pull his head onto my shoulder and bury my face in his lemon-scented hair. It reminds me of Will's baby shampoo and I start to cry. Soon I feel someone prising him away from me. I wipe my face with my sleeve and look up to see Jal's sister,

Aisha, who I met in this house once in my younger days. She was a beauty and I fell for her immediately. I begged Jal for her phone number but he warned me off, knowing only too well what I was like with women back then. She is a little weightier now but she's still handsome in pale green silk, her blue black hair pulled back loosely from her face. I offer my hand and she manoeuvres hers from underneath Daniyal who then slides to the floor.

"Billy, Billy O'Hagan."

"Yes, I remember we met once."

She smiles weakly and I can see her green eyes are shot through with grief. "Jal always talked about you Billy. Always. He loved you as a brother."

I swallow and feel myself well up again.

"We were the best of friends. Would you please give my regards to Hameeda and Mr. Akdar?"

"Of course." She nods.

I bend down and hug Danyal again.

"I'll come and see you very soon," I say, then as Aisha takes his hand and they move away I feel the soft silk of her sleeve brush against my arm.

Some time later I find myself outside in the road staring at the phone number on the huge orange skip in front of me. An elderly couple are walking past arm in arm, looking anxiously at each other, and Claire is hurrying behind them towards me. I feel dizzy and breathless and I look down at my stinging knuckles. They are torn and streaming with blood where I have been smashing them into the sharp edges of the skip. I am crying and exhausted with rage but I can barely remember any of it happening.

Claire takes me by the arm and leads me towards her car.

"I swear I'll kill them," I say as she pushes me into the passenger seat. "One day when they're out, I'll hunt them down and kill them with my bare hands, no doubt about it."

She gets in the driver's seat, takes a packet of tissues from her bag and dabs my bloodied hands. Her fingers are long and delicate, her touch tender.

"Time to get hammered," she says, looking straight ahead. When she turns the key in the ignition the radio comes on and the weather forecaster tells us to expect another overcast but mainly dry day tomorrow.

CHAPTER 19

Julie

I immediately got a sinking sensation when I saw the battered looking car parked outside as I was coming in here. A large woman with a frizz of grey hair holding a pocket dog was getting in and it all came back to me, the shiny olive green exterior, the squeaky cream leather seats and the journey home from school in Miss Barton's Beetle that awful day.

As she helped me up from the bottom of the steps and led me back into the school, I squinted through the sunlight at the other kids going through the school gates with their parents and I started shouting out for Mum. Miss Barton turned to me and put her hands on my shoulders.

"You're confused, pet," she said gently, "Your mum's still in the hospital, remember?" She took me to the staffroom toilets where she gave me a towel to clean myself up and an old P.E. top from the lost property bin. When I was done she offered me a spray of her perfume. I laughed inside. I obviously still stunk to high heaven. It was Anais Anais, one of my favourites. I'd tried the tester in Boots with Mum.

Miss Barton drove me home with the car windows open and the hot leather seats burned the back of my legs. She chatted about her boyfriend. They were going on holiday to Spain in a few hours' time and she wondered how they were going to cope in the forty degree heat over there. Despite what had just happened to me I felt special. I was in my teacher's car and she was talking to me about adult stuff. When we got to the estate she came into the house. Dad was at the hospital, dishes and plates were piled high in the kitchen sink and there was a terrible stench from the cat litter tray. I remember thinking how ashamed Mum would be.

Miss Barton scribbled her number on a piece of paper and handed it to me.

"Now, Julie, it's important you give this to your father so I can talk to him about what happened," she said, which I found a bit strange, as she and I hadn't talked about it at all.

I nodded and thanked her then as soon as the front door closed I ripped the paper up into tiny pieces. Mum and Dad were never going to know. Nobody was. Ever.

I blow my nose into the tissue that Rita has just handed me. It is Friday and we are having lunch in Wetherspoons in Chorlton, or 'The Spoons' as it's affectionately known around here. It's a beautiful listed building called the Sedge Lin which looks half-church, half-beer hall and has a lovely arched beamed roof and stained glass windows. It was once a Temperance billiard hall, which is ironic as these days the winos are queuing up for pints at nine in the morning. I come here for coffee sometimes, or a cheap lunch with Billy and the kids. Billy says what he likes most about the place is the noticeable lack of hummus on the menu and absence of the Broccoli Brigade. He's right. They wouldn't be seen dead in The Spoons.

Memories of that terrible day keep flooding back since Dad told me about his cancer.

"I can't stand it," I sniff. "I'm going to lose him like I lost her. I know it's different and he's older and everything, but I can't cope with that as well as everything else."

Rita passes me a new tissue from the packet on the table in front of us then gazes at me with contact lenses of cobalt blue.

"Your dad's a fighter," she says. "He may have cancer but he's not going anywhere just yet." She puts a hand on top of mine. "We're going to help him get through this, babe. Just you wait and see."

I've been pouring out the contents of my heart to her over a chicken caesar salad and a side portion of chips for the past hour. Who would have thought I'd be offloading to this woman that I despised with a passion a few months ago? Dad's illness, Mum's death, the bullying, Jal's death, Billy's depression, Bridget's behaviour, the poor woman's had the lot. I owe her thousands in counselling fees. I couldn't have been more wrong about her. She's a compassionate woman with a heart of gold. It's hardly her fault she ended up with a couple of psychos for nieces.

Dad came round on Tuesday evening to tell me his news when Billy was out. I've known something was wrong ever since I spotted him that time at the hospital with Rita and I've never really believed his stories about a stomach ulcer causing all that weight loss. But I've been so absorbed with the kids and Billy's problems that I suppose I tucked the thought away at the back of my mind in the way I throw toys at the back of the couch when I'm too tired to put them in their proper place.

Dad sat me down in the kitchen, drummed his fingers on the table and looked at the ceiling, the floor, the window, everywhere except at my face, when he told me. He said he had stage two bowel cancer, also called Duke's B, which basically means the tumour has spread into the layer of muscle surrounding the bowel. He said there was a moderate chance of it advancing into other parts of the body.

"Think second division cancer rather than Premiership. More like Bolton Wanderers than Chelsea," he said with a forced smile.

I burst into tears.

"I'm probably going to have to have surgery," he said, his voice crumbling. "That's why I'm telling you now. I didn't want to, what with Jal and everything, but it looks like the op might be quite soon. I've got hope though, love. Tons of it. I've got to have. I'm a City fan, remember?"

When he left I went upstairs and watched him from the bedroom window. He strode along under the glow of the street lamps in the drizzle with his usual statesmanlike elegance, his shoulders back, his head held high, not a stoop in sight, even though he's over six foot and nearly seventy. Yes, he looked thinner and maybe he did walk a little slower than usual, but he certainly didn't look like a terminally ill man carrying a time bomb around. I wondered if someone somewhere had made some kind of mistake.

Afterwards, I went downstairs and started on a bottle of Gordon's gin we still had left over from Christmas. I put Sinatra on the iPod and lay back on the couch floating in mother's ruin and memories of Dad: the time we were bird-watching in Chorlton Water Park and spotted a kingfisher; the look on his face when he held Bridget for the first time; and the look on Mum's face when all four of us got asked to leave a wedding reception because he offended the vicar. I was laughing and crying at the sentimental film of my childhood playing out in my head, then just as I was getting to the last bit, when the coffin gets lowered into the ground with 'My Way' playing in the background, Will woke up wailing.

"For fuck's sake, woman," I mumbled to myself as I stumbled upstairs, "he's not dead yet."

Rita finishes her last forkful of rice and lamb curry then dabs her fuchsia lips with a napkin. We both smile and roll our eyes when a drunk on a nearby table starts singing 'Walk the Line'. Billy's been playing Johnny Cash on a loop since Jal died. He's the man for when you're hurting. And hurting we are. I well up again. God, I miss having that lovely man in our lives.

As if reading my mind, Rita says, "So how's Billy doing now? Your dad says he's still taking it all very badly."

"Oh, you know. He's drinking like a fish, staying in bed every morning now that he's got no work. But at least they didn't charge him with that public order offence the time he hit Rufus. The thing is, Rita, he refuses to talk about any of it."

"It's hard for men like him to talk about their feelings, love."

"I know, Rita, believe me, I know. His best friend died two weeks ago and he needs to grieve. I know that too, but he really isn't the easiest person to be around when he's on a downer. He's

so moody and aggressive it's not true. It's not good for the kids."
I soak a chip in mayonnaise. "It's the memorial tomorrow night.
Jal's ex, Claire, has planned it through Friends Reunited."

She raises her penciled eyebrows. One is painted higher than
the other today, giving her a permanent quizzical expression.

"It's an internet site that connects you with old school friends,"
I say. "The same one that's organising the school reunion I was
telling you about."

"Oh yes."

She fiddles with her bra strap then finishes off her Guinness.

"I read the latest in the *Manchester Evening News*," she says.
"The little bastards will probably be out in three years. Oh, those
poor boys. And his poor wife. How's she doing?"

"We've not seen her or the boys. She's in some kind of official
mourning until the baby's born. I think they're moving back to
Rusholme for good. She's due any day now. I just can't imagine."

I start to cry again and cover my face with my hands.

"Oh, Rita. He was such a good dad, but he'll never see or hold
his baby. It's so fucking unfair. He was a good, good man."

She rubs my arm then clinks my empty wine glass with her
acrylic nail.

"Fancy another?"

Without waiting for my answer she disappears to the bar.

A few weeks ago all I had on my mind were Bridget's
misdemeanors at carpet time and Rachel Cleaver slagging me off
to the other mums, but now I lie awake worrying most nights
until the early hours. Jal is dead, Billy is paralysed with
depression, Dad's got cancer and we can barely pay the mortgage.
On top of everything else, I'm going back to work in my old
department at Manchester City Council in two weeks' time,
which is enough to make me jump, along with Billy, into his big
black hole of misery. It's only maternity cover, and I know I'm
lucky to get anything in this economic climate, but I don't want
to leave the kids for four days a week with Billy, the way he is
right now. The truth is, I don't want to leave them with anyone.

I want to stay at home with them until Will starts school. Rita's stepped in and offered to help out a couple of days a week and Dad will too when he's well enough. There's no way I could afford a nursery or child minder on the pittance I'll be earning.

I eat the last of my chips and look at some of the promotional offers on the back of the menu: 'Pint and Curry night £3.99 Thursdays'; 'Free Bottle of Wine on Mother's Day'. A queue is snaking all the way down the bar and ten minutes pass before Rita totters back with our drinks.

She puts my wine on the table and sits down.

"I know you've got a lot on your plate, but there's something you should know, Julie," she says. "You know the other day when you were telling me that stuff about Mandy and Donna?"

I nod, my heartbeat quickening.

"I made a few phone calls around the family and asked if Mandy was coming back for that school reunion in May. Well she is. She's been back in contact with her mum and she's coming to see her and going to the reunion while she's here."

I swallow.

"That's me out, then."

"Why, though? Would it be such a bad thing if you went along and met up with Mandy? Jeremy Kyle and Oprah are always saying how confronting the demons from the past are your only true path to closure."

I smile. Who says daytime TV isn't educational? "I don't think so, Rita."

"Well at least think about it. What's the worst that could happen if you go?"

"Mandy shoves my head down the toilet for old time's sake? Or I have a nervous breakdown?"

"Look, I never told you this the other day as I don't like to talk too freely about family stuff, but there are a few things it might interest you to know about Mandy."

"What things?" I take a large gulp from my glass.

"Well, I only actually knew herwhen she was about three or

four. She was my cousin John's girl, not my niece as you seem to think. John left Mandy's mum Janice when the girls were little and she brought the two of them up on her own. She was drinking then. I'd see her around the estate half cut, with the two of them in tow. Then I married Mick and I moved to Fallowfield Although I saw the girls when I was working at Priory Road, I didn't see their mum for years. To be honest, I wasn't surprised when I heard Mandy and her sisters had been taken into care. Janice was no fit mother. But years later when I left Mick and moved back here, I met up with Janice again. She was a different woman then. She'd sorted herself out and was sober. She was such a mousy little thing compared to the gobby drunk she once was. She lives on her own in one of the flats by the river. We chat at the Tuesday Bingo in the Southern pub sometimes. Once she told me how she'd tried to contact her girls but they'd refused to see her. She said she's thought of them every day since they were taken into care. I felt bad for her. She's got this look in her eyes, like she's dead inside or something."

So that's where Mandy went.

She disappeared overnight at the start of my second year in Chorlton High. I never found out or cared where she'd gone. Donna got a boyfriend and left me alone afterwards, and all I knew was that it was all over and I was free at last: no more looking over my shoulder, no more handing over money, no more taunts about my weight and clothes. For the rest of my time there I made myself as invisible as possible so it didn't happen again.

I suppose I should feel pity that she went into care, but I feel very little. What happened has damaged me far too much for that.

Rita looks at me closely.

"I can't understand why you've never told your dad about what happened, Julie. It might help."

"No," I say, slightly panicked and scrutinising her face. "You haven't said anything, have you?"

"No."

128

"I don't want to unearth it all now, with him in his condition. He's an old man. There's no point."

She takes a tooth pick from the small bowl on the table and rummages between her bottom molars.

"You're probably right, but I'll be honest with you love, you still seem a bit messed up by it. It did happen twenty odd years ago. I think you need to talk to someone."

"I'm taking to you, aren't I?"

"You know what I mean."

She thinks I'm pathetic, that I'm obsessing about a trivial spat of bullying that happened years ago. But she doesn't know the whole story. How can I tell her? She'll tell Dad.

I think about him standing at the back door that evening, calling out my name again and again. I can still hear the desperation in his voice. And all the while I was hiding in the sweltering shed ten yards away, rocking back and forth and hugging my knees.

"Eat shit pies while Mummy dies."

The smell was still there, sharp and pungent and making me gag, despite all my efforts to scrub it away in the bath and dousing myself with every perfume I could lay my hands on.

I can smell it now sometimes. Maybe it'll never go away.

CHAPTER 20

Billy

In the nineties, the Southern pub was Irish, run by Galway Mike. The fifties style juke box downstairs was packed with proper rebel songs, and a Bodhrán made and signed by prisoners of Long Kesh hung behind the bar. Mike wasn't averse to lock-ins and if we weren't clubbing in town, myself, Jal, Claire and the old crowd would drink and play pool here until the early hours then head to my flat in Nell Lane to carry on the party. They were great times. We were regulars at the comedy nights in this upstairs room too. Jal always stood at the back watching the audience reaction. I can see him now, propping up the bar, cradling his pint, discerning in his laughter. I look around. The room could do with a lick of paint, but it was the only venue we could get locally at such short notice.

I take the CDs from the box and stack them on a table by the door. I pick one up and look at it again. The cover is red with a United logo in the corner and in the centre are the words "In memory of Jalal Akbar, our wonderful friend, 1969-2008." When Claire set up the memorial page she asked for songs that reminded us of him and she made a compilation. Mine was The Happy Mondays' 'Kinky Afro'. I've just asked the girl behind the bar to play it and the memory clogs in my throat.

The pair of us were decorating offices in Stretford. We must have been twenty-one or two. We had this Friday thing. If we were on a job together we'd finish up about four, have a few shots of vodka, take a tab or two, put a tune on the ghetto blaster and have a dance. That particular time we were caught by Fat Tony, our supervisor, a bigoted lump from Wigan who dubbed us Paddistani because we always hung around together.

"What the fuck?" he said, waddling into the room and watching us leap around the paint pots and ladders, bog-eyed. Needless to say, we got the boot.

Claire and Julie have just finished placing vases of lilies and carnations on every table. Claire told me earlier he gave her lilies every year on her birthday. She moves to a table where she starts attaching cables to a lap top. A projector screen covers the wall opposite. She is tiny. She still has the girlish figure she had in her twenties and she's wearing a gold lamé dress, black PVC boots and has blazing red lips. No funereal black for her.

"I want a celebration of his life," she said when we first talked about a memorial. "I want to give him a party he would have liked to have been at."

It was the day of his burial, the day after my visit to Rusholme. We were drinking shots and beers in one of the fashionable bars in Chorlton. My hands were still stinging after their collision with the skip and we were well on our way to drunken oblivion.

"You know what the worst thing is, Billy?" she said, brushing a wisp of blonde hair back from her eyes. "When I last spoke to him we argued. We met in a cafe in town so I could give him some CDs he'd left at my flat. I called him a hypocritical bastard and he walked out. That was the last I ever saw of him." Her voice quivered, "I never made my peace with him and that hurts like you wouldn't believe."

I nodded. I knew that pain. I'd felt it acutely in the days after Da's death. The thought that I could never say sorry after we argued felt like a shard of glass in my heart and it's never gone away.

I put my arm on hers. "You were the love of his life. There's no doubt about that, and you know what? It really pisses me off you weren't allowed anywhere near the burial. You were together for twelve years, for Christ's sake. You should have had the chance to say goodbye too."

She threw her head back and downed another Sambuca shot.

"I never expected to be asked, Billy. No women allowed. It's their tradition. Plus I was his white whore, remember? His dirty little secret they chose to ignore all those years. In the end he made his own choice, though. He chose their way, he chose Islam and he chose her."

"He still loved you. I know he did."

She tried to swallow her tears but they came in floods. It wrenched at me to see her like that. I wanted to reach over and hold her and be held by her.

"How's Jason?" I asked.

She shrugged her shoulders and wiped her eyes. "Oh you know. Same old. Still hammering the weed but not getting off his arse to earn the money to pay for it. Still in the pub every night playing the celeb and getting all his drinks bought for him."

Jason Jones is the ex-bass guitarist of a well known Madchester band and a tosser of the highest order. I'd like to think Claire's judgement was impaired by all the drugs she was doing when they first met, but they're still together years later. Her fashion buyer's salary keeps him in a nice lifestyle, a skunk habit and a plush city centre loft apartment.

"Forever the rock star, eh?"

"Yep. I'm still living with Peter Pan. He won't commit. I don't give a fuck about a ring on my finger but he's still dragging his heels when it comes to having kids."

She gave a cynical laugh.

"I'm thirty-eight in a month's time and what have I got to show for it? Where the fuck did I go wrong?"

I sighed. Didn't I know that feeling only too well?

Julie comes back from the bar. She places Claire's vodka next to the laptop and hands me my pint of Guinness. We both pull up a chair to the table. Julie's making a huge effort with Claire tonight and I'm grateful. They never got on when the four of us hung around together. Too different, I suppose. Julie, grounded and feisty, was always wary of Claire's 'arty farty' ways, as she called them, the bizarre clothes, the drug-taking and the air of other worldliness.

"How many are you expecting?" Julie asks. Claire turns the machine round to check the cables and, without looking up, says, "About fifty from the memorial page, but others could turn up through word of mouth."

I lean over and slide the 'on' button on the computer. Claire laughs. "Thanks," she says.

"Some of those messages on the memorial page are well over the top," I say, helping her to get the screen in focus. "Such a public outpouring of grief. It's so bloody Lady Di. Some of them barely knew him."

Julie leans over and arranges some of the lilies in the vase.

"Oh, I don't know. His family might look at that page and see all the lovely things people have said about him and find comfort in it."

I think of the quiet dignity with which Hameeda and the Akdahs have handled the police and the press intrusion.

"I agree, Billy," says Claire. "There's definitely an element of grief tourism there." She looks at me.

"He would have hated it, wouldn't he?"

Julie clears her throat then rummages in her bag. She takes her phone out and looks at it for the umpteenth time.

"She'll be fine," I snap.

Tony and Rita are babysitting. Bridget had a stomach bug earlier today and Julie's convinced Will is going to be next. Ever since the measles episode she's become totally neurotic about the kids' health. "Kids," she sighs and puts her phone away. "They say the worrying never stops even when they're older."

A twinge of pain crosses Claire's face and I feel bad for her. Then a flash of light makes us all turn to the wall opposite where Jal has suddenly appeared, standing in a Morrissey pose outside Salford Lads' club wearing the khaki parka he never took off. His hair, long and unruly, is tucked into the hood and he's leaning against the green railings, drooping flowers in one hand, a bottle of lager in the other, a cheeky grin on his face. Claire smiles at him with a lover's gaze, Julie starts to cry and I feel numb. My grief alternates between rage and desolation to periods when I feeling nothing at all. Many of the people coming tonight will remember him as that fun-loving wild man up there. Some won't have been in contact with him since his conversion. He distanced himself from his old world and his past. They never knew the sober, Mosque-going family man he later became. I was privileged to have known both.

Five weeks on from his death I see him everywhere: kicking a football in Longford Park, sitting at our table at the pub quiz. I walked past the house in Chorltonville the other evening. Hameeda and the kids are living in Rusholme now and the house stood there like a bombed-out shell, empty of any sign of the vibrant family that had filled it such a short time ago. A punctured football lay under a bush in the corner of the lawn and the sight of it made me break down and weep. When I think about the mindlessness and injustice of it all I want to lash out and destroy everything around me.

A couple of hours later the room is thronging with friends I haven't seen in years. They've acquired thicker waists, bald heads and wrinkles. Now they're showing off photos of their kids rather than holiday snaps of raves in Ibiza. Declan has made it up from London. We cried and hugged when he arrived. The last time I saw him was at his mother's funeral in Bury two years ago. He's done well for himself in the Smoke. He's head of I.T. at an investment bank and lives in Chelsea with his Argentinean wife and baby son. He has dreams of coming back up north, though I reckon it'd be Cheshire rather than Chorlton. I'm delighted to see that a few of Jal's younger cousins have made it, but many of his immediate family are still in mourning. At around ten, Julie gets a call from Tony. Both Will and Bridget have woken up so she says her goodbyes and leaves.

Steve, Declan, Donal, Naveed and I are sitting around a long table by the entrance. Naveed is a childhood friend of Jal's from

Rusholme. In the days when our Saturday afternoons weren't taken up with family commitments we were all regulars in the Stretford End together, Declan coming up for matches when he could. We left a wreath of red roses at the graveside, a scarf and a match programme signed with goodbye messages. Initially we talk about anything but him, ignoring the empty chair beside us and the pint not ordered. Steve looks over at Claire, who is chatting to a group of women nearby, then turns to me.

"She looks good. How's she taking it?"

"So, so."

Steve's a paediatrician at Hope Hospital in Salford and recently divorced. He and Claire dated for a while when she and Jal split up. When Jal found out he refused to talk to Steve for months afterwards, even though he was engaged to Hameeda at the time. Steve's eyes linger on Claire.

"She still with Jason Jones?" I nod.

"Unfortunately."

"How are Hameeda and the boys for money?" asks Declan.

"Fine, as far as I know," I reply, thinking back to the day in the park when Jal asked me the same question. "Jal had life insurance and her parents are very wealthy."

I tear at the edge of a beer mat.

"His sister texted today to say Hameeda had the baby yesterday. Eight pounds two. Jahida, they're calling her."

A silence follows then Declan slams his hand on the table.

"I just can't get my head round it," he says. "He was out buying a pint of milk, for Christ's sake."

Six weeks ago, just before ten o'clock on a Sunday evening, Jal parked his six month old Range Rover outside a late night supermarket in a quiet Rusholme street around the corner from his parents' house. He'd just collected them from the airport after their holiday in Pakistan. He dropped them off at the family home then drove to the shop three streets away to buy milk and bread for them for the next morning. As he was getting out of the car, two seventeen year olds jumped him from behind and demanded the keys. After a short struggle he threw them in defiance into the air across the unlit street. High on crack cocaine, they dragged him onto the road, stabbed him repeatedly in the chest and face and left him to die. They were captured on CCTV and caught within days.

Steve turns to Naveed.

"Do we know anything more about them, Nav?

The papers didn't say much."

Naveed sits up, his short fat arms folded across the huge mound of his belly. He's gone from stocky to balloon-like in recent years.

"They're both from decent families in the area, but very poor. They left school with no qualifications. Rumour has it they got mixed up with a bad crowd in Moss Side and owed drug money. The families are devastated. The local Imam's round there counselling them."

I think about Danyal and Amir and wonder who's counselling them. We talk about the trial, but there are no 'lock them up and throw away the key or hang 'em' comments. We're all too left-leaning and liberal for that. We say nothing, drink some more and simmer in our shock and rage.

I've wondered what his last thoughts were. Brown or white, sliced or unsliced, skimmed or full fat? Or did he have time to think about Hameeda and the boys? He must have been terrified lying in that gutter waiting to die. Why didn't he just walk there? It wasn't raining that night and there were no heavy bags to carry. Why didn't he stop somewhere on the way back from the airport? Why did he have to play the hero and throw the keys? I want someone to tell me why.

Sometime later, Steve, Claire, Donal and I find ourselves are in the alleyway behind the pub. For once, as Steve takes the packet of white powder from the pocket in his wallet next to his doctor's I.D., I hesitate. The irony is not lost on us about the way our friend died and what we're doing now. But fuck it. We do it anyway.

There are speeches, some affectionate, some witty and well-prepared. Mine is anecdotal and rushed. Claire and some of the women make a half-hearted attempt to dance and Steve and I slip outside for a couple more lines. At times the vibe is more like a birthday celebration than a memorial, then I see someone crying and realise grief is leaking out in small pools around the room. By midnight most of the guests have hurried home to babysitters. But Claire, Declan, Steve and a few more of the hardcore among us decide to party on at the eighties night at the Irish club. It's just after midnight when we get there and the heat and the warm crush of bodies inside the club hit me after the chill night air. The queue is three deep at the bar, men are lining the edge of the dance floor cradling pints, and groups of women are dancing or sitting round tables chatting.

I spot her as I'm finally getting served at the end of the bar near the dance floor. I pass the round of drinks to Declan who goes into the Lounge Bar with the others, then I find a space near a table and lean back against the wall and watch her. I am still lifted by the drugs and feeling fully charged. She is wearing sharp heeled boots and is a head taller than anyone else out there dancing. She has seen me and she sways to Blondie's 'Rapture', her shoulders thrust backwards, hips grinding to the beat, her breasts shifting under the short gossamer dress.

I wait, knowing Rachel will come over to me, knowing I should turn away, walk out of the door and go home, but I can't. I have already passed over to another world tonight. I have lost control of the reins and I am riding into an abyss.

She stands inches from my face. Like an animal, she can smell my weakness. I can see from her eyes that she is high too. It's just like the old days.

"I heard about your friend Jal. It must be dreadful to lose a good friend and soulmate like that."

She runs a hand along my arm and I push her away.

"What do you know?"

"I know you more than you think."

"You know nothing about me."

"I do. I also know I should keep away from you, but I can't. I've never been able to."

She crushes her body against mine and whispers, "Does this make you feel better? Don't you remember how good we were together?"

The touch of her taut nipples against my chest makes me weaken.

"No one needs to know," she says. "Rufus has gone. It's over."

Her eyes still burning into mine, she moves backwards on to the dance floor and continues to dance to the Smiths tune that is now playing.

I am suddenly distracted by the sight of Claire behind her to the right. She is dancing like there's no one else in the room and I can't stop watching her. Her eyes are closed and her hair falls around her face as she twists and turns in her golden dress like a flame. She is mouthing the words,

"Oh, there is a light and it never goes out. There is a light and it never goes out."

* * *

It's two thirty a.m. on High Lane and revellers from the club are making their way home. I shiver in the sharp night air and I look up at the clear sky. I wonder if he's out there somewhere, then the realisation hits me like a falling meteorite. He's gone for good.

A cab approaches on the other side of the road and I flag it down.

She turns to me, her coat collar falling open around her neck revealing a slither of skin, silver white in the moonlight.

"This is me, then," she says.

The taxi has turned around and is now in front of us, the engine idling. We lock eyes then I move towards her and unbutton her coat. I brush my fingers slowly down the curve of her neck and press my lips there. I taste her soft flesh, then hesitate, drawing my head up and stepping backwards.

"I'm so fucked," I say, covering my face with my hands.

She moves towards me, prises them away, then pulls my face close to hers, her mouth searching out mine. She finds me and we fall on each other with a hunger I haven't known for some time. Then I follow her into the back of the taxi, in out of the cold.

CHAPTER 21

Julie

I heave the shopping bags onto the kitchen table. It is littered with scraps of paper and food, glitter, felt tip pens without tops and patches of drying glue. Dishes spill out of the sink and the basket of dirty laundry lies untouched on the worktop, exactly where I put it this morning when I left for work.

I remove my new Primarni jacket, kick off my heels and send them flying across the room. One of them lands in the hallway where a startled Will is crawling out of the living room towards me. He sits up when he sees me and gives me a beaming smile that makes my anger momentarily evaporate.

I scoop him up and press his soft cheeks against mine.

"God, I've missed you," I whisper, smothering him with kisses.

I go into the living room where Billy and Bridget are sitting on the couch watching *Horrid Henry*. Dressing up costumes litter the floor, Bridget's extended family of cuddly toys have emigrated from her room and there's a combined stench of full nappies and McDonalds' Happy Meals. With Will on my hip, I walk over and throw open a window.

Bridget doesn't look up from the screen and Billy makes a slight sideways movement with his head which I interpret as a greeting. Unshaven, he lies slumped across the couch in a crumpled black t-shirt and jeans. His face is slightly flushed and I wonder if he's been drinking. An open book lies face down on the floor in front of him beside two McDonalds boxes.

I pick them up.

"Bridget, you know you're not allowed to watch that," I say, rubbing the top of her head. She pushes me out of the way with one arm and a silence follows.

I turn to Billy.

"She hardly needs that little shit for a role model, now does she?" I hiss.

Will, no doubt tuning into my mood of mounting despair, starts to wail.

"Has he been fed?" I ask.

Billy gets up.

"He has, but it was a while ago. He might want more." He holds his arms out. "Give him to me, I'll do it."

He fixes his gaze on Will without looking at me. He seems to have forgotten how. Sadness, grief, despondency, desperation, you name it, it's all there in his eyes.

"I'll feed him," I snap, heading towards the door as the theme tune of *Horrid Henry* starts up. I turn to see Bridget leaping around the room playing air guitar.

"Na na na na na," she sings, pointing at Will and yelling, "I hate you, Perfect Peter."

Billy and I once might have exchanged a smile but now we both now look at her, exhausted. I am still raging as I return to the kitchen. I place Will in his high chair, give him his dummy and a Peppa Pig toy, then I take the kitchen scissors to the McDonalds boxes, slashing them apart like a frenzied axe murderer. I try and stuff the pieces into an already overflowing bin but they won't fit, so I throw them onto the floor. Fighting back tears I press my forehead against the glass of the rain-splattered back door.

Yes, he's grieving; yes, he'd depressed, but he's not got a note from the doctor to say he can lounge about all day neglecting his kids while I'm in that godforsaken council office eight fucking hours a day. I hate, hate, every mind-numbing data recording minute of it. But what I hate most is being away from the kids, especially on the days I leave them with him, because he just can't cope.

141

This morning, after dropping off Bridget at Broadoak, I was waiting in the queue of cars coming out of the car park. It was a beautiful, light-filled April day, with a promise of spring sunshine to come. I was checking out my swollen, sleep-deprived eyes in the rear view mirror when I saw a group of mums chatting on the pavement behind me. Envy started to seep from every pore. I was like them not that long ago, happily rocking my buggy, the whole day with the kids stretching before me. Life was lovely and simple then. Our roles were clearly defined and Billy and I were happy in them. We've never had much money but we did without so I could stay at home with the kids: no foreign holidays, supermarket clothes, a ten year old car. We were content, but now my wage is barely paying the mortgage, never mind the food bill, and if interest rates get any higher we'll lose the house.

I heat up a jar of food in the microwave for Will, load the washing machine, then I sit down next to him and start to feed him. I am exhausted and I can barely find his mouth with the spoon. Not long afterwards, Billy comes in and starts on the washing up. Without looking up I ask, "What happened to the washing?" He looks over at the basket.

"Sorry. I forgot."

"How could you forget? It was staring you in the face on the worktop all day. She's got no clean uniform for school tomorrow now."

"Sorry. Like I said, I forgot."

"You didn't forget to read your bloody book, though."

He says nothing. I've been treading carefully around him for so long but now I've had enough. My simmering anger and frustration are about to explode.

"Look, Billy, I know you're still grieving but I need you to think about us more. About me and the kids. I need you to... "

"How many more times?" he growls. "I said I'm sorry. I had a bad day today, that's all."

I leap to my feet, the jar and spoon still in my hands.

"*You* had a bad day?" I yell.

He slams a colander onto the worktop and turns towards me.

"For fuck's sake," he says, "will you get off my back, you patronising bitch?"

I explode.

"What the fuck, Billy? Why am I doing it all? When you came home from work, you came home five days a week to a cooked dinner, a tidy house and washed and ironed clothes. But on the *two* days you're looking after the kids I have to return to this... this pile of shit."

"Cooked dinner, my arse. I came home to an awful lot of takeaways."

"Well at least you come home to *something*. But go on, you haven't answered my question. Why am I doing it all?"

"You are not doing it all."

"I fucking well *am* doing it all."

He throws down the tea cloth he's holding.

"Oh for Christ's sake, just listen to yourself, the weight of the world on your shoulders, just because you're doing a few days' work at last. Now you know how easy you've had it all this time."

"Easy? So raising two kids, day in day out, is easy, being married to a useless bastard like you? Well if it's so fucking easy how come you can't manage it?"

He moves towards me, jabbing his forefinger threateningly close to my face.

"Do you think for one minute I want to be out of work, to be hanging round the park and in baby groups being ignored by the stuck up bitches of Chorlton? Do you?"

I shrug my shoulders.

"Seems to me you don't mind the company of a lot of those stuck up bitches." I lower my voice, "I think you'd love a bit of yummy mummy." I cock my head to one side, "A bit of Rachel Cleaver, perhaps?"

He turns and faces the window, gripping the edge of the worktop, his shoulders rising and falling. Will starts to bang his toy on the side of his high chair and I take it from him.

"If you hate being with your kids so much then get a job, Billy. Any fucking job."

He swings around, rushes at me and pushes me up against the back door. I drop the bowl and spoon in my hand and he pins me there, my arms above my head, his face inches from mine. I am filled with terror, the way I felt in Priory Road. It all comes back to me. I stare at his face that is full of untethered loathing, a face I no longer recognise.

Will starts to wail.

"There are no jobs out there. Don't you understand? There are no jobs, you stupid cunt."

He lets go of one arm and slowly but surely raises a clenched fist. I hear myself gasp.

"Daddy, stop it."

We both turn to see Bridget clinging onto the edge of the kitchen door. She is trembling, moving one leg back and forth in agitation, her eyes wide with fear. He releases his grip on me.

"Bridget, sweetheart," he says, his voice anxious and cajoling. He steps towards her but before he can get anywhere near her I've grabbed Will from his high chair and I'm dragging Bridget behind me out into the hall then upstairs.

"Bath time," I say in a singsong voice, trying to normalise my fear. I hurry them into Bridget's bedroom, shut the door behind us then huddle on the bed with both of them.

"Let's play hide and seek with Daddy," I whisper in a cracked voice. I am shaking and taking deep breaths. Bridget is whimpering with her thumb in her mouth. I hear the front door slam and I slump back against the wall in relief.

Half an hour later the three of us are standing outside Dad's front door in the rain with a large suitcase in tow.

CHAPTER 22

Billy

I watch her from the doorway of the living room as she smooths the ruby lipstick carefully around her mouth in the hall mirror. The front door is ajar and she is waiting for a taxi to take her to her school reunion. It's a warm June night that cries out for a beer garden, chilled white wine and cold beers. I'd like nothing more. Just the two of us, but she'd laugh in my face if I suggested it.

It's been seven long weeks since I moved out. I love the days I have the kids while Julie's working, but I can't relax when I come over in the evenings. I am an unwelcome guest in my own house and the tension is palpable. I circle silently around the wife I still love until the kids are in bed, but she treats me no better than an irritating fly. At about eight I return to Steve's chrome filled bachelor flat in Didsbury, where I read a lot and flick through the channels on his forty inch plasma. He's not around much as he does shifts at the hospital and often sleeps over. His divorce papers came through the other day. He's relieved and glad to be single again, but then he has no kids. I'm terrified of ending up like him, approaching forty, living in hollow rooms and trawling bars for sex. I've done enough of that in my time. I want my family back. I yearn for their clutter, for the sound of Will's hungry cries and Bridget's chatter. I long to pull my kids onto my knee and kiss them whenever I want to, to watch *Corrie* with Julie's head on my shoulder, to empty the kitchen bin last thing in the evening.

Regret, longing and antidepressants keep me awake for most

of the night in Steve's spare room, and when I finally do get to sleep I wake up a few hours later listening for the sound of my wife's breathing then I reach out in the bed to the place where her shape should be.

The morning after she walked out I heard the key in the lock downstairs, then I heard her moving around. She eventually came up to the bedroom where I lay crushed by a brutal hangover. I'd spent the rest of the previous evening in the Spread Eagle drinking with Lee Coppull and his mates, for once refusing his invitation to party on elsewhere. Christ, I am such a model of restraint. Without looking at me, Julie took a holdhall from the top of the wardrobe, threw a few things in it from the chest of drawers, then stood at the foot of the bed. Her hair was dishevelled, dark red shadows hovered under her eyes and she was ghostly pale. I froze and filled with fear as I knew what was coming. She spoke tonelessly, like she was giving a prepared speech at a business meeting.

"You were about to hit me, Billy," she said. "You were about to hit me in front of the kids. I know you've just lost Jal and you're grieving but I can't forgive you for that. I just can't take your moods any more and I want you to leave. I'd go myself but I can't stay at Dad's in his condition. It's not fair on him and it's not fair on the kids."

I pleaded and said I was sorry. I said I'd never hurt her, that I had problems and I needed help. I even cried. But I could see something had changed by the way she looked at me. She'd closed herself off, the door was shut and I was no longer welcome. She stood stock-still as I spoke, her arms folded, her features expressionless. When I'd finished she moved towards the door.

"No one bullies me," she said. "Not you, not anyone."

Then she left the room like an icy gust of wind had swept through it.

I knew it would happen one day. It was just a matter of time before she saw the true side of me, the monster I've tried to keep

146

caged and hidden for so long. Would I have hit her? The thought stabs me with shame. I hope to God not, but my past form indicates differently. I thought Rachel Cleaver might be the one to destroy us but it looks like I've managed to do it all by myself. I've never really felt worthy of Julie. It was too good to be true. A happy marriage was always too much to ask. Damaged types like me always destroy what's good in our lives. We all know it'll happen sooner or later. And that isn't self-pity talking. It's fact. People like me simply don't do happy endings.

I step into the hallway.

"Nice dress," I say tentatively.

"Charity shop," she replies, not moving from the mirror.

I wince. Is that what it's come to? Secondhand clothes for a school reunion? She puts the lipstick in her bag and takes her jacket from the banister. Charity shop or not she looks beautiful. Auburn pre-raphaelite curls tumble onto green velvet and an emerald necklace nestles in her cleavage. The dress hugs her figure. She's lost weight since I moved out. We both have. The taxi horn sounds outside. She picks up her bag and keys and shouts goodbye to Bridget.

"Will shouldn't wake up. I'll be back about twelve."

I listen out for a kind word or a mellowing in her voice but she's already disappeared out of the door. I return to the living room and to Bridget. It's strange how self-conscious and nervous I feel around Julie now. She can break me or elate me with a look or a word. It's like when we were first together. No other woman has ever had that power over me before or since.

When we met in 2000, I was in a relatively stable period of my life. I was only drinking at weekends, cutting out the charlie and speed and doing a few tabs here and there. I was also in a relationship that had lasted four whole months. She was an actress called Debbie, an Audrey Hepburn lookalike with a taut dancer's body, an upcoming role in *The Bill* and a tendency for melodrama that was starting to grate.

It was Indie night at The Carlton, a dusty former cricket club in Whalley Range where you got free tequila shots on the door, danced under cobwebs and drank from cracked glasses.

I was queuing for the cloakroom at the top of the stairs at the end of the night. Julie was in front of me with a friend and Debbie was chatting to friends down in the foyer.

I'd noticed her earlier in a pink mini skirt bouncing around to The Pogues' 'Sally McLennan'. Bounce, jump, leap, vault are all word that come to mind to describe the way Julie dances. She throws herself around like a bucking bull with commendable energy and enthusiasm but with little reference to rhythm or beat. That night as I watched her I was touched by something about her, something unselfconscious and childlike, something that warmed me and made my lips curl into an involuntary smile. She also had incredible breasts, large but firm-looking.

She dug around in her bag for her ticket as the cloakroom attendant looked on impatiently.

"Hurry up, Julie," urged the friend, a pleasant looking blonde.

"Yeah, come on ginger," I said. I stepped up a stair with a wink, ready to sharpen the killer brogue if need be. She turned round, her lovely blue-grey eyes ablaze.

"Who the fuck are you calling ginger?" she growled, giving me a prod in the chest that caught me off balance and sent me flying backwards. Down the stairs I went. I heard gasps as a sea of people opened up behind me and I rolled and bumped until I crashed at the bottom, ripping my chin on the iron banister as I landed.

Dazed, I opened my eyes to see Debbie and the redhead leaning over me.

"Oh my poor, sweet darling, you're bleeding." Debbie stroked my cheek theatrically, glancing around at the audience that had gathered. The redhead was wide-eyed and serious one minute, struggling not to laugh the next.

"I'm so sorry," she said as I tried hard to avert my eyes from her magnificent cleavage in case she gave me another thump.

Later in the A and E waiting room at St Mary's, I dumped

Debbie, her Florence Nightingale role having tipped me over the edge. She cried and pleaded and gave a melodramatic performance worthy of the Old Vic.

"You selfish, fucked up bastard," she yelled, slapping my cheek. "At least you'll get an anaesthetic for your pain." I winced then I laughed. I really did. Jesus, I was a brutal piece of work back then.

The nurse had difficulties sewing up my chin.

"Keep your face straight", she said, "I'll have you in stitches if it kills me."

But I couldn't stop smiling at the thought of the sassy redhead with the button nose.

The hair, the half-mocking smile, the cleavage, they all kept appearing uninvited in my thoughts. She'd floored me in more ways than one. I was thirty years old, I didn't do crushes and the L word had never crossed my lips. I'd barely spoken to the woman and she had, after all, committed an act of violence against me, but I just couldn't get her out of my head. Without explaining why, I dragged Jal and Claire back to The Carlton Club every Thursday for the next two months in the hope of seeing her again. No luck. I had no phone number, just a memory, a first name and a small scar on my chin. That was it. I resigned myself to never seeing her again.

Then one Saturday morning she appeared to me in the frozen food aisle in Safeway in Chorlton. As I lifted my head out of the freezer she was standing there with a bag of oven chips in her hands. Reddening like a schoolboy and my heart pounding, I lifted the bag in mine.

"Peas," I said.

Peas? After all the silver tongued rhetoric I'd delivered to women in my time, now, when it mattered, I was reduced to a monosyllabic vegetable.

"Chips," she grinned in return, pointing to her own bag, and I was delighted to see the colour rise in her face too.

"How's your chin?" she asked.

"Grand," I smiled. "Well it is now, anyway."

"Sorry. I can't believe I did that."

She looked coyly down at the floor and I wanted to kiss her there and then.

"No harm done," I said, "honestly."

Minutes later I watched her scribble down my number, taking in the creamy skin, the freckles, the curves of her neck and, of course, the breasts.

Ours was a real courtship. We went on dates and walks and she refused to sleep with me for two tortuous months. By the time she did stay over I had fallen deeply in love with her and she never left. We married quietly at the registry office in Manchester Town Hall the following year and Bridget arrived in 2002. I was taken aback by the speed with which it all happened, but it felt right. I was adrift before I met her, an unmoored boat on a dangerous sea. She and the kids gave me the love and stability I never imagined I deserved and they anchored me in happiness.

I stand at the window with Bridget, who waves as Julie gets into the taxi, then we watch it drive off. Afterwards I turn on the *X Factor* and we cuddle together on the sofa. I pick up my book. I'm half way through a Raymond Carver short story where a group of friends are enjoying a booze-fuelled evening and talking about the nature of love. I thought I might learn something but I put it down. The story is soaked with gin and tonics and cold American beer and the urge for a drink starts to sings to me like a siren. But the cupboards are empty. I've made sure of that. Not a drop has touched my lips since I started on the antidepressants. I'm feeling better in some ways but the hangovers have now been replaced by the side effects: agitation, dizziness, nausea and dry mouth. I've certainly taken better drugs in my time.

I pick up my book again and try to concentrate but I keep thinking about the sight of Julie's black-stockinged legs and heels climbing into the back of that taxi. I start to panic. She could technically consider herself single. She could have a fling. You hear about it happening all the time at these reunions. I imagine the dress sliding from her shoulders, a mouth moving down her neck towards her breasts. I try to block the image out and concentrate on the dog jumping through hoops on the TV screen. She spent so long getting ready. She could hook up with anyone, an ex or even an old friend.

Just like I did.

I think of Claire's small naked body curled beside me on the Indian rug of her living room, our clothes scattered everywhere, the Manchester skyline looming outside the huge glass windows. I was truly lost when I got into the cab with her that night. We both were. Stoned and consumed by grief, we fucked in desperation on her floor as soon as we got in the door. It came from somewhere deep and visceral, a raw and brutal need rather than sexual pleasure. We both knew it wasn't each other we wanted. It was a fucked up need to be close to Jal through each other. When she was in the bathroom I got dressed quickly and left. I skulked home through the empty streets like an urban fox, feeling hollow and full of self-loathing, the way I'd felt so many times in the past. I was self-medicating again, losing myself in sex and drugs to ease the pain, this time the pain of Jal's loss. I knew Claire would find it hard to get over his death. As I was about to leave the flat I looked back and noticed that all around the open plan room were bottles and vases filled with lilies.

CHAPTER 23

Julie

She was standing beside the curtain in her yellow pyjamas, clutching her pink teddy, when I left. Billy had his hands on her shoulders and she raised her hand in a shy wave. She cried earlier when I said I was going out. She's been doing it a lot since he left even though he comes round most evenings and only leaves when she's asleep.

The moment Billy raised his hand to me, something moved deep in my core like those plates at the bottom of the sea before a tsunami. Waves of strength rose up inside me and I knew then it was the end of so many things. I would no longer put up with his moods or accept his refusal to confront his problems. I would no longer carry him and be the one to do everything at home and work as well. I know he's grieving and he's out of work but I'm juggling a job, the kids and trying to do my best for Dad. When I needed strong arms to hold me up he offered me a fist in the face. I surprised myself when I found the strength to say "enough" and asked him to leave.

What happened between us has been the driving force that led me here to the reunion tonight. I am strong enough to confront Mandy Sherburn now. In the words of Rita and Jeremy Kyle, it really is necessary to confront the demons of the past in order to move on. I'd really like to think I might finally have found my backbone, but right now I feel like jelly. My stomach is doing somersaults and a grim nausea is swilling round my insides.

High-pitched laughter floats up from a group of women coming up the stairway behind me. I stop and grip the brass banister which is cool under my hot, sticky palms. My breathing quickens and to steady myself I try to concentrate on the words of the Madonna song coming from the function room above. I pretend to rummage in my bag for something and let the women, none of whom I recognise, pass. I look up. It's probably only about twenty or so steps to the top but it seems like the tip of Everest to me.

I finally make it. A well-built blonde in a red wraparound dress is sitting at a table at the entrance stacked with t-shirts in cellophane and a box full of name badges. Denise Jones runs a scarlet acrylic nail down the name list, efficiently ticks me off and hands me a name badge.

"Hi Julie," she says with a botoxed smile. Former Head Girl and county long jump champion, Denise disgraced herself when she seduced fourth year Andrew Roberts. His parents were pushing him into vicarhood but rumours abounded around the school about him and Denise having moonlit sex in the Merseybank allotments when he should have been swotting up on Mark, Verse One, Chapter Nine.

I return her fixed smile and go inside, convinced she has no idea who I am.

I head straight for the bar and order a swimming pool sized glass of Chardonnay. I've been to so many parties in this room. Chorltonites are christened, married and buried in the Irish Club.

People are pointing at each other's name badges, hugging and shaking hands and squealing "Oh my God!" and Mick Hucknall is singing about 'Holding back the years'. A huge banner across the back wall welcomes us back to Chorlton High and to 1986.

They weren't bad years after Mandy left. I liked my lessons though I was never academic or in any of the top sets. I kept my head down and made a few friends but not many.

I stand at the bar feeling conspicuous. I take a few gulps of wine and scan the room. I recognise a few familiar faces but I don't have enough courage to go over just yet. I don't know if I'll even recognise Mandy. I obliterated her and Donna's faces on the only class school photo I had from Priory Road. There are no photos of her on the website so I only have snatches of memories to go by: the greasy lank hair, the collar of her school blouse lined with dirt, the small rodent-like eyes. I pored over her entry on the Friends Reunited website earlier, dissecting every word as I had many times before.

"Living in Leeds with my partner and our gorgeous labrador, Buster. Working for a charity and still a mad City fan."

She sounds happy. So am I tonight. My life is hunky dory. My husband's got a successful business and I don't have to work, we live in a secluded cottage just around the corner from Manchester's bohemian enclave and we've got two beautiful, extremely well-behaved kids.

"Hey, Julie."

I turn around, then smile with relief at the sight of Cathy Foreman and Amy Broadbent waving me over from the other end of the bar. Cathy was in my class in Priory Road and Chorlton High and the closest thing I had to a true friend. As I approach I am reminded of her deep set eyes that disappeared into her face when she laughed. I was so envious of her waist length white blonde hair that's now cut into a neat bob. The three of us find a table and soon we're swapping family photos.

"Oh, Julie," says Cathy. "Your husband's a dish. Look, Amy."

She hands over a photograph of Billy taken when we first got together. He's sprawling on a bean bag in the living room of his old flat in a white shirt and faded jeans, his arms behind his head, his hair black and tousled. He's grinning at the camera and there's not a trace of the darkness that has taken hold of him since. I look away, feeling sad to the core.

I get choked up when Cathy asks me about Dad. I tell her about the cancer and his op next week to remove the tumour. Amy listens for a while then starts to look bored and scans the room, so I ask her about herself. She has acquired a cut glass accent which couldn't be more removed from the grim corner of the estate where she grew up. It stabs and slices as she talks about her stockbroker husband, the Bedfordshire village where she lives, the villa in Tuscanny and her horse-loving daughters. I watch her, mesmerised. The tailored salmon suit and pearls say, "I'm smart, I've made it and I'm much better than you." She always did have a ruthlessly competitive streak when we were kids. Shoes, boyfriends, records, she always fought to be number one in Chorlton High. I can't say I like the caricature she's become but at least she got out and made something of her life.

The party starts to warm up. Cathy and I drink and reminisce and Amy wanders off to talk to a group of men by the bar. Before I know it an hour and a half has passed and I'm enjoying myself so much I haven't given a thought to the reason I am here. People start to dance. Denise Jones glides across the floor with Andrew Roberts to 'Lady in Red'. He's wearing an open-necked Hawaiian shirt and there's not a dog collar in sight. I point out Denise's remarkably muscular biceps and calves to Cathy then I splutter on my wine when she tells me she is last year's North West Women's Body Building Champion. We watch a group of Set One girls moving languidly to Diana Ross' 'Chain Reaction' and try to remember their names.

"Look how slim and young-looking they all are," I say.

"I thought that too," nods Cathy. "It seems the lower the set you were in, the worse you've aged. Like our destiny was mapped out early on."

She nods over to the bar at Amy, "Except for Mrs. Thatcher over there."

She suddenly jumps to her feet.

"I love this one. Come on, let's dance."

She throws her arms into the air and starts singing to 'Spirit in the Sky'. Laughing, I follow her on to the dance floor.

Then I see her.

I stop in my tracks. She is leaning against the wall near the entrance next to a woman I do not recognise. Trance like, I start to walk slowly towards them, the noise of the room floating away behind me, distant and gnarled. Was she really so short and slight? She was always dinosaur high in my eleven year old eyes. Her trousers are grey and sensible, her shirt crisp and white, her hair cropped short. She looks like a young boy who's been reluctantly scrubbed and forced to smarten up. In contrast, the woman beside her is beautiful: creamy-skinned with an abundance of deep auburn hair, loud red lips and is dressed in a flame-coloured, fifties-style floral dress. She leans forward and whispers something to Mandy, and there's something about their proximity and about the way Mandy looks back at her – a searching, a locking of eyes – that tells me that Mandy is gay. I stand in front of them.

"Hello, Mandy."

"Julie." She nods and gives me a wary smile. Her face is withered and she has aged way beyond her years.

"You remember me, then?"

"Yes. Julie Pattenden. Priory Road, Miss Barton's class."

I shift from one foot to the other, staring, saying nothing. She and the girlfriend exchange a look.

"Do you remember what you did to me, Mandy?" I try to suppress the tremor in my voice.

She cocks her head to one side. "Remember what?"

How many times have I practised this script in my head? How many times have I reworded and rewritten it as the years went by? I move closer so she can hear me.

"I was eleven years old and you made my life a living hell. You tormented me for over a year at Priory Road then another at Chorlton High. That last day at Priory Road, the stuff you did to me."

I search her face for some kind of guilt, recognition even, but there's nothing there.

"I know we messed about a bit but I don't... "

"Messed about? You fucking tortured me. I think you know what I'm talking about."

She reddens and I jab my forefinger at her.

"You fucking liar."

The girlfriend steps towards me and holds up a hand that has rings on every finger.

"Hey, come on now," she says in a deep American drawl. Mandy touches her arm.

"No," she says, looking at me, "I have to deal with this stuff. Go on."

I take a deep breath.

"My mum was in hospital that last day of Priory Road. She was sick and in a coma and dying." I try to look her directly in the eyes but my vision is blurred with tears. "She died alone because of you."

Hearing the words out loud is too much to bear and I can't go on. I run back to the table, grab my bag and jacket and run out of the crowded room down the stairs and out of the foyer.

Some minutes later I am leaning against the railings at the top of the steps, crying, when I feel an arm around my shoulder.

"Julie?" says Cathy. "Whatever's up? Come on, let's sit down. Let's talk about it."

She leads me over to a free table in the beer garden and I slide into the bench. While she's getting a drink from the downstairs bar I open my bag, take out a tissue and a mirror and sort out my face. It's still and warm and the gentle evening light falls on the weeds that fill the cracks in the patio. A fug surrounds the smoking shed like a grey halo and the guests from a wedding party in the downstairs function room are standing around chatting in groups. Upstairs at the reunion they are playing 'A Night to Remember'.

Cathy places a wine glass in front of me.

"Do you remember the last day of Priory Road, Claire?"

"It was so long ago." She looks down and slips into the chair opposite. "I do remember seeing you lying at the bottom of the steps in the playground, though."

I feel relieved. I was starting to believe I'd invented it all.

"Go on," she says. "I'm listening."

"Do you remember Mandy and Donna Sherburn?"

"Vaguely."

A young boy in a page boy suit runs past into the car park and starts to chase one of the bridesmaids.

"When the bell went that day I got my things and hurried out of class. Mandy and Donna usually waited for me at the gate and followed me home."

"Sorry? You've lost me."

"Mandy and Donna. I was bullied for ages before that day. I thought everyone knew."

"Oh, Julie. No. I had no idea."

"It carried on in Chorlton High until she left. Anyway, I was determined to get home quickly that day because we were due at the hospital. Mum was going downhill rapidly."

"Tumour, wasn't it? I remember now." I nod.

"She'd been in a coma for three weeks by then and I'd already had quite a bit of time off school. Dad thought it was better if I went back. Anyway, the bell had gone and there I was, desperate to get out, but it was chaos. Everyone was shouting and running, standing round in groups, writing on each other's shirts and blocking the way in the corridors. Mandy had written me a note earlier in class saying they had a special surprise for me, so I was crapping myself. Then just as I was passing the girls' toilets, Donna was coming out and she grabbed me. I struggled as best I could but she and Mandy pulled me in. I had no chance."

I take a slug of my wine.

"Donna looked into all the cubicles and found one that wasn't flushed then they pushed me into it onto my knees and held my head in the toilet bowl, yanking me out by the hair then putting my head back in again and again."

Cathy gasps.

" 'Eat shit pies while Mummy dies'. That's what they said, and they laughed hysterically. Then they ripped off my blouse, smeared my arms and chest with shit and pushed me out into the corridor."

Cathy puts a hand to her mouth.

"Oh God, Julie! We were eleven, the same age as my Lucy is now. I really had no idea."

"I tried to get away so I ran out of the toilets and through the nearest exit which was at the top of the steps near the gym. I remember pushing through the other kids and into the blinding sunshine and looking down into the packed playground. I also remember the smell. Oh God, the smell. It was everywhere, sticking to me, making me gag, making me sick. Then I felt a massive blow to my back and a shove, and down the steps I went."

Claire puts a hand on my arm.

"Miss Barton helped me to clean myself up and she took me home. Dad was at the hospital. He was due to pick me up and take me in with him. I found out later that Mum was deteriorating by then and he was spending every minute possible with her as he wanted to be with her when she died. When Miss Barton had gone I scrubbed myself in the bath until my skin hurt then I went downstairs into the kitchen. As soon as I heard Dad's key in the lock I panicked. I couldn't face him so I ran out of the back door and hid in our garden shed. I sat there for over an hour. I couldn't move and I was numb with shock. Post traumatic something or other they'd call it nowadays. I knew we were due in at the hospital, but I was a wreck and couldn't think about anything. When I finally did go into the house, Dad was putting the phone down in the hall. He didn't even ask me where I'd been or why I'd been crying or anything. He just grabbed his jacket and said to get in the car. He dragged me by the hand through the hospital corridors, then as we reached Mum's ward, one of the nurses who was also Mum's friend, Carmel, was walking towards us. She knew Mum well and tears were pouring down her face so we knew it was too late."

I cover my hands with my face.

"She died alone that night when me and Dad could have been there with her. It was all my fault, Cathy. I've never told a soul except you and I've never been able to forgive myself."

CHAPTER 24

Billy

Tony puts his palms on the bed, inches himself up against the pillows and takes a sip of water from the paper cup on the patient table in front of him.

His face is hollow-cheeked and pewter-coloured. He yelps in pain as he lies back down again, careful of the drip in his arm.

"More cables and tubes down there than in the back of my telly," he says, patting the blanket covering his lower body. "Six days and counting. I can't wait until I'm out of this godforsaken place."

I fear he just might unplug himself and go for The Great Escape sooner. The op to remove the tumour from the bowel lining has gone well enough, but he's finding the recovery hard and he has transformed from a lovable eccentric into a belligerent old bastard. He had a go at the hospital chaplain earlier. The poor man was chatting to one of the nurses in the middle of the ward, minding his own business when Tony leant forward and yelled, "Well hello, Reverend. You hovering round the sick and the vulnerable again?"

The chaplain and the nurse glanced over at him, rolled their eyes then continued with their conversation, but he didn't leave it there. "It's the only time your lot get any attention, when the grim reaper's calling. That's when you start the scaremongering and they all come running. Your bloody churches are empty the rest of time."

I told him to hush, that the man was only trying to get a job done.

"Bloody vultures," he scowled, picking up his crossword book.

I smile. I've missed the craic and the old familiar banter with him. I've rarely seen him since I left the house.

It's mid-week visiting time and the ward is quiet. A teenage goth sitting by the next bed is showing her grandfather pictures on her mobile, her black lace fingerless gloves moving deftly over the screen. An obese man opposite is moaning quietly to himself and a pretty, raven-haired nurse with hazel eyes is hurrying down the ward with a tray of medicines.

Tony runs his bony fingers along the silky edge of his blanket then clears his throat.

"You know I've always thought well of you, Billy, don't you?"

I shift in my chair feeling nervous about what's coming next. I haven't seen him because I've been avoiding him, to tell the truth. Julie said she hasn't told him the details of what happened between us and he just thinks we're having time apart. I don't think I could ever face him again if he knew I'd raised my hand to his daughter.

"Look, lad," he says, "I've never tried to interfere between you two and I don't know what's gone on now."

I look away, my eyes resting on an elderly woman in lilac further down the ward, tucking blankets into her husband's bed.

"But I do know you both still love each other."

I look back at him.

"I think it's fair to say she hates the sight of me right now, Tony."

"She hates the way you carry on, the moods and the depression, not you. Sort out whatever it is inside you that's rotten and she'll have you back."

Pull yourself together. Sort yourself out. Get a grip. If only it was so fucking easy.

He leans back on his pillow and closes his eyes. "True love doesn't come along many times in a lifetime," he says hoarsely, "so treasure it when you've got it."

I look at this sick old man I love, lying in a hospital bed talking

161

about his love for his dead wife and I just don't know what to say. I feel guilty because I'm not choked up or crying or something, but I don't seem to feel things the same way I once did. That's the antidepressants for you. My everyday emotional highs and lows are neutered, all life's lurid colours have gone and I'm living a pastel existence. But it's a price I'm willing to pay to get my family back.

The girl goth calls over the nurse and asks her about the pay T.V. The nurse then reaches up over the bed and pulls it down. She has a neat little body and her uniform bunches up around her breasts, revealing a glimpse of black lacy bra and cleavage. My groin aches and I imagine fucking her over the bed. I don't think the pills have got to my mojo yet, but then I'd need the opportunity to find out.

I ventured out for the first time in ages last Saturday. Steve was meeting a date at the eighties night at the Irish club so I tagged along. I had no stomach for it though and after a couple of pints I left early. I was waiting for a taxi outside when I spotted Rachel Cleaver by the smokers' shelter. She had her back to me and she was standing close to one of the Broadoak dads, Amy's husband, a nifty dresser who owns a sky blue Lambretta. I watched Rachel as she lifted her cigarette in her right hand, stretching her neck upwards and inhaled. Then she brushed the fingertips of her left hand briefly along Amy's husband's arm. He turned to her, whispered something, and touched the arch of her back. If I'd blinked I might have missed it.

Tony farts loudly.

"Better out than in," he says, grinning. "As soon as I'm out of here and I'm well enough, I'm taking you all on holiday: Rita, the kids, the lot. You and Julie can have some time together to sort yourselves out."

"We'll see," I sigh, unable to imagine the scenario.

"When's your sister getting married in Galway?"

"Last week in August."

"We'll go for that if she'll have us. We'll stay for a week. I should be able to travel by then."

I said I'd give Jenny away. She's marrying into money and it'll be a huge church wedding. The mere thought makes me panic. I'm dreading it.

"We'll see now, Tony. You need to get better first." He groans and puts a hand under the blanket to manoeuvre a tube, his fighting spirit punctured again. He whimpers and I get up and go to his aid, afraid he'll shoot me if I put my hand down there. He rolls his eyes, waves his hand at me to sit down then turns his head to one side and takes deep breaths.

"If the tumour comes back and it's bad, I want out," he says, almost inaudibly.

I move my chair nearer to the bed. "What's that?"

"You heard. I want out. I want to end it."

"Jesus, you're a bundle of laughs today."

He frowns.

"I mean it, Billy. It's stage three bowel cancer. Fifty percent survival rate for five years after surgery. There's a good chance I'll suffer before I go."

He runs his tongue along his lower lip.

"I've thought long and hard about something like this happening. You do at my age. I don't want to end up a rotting vegetable like a lot I've seen. I don't want my family to see me suffer. I don't want you to remember me like that. I want some dignity."

"Don't be talking like that. You're just having a bad day, that's all. You'll make a full recovery."

"I might not. And there's no point hanging around if all that's left is pain."

A sudden clatter of feet makes us turn towards the ward entrance. Bridget is charging towards the bed waving a piece of paper in the air.

"Look, Grandad, I did a picture of Old Trafford on fire for you," she cries.

Tony's face brightens and he manoeuvres himself round to see her. She tries to scramble onto the bed but I pull her off before she untubes him. I sit her on my knee.

Julie enters carrying Will. She is wearing a short, pale blue summer dress covered in small white flowers that I haven't seen before. She absorbs the bedside scene and smiles at me. It's just a scrap from her table but my heart accepts it with delight.

"Come and give Grandad a kiss, then," Tony booms, holding the picture up and smiling. "Oh, that's smashing, that is."

*　*　*

Back at the house after putting the kids to bed, I watch the news then I go into the kitchen to wash up the tea things. I keep thinking about what Tony said about suffering and staying around if there's only pain. How can you tell a man in his condition that you think he's right?

I'm drying off the cutlery when Julie comes in. I hear the fridge door open and when I've turned round she's pouring a glass of wine.

"Want one?" she asks, then she looks at me like she's seeing me again after being so invisible to her for so long. First the smile earlier, now this. I'm not sure what I've done to deserve it. I hesitate, wondering if I can stop at one drink and drive back to Steve's but I take a glass from the cupboard. She fills it then moves over to the window, the late evening light falling on her face and lighting up the copper streaks in her hair. I watch her lips curl around her glass and imagine mine touching them again and feeling the crush of her body against me. She turns to me.

"Thanks for going to see Dad. I know he was really looking forward to your visit. He's so grumpy. I don't know how Rita puts up with him."

She looks out into the yard and runs a finger along the window pane.

"Has he told you he wants to take us all to Jenny's wedding?"

"Yes." I step towards her, "Would you like that?"

"Maybe," she says, picking up a milk carton that's fallen out of the overflowing bin.

"Leave it, I'll tidy up." I take it from her. "I'll come in when I'm done."

When she goes into the living room I watch her shape shifting under the silky material of her dress.

I clean up the kitchen, tie the handles of the bin liner and take it out into the yard. It's a pleasant July evening with a light breeze and there's the sound of laughter and people sitting out in one of the yards further along. The forecast is good for the weekend too.

I heave the black plastic into the three-quarters full bin, turning it on its wheels to get a better angle. I shut the lid and as I am wheeling it back I notice a child's toy half hidden in the crevice between the bottom of the fence and the paving. I pick it up and turn it over slowly in my hand. Luke Skywalker. My chest tightens. I turn it over in my hand again then drop it to the floor as if it were a burning hot coal. My breathing quickens and I start to shake, so I stand with one hand against the wall to steady myself.

"May the force be with you."

He is standing with his back against the classroom window, his black bulk blocking the light. He is looking directly over at me.

"Watch your mouth, kid, or you'll find yourself floating home."

"Aren't you a little short to be a storm trooper?"

He knew every line in that film.

Luke Skywalker, Darth Vader, Princess Leia and Yoda, those figures were way beyond our pocket money budget and impossible to get hold of, but he had the whole set in his desk drawer. Brian Meehan and Keith Carney told me so. It was a great secret, they said. Only the clever lads chosen for extra Irish were allowed to see them.

Da was delighted when I told him about the lessons.

"It's about time someone recognised your potential at that school," he said.

Da liked Brother Mullaney. That time after the nativity play when he recounted that story from his childhood, the one about the crazed donkey, I was standing between them. Da was doubled over with laughter as Mullaney's plump hands squeezed down on my shoulders.

"Didn't he make a great angel," he said, running his fingers through my curls. "How could we not have such a handsome fella up there on the stage? And such a clever one too? I tell you, this one's going to go far."

Da was beaming. Later I realised I wasn't the only one being groomed.

I gag, the hot bile making its way up through my throat. I throw up again and again until I am empty then I look at the mess on the ground. So much bile inside me.

Julie comes to the back door and I shield the vomit-splattered fence. I'm panting and sweat is pouring down my face.

"Are you OK?" she asks.

I push past her into the house. I'll never let her see me like this. Never. I shout out from the hallway.

"I'm not feeling too good. I need to get off."

I rush to the van, almost knocking a passing gangly teenager off his feet, headphones in, lost in his music. I manage to drive round the corner and pull up.

I sit, bent over the wheel, taking deep breaths, waiting for the panic to subside. I've tried to shut Brian away but he keeps turning up in my dreams. He was the youngest of eight and a great little footballer. I am running beside him on the field, his strawberry blonde curls blowing behind him. His expression is determined, his arms are up and he is hollering for the ball. They found his three day old body on a Dublin estate after years of heroin addiction.

I put my foot down, drive into Chorlton and pull up outside Bargain Booze. I open the door and put a foot on the pavement, but then I stop myself. Maybe it's the thought of her in that blue dress in the evening light or the thought of Brian's scrawny body hanging from a ceiling beam. I don't know. Somehow or other I make it back to Steve's sober.

166

CHAPTER 25

Julie

"Let's sort his things out while he's asleep then I'll make a brew and you can read it to me."

Rita takes a handful of thrillers and a crossword book out of Dad's black holdall and places them on the sideboard. I grab the dirty laundry, go into the freshly scrubbed kitchen and load it in the washing machine, pausing for a moment when I see speckles of blood on one of his vests. I think about the time I got my first period. Dad made such a fuss. It was like he'd been preparing for it with great care. He insisted I stayed off school and he put me to bed with a mountain of chocolate and hot water bottles. But he's not coping too well with the role reversal now he's the one who needs looking after.

When I return to the living room Rita is sitting on the sofa, leaning over the coffee table, taking multiple pill bottles out of the white chemist's bag. The zip on her lemon velour track suit top is pulled low revealing a wrinkled cleavage; the sunglasses on her head fall slightly as she reads the label. I perch on the sofa arm.

"Don't you get any ideas about selling those on," I say.

She grins and holds a bottle up to the light, running a nail along its side.

"I do remember these giving me a pleasant little high."

Rita had her womb removed two years ago when they found the early stages of ovarian cancer. She's something of a specialist in the disease. She knows the ins and outs of the system and has done volunteer work at Christies, the cancer hospital.

"I don't know how I'd have managed these past few months without you. You've been so good with the kids as well as everything you've done for Dad." I lean towards her and give her a long hard hug. "Thank you so much."

"No worries, love." She puts the pill bottle down. "So how are things? Your Dad was hoping Billy might be back home by now."

I slide onto the sofa next to her, "Oh, Rita. I don't know. I think he's really changed, you know. He hardly drinks, the antidepressants seemed to be working and he never misses an evening putting the kids to bed."

"So?"

I look down and twist my wedding ring absently. Despite everything I've never taken it off.

"The other day, after he visited Dad in hospital, he came back to the house and I opened a bottle of wine. I thought we were going to sit down and talk but then he changed his mind and buggered off, making some excuse about not feeling well. And now he's retreated into himself again. I'm not even sure if he wants to come home anymore."

She pats my knee.

"Don't be daft. Of course he wants to come home." She gathers the pills in her hands and moves over to the window sill where she places them next to the other boxes and bottles piled there.

"It's looking more and more like Keith Richard's bathroom in here every day," she says, then she turns to me. "He's obviously got issues, love."

"I really have no idea what's going on in his head and I've given up asking. One minute he's all up for us going on holiday to Ireland then bang, he's back on his knees, on a downer again"

"I keep saying it, but men find it hard to talk about their problems, even intelligent ones like Billy." She hands me Dad's tartan toiletry bag.

"You put this in the bathroom, I'll go make that brew and we'll get on with the email."

I nod and go upstairs. I should probably feel threatened by the fact that she's taken over everything to do with Dad but I don't, partially because I like her so much, but also because she's doing a far better job than I ever could in my present circumstances.

On the landing I can hear choking snores coming from Dad's bedroom. I put my head around the door. He is in a deep sleep, his head cocked to one side on the pillow, his glasses falling off his nose at a comical angle. I tip toe inside, carefully remove them, smooth down the duvet and ever so gently kiss the top of his head.

Back in the living room I take the neatly folded piece of paper from my jeans pocket and sink into the armchair. The email arrived in my Friends Reunited inbox last night and I've already read it quite a few times.

When Rita puts down the tray of tea and bourbons she gives me a nod and I begin to read:

"Dear Julie,

Hi, it's Alex Durkan here, Mandy Sherburn's partner. We met briefly at the Chorlton High reunion.

I hope you don't mind me writing but I felt I needed to after what happened back there. Mandy doesn't know that I'm contacting you but I know that she is very troubled by the things you told her that night.

I think you deserve to know some things about Mandy that may help you to understand what happened when you were children. Mandy has told me that she has only vague memories about some of the things that happened at school involving you. This is because she has blocked out a lot of events from that period of her childhood, something very common in people who suffer trauma on the scale she has.

You probably remember her sudden departure from Chorlton High School. I don't know if you knew at the time but she was pregnant. The pregnancy was the result of physical and sexual abuse inflicted on her by the boyfriend of her alcoholic mother from the age of nine until she was twelve. He raped her on a regular basis and took her to various locations in Manchester where she was forced to have sex with a number of other men. Mandy is convinced her mother knew about the abuse but she did nothing, remaining financially and emotionally tied to this man who was never prosecuted for what he did. A few months into the pregnancy, Mandy told a teacher at the school everything and consequently she and her younger sister Joanne were taken into care. It transpired that Joanne was also being abused. Mandy gave birth to a baby boy, David, who was given up for adoption and she and Joanne spent the rest of their childhood in and out of foster homes, always together and always close. Throughout her life Mandy has had intermittent alcohol and drug dependency problems and has attempted suicide three times. Her beloved Joanne died in a car crash in 1990.

I met and fell in love with Mandy when she was volunteering at a drug dependency unit in Leeds that I was managing at the time. She had been sober for two years and I was married with young children. Nine years on, our love is as strong as ever and we enjoy a happy family life together. Mandy still suffers panic attacks and bouts of depression and not a day goes by without her thinking about the son she gave up for adoption. She lives in hope that one day David will come and find her.

Mandy has come through the darkest of times and is now a beautiful, sensitive human being. The day after the reunion she told me that the thought that she may have physically abused another child horrified her and I know it plays on her mind.

When Mandy came back to Manchester that weekend she was looking for some kind of closure with her family and, twenty-five years later, she had an emotional reunion with her mother. She wanted to confront her past and to move on. Maybe you were looking for something similar at the reunion too and I hope this letter helps you to find it.

I know Mandy is truly sorry for any pain she caused you and I hope you have it in your heart to forgive her.

Alex Durkan."

Rita's eyes are bright with tears as she puts her coffee down and reaches into the leopard skin handbag at her feet.

"Come outside love. I need a fag."

We sit on the low wall at the end of the garden. The sky is cloudless and a similar grey white colour to the roofs of the maisonettes opposite. A woman in stonewashed jeans with enormous hoops in her ears is walking up the drive of one of them. She is weighed down by Iceland bags and she glances up at the open window where a St George's flag flutters in the breeze. Two doors down on our side, Beyonce is playing through an open window and a girl of seven or eight in a red, gingham school dress is jumping on the trampoline in the tiny garden next to two white plastic garden chairs.

Despite the lack of sun, Rita's face is hidden behind her large, dark Jackie O glasses. She inhales on her cigarette hungrily.

"Jesus, I had no idea. That poor little mite. And Jackie let it happen because he was paying for her next drink. Good God almighty." She looks up and down the street. "This shithole estate has got a lot to answer for," she sniffs. "Stuff like that is still going on around here and Social Services are not on to it. They're too scared to risk their own necks or too disorganised to get involved half the time."

I watch the mountain of ash gathering on the end of her cigarette.

"I had no idea about Mandy either," I say.

"At least now you can move on now, though."

I stare down at a Coke can that says 'make it real' on its side.

"It's not that simple, Rita."

The mountain of ash drops off onto Rita's thigh and she brushes it off.

"What do you mean?"

"I feel for Mandy. I think I do, for what happened to her, but it doesn't wipe away the damage she did to me. It won't go away overnight."

"Come on now, Julie love. Mandy was an eleven year old child who was being raped and abused when she lashed out at you. No offence. It wasn't nice what she did but there's really no comparison between what happened to you both, now is there?"

I clear my throat, feeling my anger rise.

"No, there's no comparison, Rita. But she didn't just lash out. She systematically tortured me, mentally and physically. Why don't people see that bullying is also abuse? Just because it's done by another child and not an adult doesn't mean you can dismiss it as child's play. The psychological scars still stay with you, you know. For life."

I lay awake last night for ages after reading the email, trying to work out how I felt. Of course I feel for Mandy and the horror of what happened to her, but it doesn't change the fact that Mum died alone.

I fold my arms tightly across my chest.

"She could have written to me herself and apologised if she's so troubled."

"For something she can't remember doing?"

"If she can't remember. Could she really block out what she did to me for so long?"

Rita shakes her head and looks at the white van pulling up outside the house next door. A well-built twenty-something with floppy blonde hair and a paint-spattered jacket hops out. He smiles over at us but gets no response. Rita grinds her cigarette out with her foot, crushes the lighter back into the cigarette packet and turns into the gate.

"It really is time for you to move on, Julie." She is sharp and scolding. "That poor kid suffered things you and I couldn't possibly imagine. Besides, you've got other things to worry about now." She gestured up to Dad's bedroom. "He should be awake any minute."

Stung, I slope inside after her, feeling self-indulgent, callous and small. I hate the fact that she thinks so little of me when I think so highly of her. But there's also a big part of me that feels like I am eleven again and she just doesn't understand. She's the dinner lady who did nothing when I told on Mandy, the teacher who dismissed it all as a silly prank. None of them saw beyond the child's play to the cruelty beneath and the damaging, far-reaching consequences.

The thing is this. I have no monster any more, no bogey man to blame. Mandy is the victim now, not me. So much for my search for closure. Instead, I find myself in a kind of limbo. I was almost at the finishing line but suddenly I've tripped and I'm rolling on the ground in despair and frustration.

We go inside. Rita goes upstairs to Dad and I start to prepare some salad in the kitchen. Out of the window I see the girl who was on the trampoline earlier skipping past in her school dress, her long hair trailing behind her in the breeze. She looks so carefree and happy, like girls of that age are supposed to be.

CHAPTER 26

Billy

"I reckon Rachel got fed up of standing him on a box when they wanted a snog. He's got at least six inches on Rufus."

"Maybe getting up at 6.30 every day for the consignments of Polish cabbage was the final straw."

"He's not bad looking in a faded rock star kind of way. He could lace those army boots up, though. He could do with a wash as well. Just like Rufus. She must like them mucky. Dirty bitch."

"Enough," I laugh, starting to feel uncomfortable about Julie's running commentary on Rachel Cleaver's new man. We are sitting on a bench in Chorlton Park pretending not to watch her cavort by the swings with him. She looks happy. Tanned, in a white figure-hugging t-shirt and faded Levis, she has a dishevelled, sex-satiated air about her. She is multi-tasking, stroking and caressing her man while trying to entertain Tabatha on the swing. She seems too absorbed to be taking much notice of us. I thought for a moment she might be embarrassed after coming on to me in the Irish club that time, but Rachel is ice cool. She doesn't do shame.

I think about Claire and the email I got from her yesterday asking if we can put what happened behind us. Isn't that the only place for it? I wanted to reply. She and Jason are going to Relate and her counsellor is also working on her "grieving issues". I'm glad she's getting help. I wish to God I had the courage to do the same. I come across painful reminders of Jal every day. I bumped into one of Tony's friends from the pub quiz in Chorlton the other day. A nervous Cork man who always dresses in a suit and tie,

Tom Joyce enquired after Tony's health then asked me why I wasn't going to the quiz any more with my mate.

"Standards are going downhill," he said, his face suddenly turning a dark shade of puce. "Oh Jesus, I am so sorry. It was your friend who was killed in Rusholme, wasn't it? Oh what a fecking eejit. Oh I am sorry."

He put his hands into his pockets and looked down at the floor.

"No worries, Tom," I said, touching his elbow before he shuffled off.

I could never go back and sit at our table next to that empty chair or bear the silence where our laughter should have been. I still have the photo on my phone of him and the kids climbing the lilac tree in Longford Park. He's larking about in a Tarzan pose against the evening sky, the world at his feet. I look at it constantly and ask myself if any of it really happened.

I lean over and gingerly remove Will's dummy from the side of the buggy where it's fallen when he drifted off to sleep. Jal will never do this for the daughter he never met. He'll never see her or the boys graduate, or marry, or have kids. The trial will be coming up soon and we'll all have to relive the whole thing. I'll have to attend, but I don't know if I will be able contain myself with the pair of them in the same room.

Chorlton Park is busy this afternoon. Sunday league footballers trudge round the fields behind the playground and there's a standoff between a mother and toddler in the queue by the ice cream van. Kids are whizzing around the skateboard park and I've been watching a burly, middle-aged biker having a lesson from a couple of teenagers on the path nearby, and applauding his determination to keep getting back on. It was a warm and promising morning when we set out but now the sun has disappeared, clouds are starting to gather and I feel a sharp breeze through my thin cotton jacket.

Bridget is on the roundabout with Tobias, Rachel's boy. She's excited to have him here, a little over-excited perhaps. She's been stalking him since we got here. When he changes seats she manoeuvres herself next to him. Other kids are circling, wanting to get on.

"See how possessive she is?" Julie says. "She's like that a lot around other kids. She has such difficulties making friends that there's a desperation about her when she does get someone to play with." She stretches her legs out, puts her fingers in her jeans pockets and sighs. "It breaks my heart."

"You worry too much about her," I say.

Once I could have put my arm around her and that would have been comfort enough. Though things are improving between us, we're not in the place where I can do that yet. Will we ever be? I don't know why she just doesn't be done with it and tell me it's over.

She suddenly gasps and leaps to her feet. "Shit. Did you see that?"

"What?"

"She's just kicked that little kid trying to get on the roundabout. Oh, God."

Julie dashes to where a small blonde boy of about four in an England strip is writhing on the ground wailing and clutching his stomach. I watch as his dad, wiry and shaven-headed in a white hoody, appears behind him and scoops him up, a look of fury on his face. Julie stops the roundabout, grabs Bridget by the arm and drags her off. By the time I've arrived with the buggy the dad is yelling and shaking his fist at Bridget, and Tobias and the other children are scarpering back to their parents like scared kittens. Soon every adult in the playground is calling out for their kids, one eye on the unfolding scene.

"Little bitch." He paces up and down ignoring the sobbing boy on his shoulder.

"I'm so sorry." Julie looks down at Bridget. "Bridget, say sorry." She tightens a protective arm around her shoulder. Bridget shifts from one foot to another, a terrified look on her face, then suddenly breaks free and makes a run for it. I reach out and try to grab her, but she dodges me and runs to the other side of the playground where she disappears inside the small enclosed space underneath the slide.

"She wants belting, she does. Look at him. He's half her size." The dad rages on and on, his oversized pupils darting in all directions and I wonder if he's drunk or high or maybe just enjoying having an audience. "If she ever goes near my kid again I'll fucking land her one."

I step forward.

"Now hold on, mate," My fist curls and clenches.

"Don't you mate me, you Irish cunt."

I want to smash my fists between his tiny ratty eyes but I feel Julie watching me, then feel her restraining hand on my forearm. Behind her in the distance I can see Rachel clutching Tobias.

Feeling like a magnet that's being pulled away from its natural force, I somehow manage to turn and walk to the other side of the playground. When I eventually do look back, the man and the boy are leaving through the gate and children are being released from the clutches of their parents, who are giving me approving looks. Julie hurries towards me with the buggy. She is visibly shaken.

"Let's get her and get out of here."

"OK."

I head towards the slide. Trying to keep up the good parent act, I call out Bridget's name as calmly as I can when I actually want to shake her and give her the hiding of her life. A long list of threats and punishments are rushing to the tip of my tongue as I call for her again. She doesn't answer. I look under the slide but the space is now taken by a plump blonde girl with freckles, in conversation with a Barbie doll. I scan the playground then look over at Julie who is kneeling by the buggy giving Will a beaker of water. She stands up quickly and looks around. Bridget is nowhere in the playground.

I walk towards the hedge that separates the playground from the field behind. There are tennis courts on one side and a copse of trees and bushes on the other. I look for the head of copper curls and blue striped dress. Or was it green? I exit through the gate and call out for her. Julie is now running towards the other side of the playground calling her name. I go into the wooded area. Branches and crisp packets crunch under my feet and brambles spike my face as I make my way inside. She'll be here curled up, hugging her knees and sulking somewhere. That's what she does when she knows she's in for a telling off. She runs away and hides. I search deeper into the darkened copse for a good ten minutes. Nothing. Then I make my way back out. When I look up, Julie is running frantically towards the tennis courts, her long cardigan flapping behind her in the breeze. She stops and gestures wildly at a group of teenagers leaning carelessly by the fencing. In the playground, Rachel Cleaver is rocking Will's buggy and I can see her boyfriend and some of the other parents searching the area and paths at the area near the road.

I run towards the tennis courts, panic starting to kick in. To my right a young couple are getting up from the grass and dusting themselves down. I ask if they've seen my little girl.

"About that tall, a pretty redhead with freckles," I gush.

"Sorry. Your wife already ask," replies the olive-skinned girl in a foreign accent, the look of compassion on her beautiful face filling me with alarm. I look at my watch. Nearly fifteen minutes have passed. I am missing my child but I refuse to believe she is missing. But then I glimpse a future with no Bridget in it, a gap, a gaping wound somewhere, and my heart misses a beat.

Julie runs towards me.

"Someone's rung the police." She is panting and shaking, "Oh, Billy, have they taken her? Please tell me they've not taken her like they took Maddie. Please tell me they haven't taken her."

She lets out a low moan, her legs buckle and she falls against me. I can feel pin pricks of rain on the back of my neck as I grip her arms and pull her up. I have to be the strong one now.

"We'll find her," I whisper, holding my wife for the first time in months, "She's here somewhere. I know she is."

There's a faint sound of sirens in the distance. "Wait here," I say, running back towards the playground.

A curtain of rain is suddenly sweeping down over the park. People are hurrying out through the gate and some are sheltering under the municipal building behind the tennis courts. Then, as I turn towards the copse, I spot her, climbing down from the low branches of a tree.

Julie gets to her before I do, lifting her up into her arms before her feet can touch the ground. Through the sheet of rain I watch her kiss and hug and shake our daughter, leaving her flopping around like a wet rag doll.

My knees suddenly feel weak and I crouch on the ground. As I raise my hand to my face I feel a gentle tap on my shoulder and the buggy appears next to me with Will asleep inside. I look up to see Rachel walking back to the playground. When I turn around Bridget is taking slow steps towards me.

"Has he gone, Daddy?" she asks tentatively, glancing around, rain drops dripping from her button nose "Has the naughty man gone?"

"Yes, sweetheart, he's gone." I swallow and pull her towards me, feeling the dampness of her hair against my face. It's like I've been gasping for breath for the last fifteen minutes and my oxygen supply has returned. The sirens are screaming now and I watch the blue and yellow squad cars pull up by the main road.

Julie and I say very little to each other on the way home. We watch Bridget closely as she skips along, holding on to the buggy handle as if nothing had happened. I try to put myself inside her head. Was it fear of the boy's father that kept her up in that tree for so long? Couldn't she see us searching frantically? Yet she still refused come down? Julie and I are too emotionally shattered to get to the bottom of it right now and we agree to deal with her tomorrow.

Back at the house we go about the evening routine, the tea, the washing up, the tidying and the kids' bath time, but I sense something has changed between us. We looked over a precipice today and glimpsed a horror. Now we've stepped back from it we've moved closer together.

I look in on a sleeping Bridget when Julie is putting clothes away in Will's room. I take in the pale skinny legs strewn on top of the pink duvet, the mop of hair against the white pillow and the serene look on her face. I inhale it all. I don't know to whom or to what but I am feeling eternally grateful. Julie appears by my side, we both look at our daughter for a while in silence then I feel her fingers searching for my hand.

"Stay," she says, then she rests her head on my shoulder.

CHAPTER 27

Julie

"Mmm. Lovely." Dad wipes the froth from his lip and places his pint of Guinness on the table. "It's true. It definitely tastes better over here, smoother, more velvety somehow."

We're sitting outside Lydon's pub overlooking the stream that runs through the village where Billy was raised. I can hear the rush of water running over stone, and further down a group of Italian tourists are feeding the ducks and taking photos in front of the grey dry-stone wall.

Dad sits back and smiles, an arm draped around Rita. Eight weeks after the op he's put on weight, he's got a healthy blush in his cheeks and his curmudgeonly ways have disappeared. The tumour is behaving itself and, fingers crossed, he's on the road to recovery. The doctors were reticent about giving him the go ahead to travel at first, but they relented when they saw how determined he was.

"Could you get a more beautiful view or a better day for a wedding?" he says looking upwards with a grin. He undoes the top button on the wafer crisp shirt that Rita ironed to perfection this morning, then loosens the tie I bought him, burgundy to match the corduroy jacket that's folded carefully over the arm of the bench.

"It definitely beats looking out at the knackered old sofa in next door's garden," says Rita, stirring the lime green and lemon umbrella in her cloudy cocktail.

Dad's right. It's perfect. I look up at the cloudless blue sky, the Connemara mountains rising and falling like gentle waves in the distance and various shades of green – olive, pine, sea, avocado and jade, all woven into the landscape. Forty shades of green, so the song says. Dad sang it in the car yesterday when we were driving to Mum's village with Bridget. It was a stinging hot day then too.

"Your mum liked the Foster and Allen version but I always maintained you couldn't beat Johnny Cash," he said, gazing out of the car window into the passing fields like he was unearthing something there.

I'd already fallen for Billy when I discovered that he was born and raised twenty miles from Mum's homestead, but the fact did reel me in further. As strange as it sounds, at the beginning it was like a bit of her spirit was in the room with us at times. He used to tease me about inbreeding in the west of Ireland, about the possibility of us being distant cousins and having kids with two heads. I said I didn't mind just as long as they were his kids.

When we arrived at her village I parked up to get an ice cream to placate madam, who was hot and irritable in the back of the car. I barely recognised the place from my childhood holidays, but then the entire country has changed radically, even from the time I came over with Billy when Bridget was born. I wonder what Mum would have made of the pastel coloured mansions that have sprung up everywhere like icing decorations on a cake, or the four by fours parked on gravelled drives behind gilded gates. Billy's mate Davy has a neighbour whose garden is the equivalent of a small playground in Manchester, with swings and benches and sophisticated climbing equipment. Then there are the trampolines. I've never seen so many in my life. At any given moment a large percentage of the Irish population must be in mid air. On the way to the ice cream shop in the main street I spotted a Michelin starred restaurant and deli with a special in the window on Spanish cheeses and cold meats. Mum was too down to earth to have been impressed by the deli but she would have loved the twenty-four hour Tesco on the road into the village, and the Chinese restaurant called Paddy Fields.

Davy says it's all only an outward show of wealth and the economy is about to crumble. He says there's talk of boom and bust. Lots of the houses are up for sale or for holiday rental and the pubs and restaurants are only half full, even though it's still high season.

We left the village and drove a couple of miles to the hill top spot where Dad was adamant Mum's family house had been, but we couldn't find it anywhere so we returned to the village. Bridget and I popped into the souvenir emporium and asked the chic elderly woman folding Aran sweaters if she knew Mum's family. She did, of course. Everyone knows everyone in villages like this. Not only did she know them but it transpired she had actually been at school with Mum and had been friends with her as a teenager before she left for England. She said Mum's nephew Conal, an architect, had inherited the house, demolished it some years ago and built his own further back off the road.

As we were leaving, she handed Bridget a leprechaun key ring and said, "You look just like your Granny. Bridget was lovely, God rest her soul."

"She's named after her," I beamed.

On the drive over to Conal's house, I recalled Mum reminiscing about her own childhood as she bathed me when I was little. I could feel her fingers running through my shampooed hair and hear her silvery voice telling me how she walked to school through the fields with rags on her feet in summer and boots that were too big and let in the rain in winter. I saw her sliding down haystacks with her brothers and sisters when they should have been making hay and her stern father chasing them with a pitchfork. She is forever framed in my mind aged seventeen leaving for England, carrying a small suitcase and dressed in a navy coat with a fur trim which her cousin had sent down from Dublin.

It was six o'clock by the time we finally arrived at Conal's house, an uber modern, glass-fronted construction with solar panels and tall electronic gates. I was hoping to meet him and his family, but we were greeted instead by an Eastern European sounding au pair over the intercom. She told us Conal and his wife wouldn't be back from work until seven. We explained who we were and that we wanted to visit the spot where the old house stood.

"Yes, yes, is good. No problem," she shouted over the cries of a young child in the background.

Dad touched my shoulder.

"Come on, let's just go. I think I remember how to get there from here."

We set off up a narrow stony track by the side of the house. I took Dad's arm and Bridget skipped on ahead through the brambles. Soon the path steepened and Dad slowed down, bent double in a coughing fit. Bridget ran to him and patted his back. "You sure you want to do this?" I asked.

"It's what I came here for," he said wiping his forehead with the tissue I'd just handed him, "I came to see her one last time."

We trudged on in silence until we came to the top. "There it is, over there." He was pointing, breathless with excitement this time.

I immediately recognised the field to the right of us where the house had once stood. How could I ever forget that view? The mountains dropped down like a steep curtain under the flushed evening sky and the lough glistened like a sequinned dress below. The ground was rough and stony with patches of dry yellow grass; a few boulders of the old house remained alongside pieces of farm machinery and the remnants of a tractor. I'd spent happy sunlit days playing outside there with my cousins. Laughter and chatter had floated out of the whitewashed farm house where a stream of visitors and children flowed in and out. It had been heaven for an only child like me. I was devastated to see it all gone and I could see from his face that Dad was too.

We made our way slowly to the tall cedar tree where we'd scattered Mum's ashes with her family on that breezy August day twenty-six years ago. I remember the sound of sobbing and the gulls crying overhead.

Bridget ran over to play on the tractor and I held back as Dad walked towards the tree that stood unchanged and in full leaf. I watched him, an old man on a hill top talking to a tree in the evening light, and tears poured down my face. After a while he turned away and went over to Bridget and it was my turn.

I knelt down near the sprawling roots, the coarse grass chafing my bare knees as I placed in a row the five roses I'd brought. One from each of us, I said. I told her how the kids were doing and how Billy and I had been through a bad patch and how we were still trying to work things out. Then I paused and swallowed, the words coming out of my mouth slowly, like hostages released into daylight.

"I'm sorry, Mum," I said. "I'm sorry for what happened that day. I know you've forgiven me long ago but I've had trouble forgiving myself."

I had a little cry then I felt Dad's hand on my shoulder. I looked up at him. I knew if I was ever going to tell him then this was the moment. But his face was full of a serenity I did not want to disturb and I knew the moment had passed.

We walked around for a while inhaling the view and reminiscing. I told Bridget about her grandma's family, how she was one of twelve, and how lost she'd felt when the older ones had emigrated to America and England one by one. I told her how playing nurse to her younger siblings had inspired her to become one herself and that she'd never really wanted to leave Ireland and her family but she had no choice. It felt so right, passing on her family history in that spot.

We made our way back down the narrow path. Bridget spotted a blackberry bush and we picked handfuls and washed them with the bottled water I had in my bag then ate them. She skipped ahead in her yellow dress with a smudged purple face and I took Dad's arm again, feeling lighter and more clearheaded than I'd felt for some time.

The heat is searing through my lace dress into my back and shoulders and I edge further under the table umbrella into the shade. I am pale, I am ginger. Twenty-nine degree heat and blazing sunshine are my sworn enemies. Dad leans over to the bench on the next table picks up a newspaper someone has left behind. He holds it up and points to the headlines.

BISHOP TO RESIGN OVER ABUSE REPORT CALLS FOR APOLOGY FROM THE VATICAN.

"It's everywhere you look," he says shaking his head and turning the pages. "Pages of it, editorials examining the country's psyche, the victims' stories."

Rita rolls her eyes.

"Not today, Tony. We've heard enough of your rants against the Catholic Church in the pub every night. I'm proposing a truce for a day."

"Here, here," I say, lifting my glass.

He feigns a hurt expression then carries on reading.

This past week both Dad and Rita have acquired the status of minor celebrities in the village. They've been in the pubs every night and yes, he has offended some with his anti-Catholic rants, but they've been mostly taken in good humour and softened by intervals of Rita's singing. She's been gigging most nights, sometimes alone and sometimes accompanied by session musicians. Last night Dad said there was a slow handclap and cries of "Rita, Rita", until she got up to the mic. She had the American contingent of Billy's family weeping at her rendition of 'Danny Boy'. She looks magnificent today in a gold lamé dress, a brimmed veiled hat and long lace gloves. Billy's been making bee-keeping jokes all morning, but she's taken it very well.

"Here they are," she says, nodding towards the road where Billy and Davy are crossing. I fill with pride. Billy looks gorgeous in a pale pink shirt and the beige linen suit I spotted in Chorlton Oxfam. He's got a bit of Mickey O'Rourke stubble, a light tan and looks healthier than he has for years, all the result of cutting down on drinking. He stands behind my chair, his hands lightly touching my shoulders. It feels nice. Since that day in Chorlton Park when Bridget disappeared, he's stayed over at the house quite a few times in the spare room. We've made an effort to spend time alone since we got here, going for long walks and talking things over while Carmel, his mum, has had the kids. We're communicating properly again and things are looking positive, but neither of us are quite ready for him to move back in just yet. We're taking it slowly.

When the men approach, Dad stands up. "Time for a swift one, lads?"

"Better not," says Davy. "This priest is a stickler for starting on time. We need to get the mini bus straight after mass too."

"What's happened to the old Ireland?" asks Dad, "The one where no one watched the clocks?"

Davy leans forward, a hand resting on the bench near Rita, a thick gold watch glinting in the sun.

"It moved on, Tony, along with the horses and traps," he grins.

Davy McConnel is Billy's childhood friend. Next to Billy's towering stature, he is short and squat. He has a pleasant boyish face and deep-set green eyes.

He runs a limestone quarry in the village which he inherited from his family and you often see the lorries rumbling around the quiet country roads. It's touching to see how fond of Billy Davy still is. It reminds me of Jal. When I told Billy this we both cried. Davy is warm-hearted and incredibly generous. He won't take a penny for the house he owns that we've been staying in and his lovely, eighteen year old twin daughters are babysitting the kids again today.

I finish my drink, we gather our things and the four of us make our way to the church along the main street. Billy and I walk ahead. The sun is pounding onto the narrow pavements, and women in extravagant hats and designer heels walk alongside scrubbed-up husbands, greeting us whether we know them or not. Billy returns their smiles with a cheery comment and a grin. I'm impressed with the act. I know he's shaking inside and the rivulets of sweat streaming down his face aren't just down to the heat.

187

"You'll be fine," I say, taking his damp hand in mine. He's terrified about giving Jenny away in that church then standing up in front of two hundred people at the wedding of the year to make a speech. Who wouldn't be?

CHAPTER 28

Billy

The church is stifling hot. Bodily odours mingle with the scent of Dior and Chanel, women are fanning their faces with hymn sheets and I hear a cormorant cry through the open window. I battle to undo the top button of my shirt and yank it off in frustration, watching it fly into the air and disappear under my mother who is kneeling beside me, eyes shut tight in prayer. I stare down at the movement of the grain in the wood in the pew in front. It is fluid and free. I wish I was. How I'd love to bolt out of that door and run into the shade in the woods behind the church, just me and the smell of the hawthorn down there.

Blessed are those who come in the name of the Lord.

He glides around the altar in front of Jenny and Tom, the swish of his emerald and green robes and the clacking of his glossy brogues magnified in the silence. He is young and Polish. No one wants to be a priest in Ireland any more. The altar boy follows, eyes lowered. I try to control the tightening in my chest and ignore the nausea. Not much longer now.

I distract myself by thinking about the speech I wrote in my old room yesterday. As I put pen to paper I could still feel Da's gentle presence around the house and hear the stutter of his lorry in the yard as he arrived home every evening. He'd appear at the back door, arms outstretched, lifting us high one by one for hugs and kisses. His affection and warmth filled the gap of Mam's aloofness like a draught excluder keeping out an icy chill.

As I wrote I thought of the loving words Da might have said about Jenny and the restrained ones he'd have used about Tom.

Never one to suffer fools, I know that he too would have found Jenny's choice of husband arrogant and whimsical, someone who's had everything given to him on a plate: the palatial house, the family building business, the Porsche. Everything except Jenny, that is. He chased her for years before she finally agreed to have him.

Go in peace in the name of our Lord Jesus Christ, Amen.

As the newlyweds walk down the aisle into the sunlight, I turn to Julie who is looking straight ahead, her eyes brimming with tears. We inch our way outside through the crush of bodies, out into the air and light where I can breathe again. How I got through that without some kind of attack I'll never know.

* * *

As I relax into my seat after the speech people make their way over and congratulate me, squeezing my shoulder and shaking my hand. Not Mam, though. She sits beside me uptight and button-lipped in lilac. She's such a fucking ice queen, I doubt a flicker of emotion crossed her face throughout, not even at the mention of Da. She was probably deep in prayer and not even listening. She's one of the few remaining defenders of the faith left in Ireland these days.

I glance around at the opulence surrounding me. In my day, this hotel was a spit and sawdust dance hall packed with drunk teenagers. Millions of euros later it's a four star golf and spa venue staffed by Eastern Europeans and popular with East Coast Americans.

Julie puts a hand over mine.

"You were brilliant," she says, dusting down the shoulder of my jacket. "Funny too." Her eyes are bright and she looks sultry in a dark blue lacy dress that clings to her curves.

My cousin Ted pulls up a chair between us. "Wow. Great speech, cuz. Moving tribute to your old man too. He was such a nice guy."

Ted is my Aunt Julia's son. Julia emigrated to Long Island, New York, in the fifties. To the horror of her family she married an outsider, a good looking, happy go lucky Italian, Ted Senior. They produced two olive-skinned, ebony haired children and returned to the village with impressive regularity. Their summer visits figured largely in my childhood and I remember how we hung around the house for hours waiting for their arrival. My sisters fizzed with excitement at the sight of the hired car turning into the yard.

"Mammy, the yanks have landed!" they'd yell and I'd watch from the window as Ted Senior wheeled two gigantic suitcases along the gravel, wondering if there were any New York delicacies in there for me. The weeks that followed were spent in the fields and the village with my exotic-looking cousins, my head filled with words like sneakers, sidewalk, skyscrapers; and diners with ice creams the size of footballs. I was given glimpses of beach houses with verandas, something called the Subway and powerful showers in bathrooms where no one shared the bath water. Three years older than me, Ted gave Davy and me our first drink in the woods when we were thirteen, bottles of Budweiser stolen from his father's stash under our sink. I fell in love with alcohol that day. I loved the escapism and the lofty feeling it gave me. I felt like the Incredible Hulk as he ripped through his clothes. I loved the way it made me become someone else, someone cool and confident, not the jittery, introverted teenager I had become. Ted is now an NYPD cop turned detective who has recently divorced from his Cork born wife.

"So, when are you guys coming to New York?" he asks, looking straight at Julie. "I'm not far from the beach, there's a small pool for the kids."

"Sounds great, Ted," I reply flatly. Go to New York? What fucking with?

I wonder if I'd have the pool and the beach house too if I'd joined my sister Clodagh in New York when she'd asked, instead of scarpering to Manchester. Or what if I'd stayed put? How big would my piece of the Celtic Tiger be? Six bed mansion, two four by fours big? What have I got to show for myself instead? A few paltry crumbs from the Englishman's table?

"We'd love to come when the kids are a bit older," Julie says, making up for my lack of enthusiasm. "You should come to Manchester, Ted," she giggles, playing with her hair. "There's loads of crime there for you to solve. We've got a Frankie and Benny's in Salford as well now."

Ted laughs a little too enthusiastically for my liking and I put my arm around the back of Julie's chair. He tells us about his detective work then the conversation moves on to the London bombings, then on to 9/11.

"I wasn't in New York that day," he says. "I was on a cruise."

He picks his Guinness up from the table and drinks slowly, "I lost over twenty good friends," he says quietly, "and in the weeks that followed I attended so many funerals I couldn't remember each one individually. They all merged into one."

"Were you involved in the rescue operation?" I ask.

He nods.

"Oh yeah. I have the dry cough to prove it. We all volunteered. But there wasn't much there, just, you know."

A flinty look crosses his face.

"Fucking towel heads. They should send every one of them back home. Guantanamo is too good for them."

I bristle.

"Not all Muslims are terrorists, you know," I say. "A good friend of mine, he... "

"You have friends who are towel heads?" He looks incredulous.

"I did have a Muslim friend. Yes. He died."

"Yeah? Well so did a lot of my friends, buddy. They died too."

My fingers grip the back of the chair. I want to leap to Jal's defence but when I look at the expression on Ted's face as he stares into his drink I imagine he's probably back there in the horror looking for body parts in the rubble and the dust and so I say nothing. "I'm going to find Davy," I say kissing Julie and leaving. As I make my way to the bar to Davy, I congratulate myself. Once again, I've managed to walk away from a potentially inflammatory situation. Things are looking up.

Davy is surrounded by a group of men and as I approach he puts his two fingers to his lips in a smoking gesture and nods towards the door. I give him a thumbs up and follow him through the hotel lobby outside. A crowd of smokers jostle on the cramped terrace that leads out on to the narrow street. Davy hands me a cigar and holds his lighter out to me.

"Looks like thunder," he says.

He's right. Plumes of dark clouds roll low against a magnificent mauve sky. I watch him inhale his finest Cuban. He looks very much like a man who might enjoy a fine cigar these days: the ruddy jowls, the made to measure shirt tugging round his portly middle, the soft leather Italian shoes. Davy this, Davy that. I've heard nothing else from Julie and my sisters since I got here. Davy says we can go in his box at the Galway races, Davy says we can stay at his villa in Bulgaria, Davy says he knows people in Manchester who might have work for you. Don't get me wrong, I love the man. I'm just fucking sick of hearing how wonderful he is, that's all.

I am about to ask him if he knows the score in today's United match when shouting erupts from the other side of the street. Heads turn to where a group of shirtless teenage lads with cans in their hands are jumping down from a high wall. In front of them is an elderly man. Despite the heat he's wearing a long dark overcoat and a flat cap pulled down over his face and is trying to pass through them clutching a carton of milk to his chest. I can't make out what they're shouting, but they are dancing chimp-like around him and taunting him. One of them takes the cap from his head and skims it out into the road, leaving him shielding his face with his hand. I look around. People are mumbling to each other but nobody on the terrace moves. I fling my cigar to the floor and I'm about to dash over to them when Davy grabs my arm.

"What?" I say, looking at him with incredulity, "He's an old man, for Christ's sake."

"It's Mullany." He still has a grip on my arm and he's looking anxiously at me. "Remember? Brother Damian. From school."

Not fully registering, I push blindly through the smokers and step out onto edge of the pavement. The boys are still doing a war dance and refusing to let him pass when a small blue Golf pulls up beside them and sounds its horn. The driver, a silver-haired woman in pink, leans over and opens the passenger door. Before he gets in, the old man lifts his head up and glances up and down the street. I can see his face clearly.

Time stops. It's him without a doubt. Unable to move, I watch the car drive off and the youths saunter away. Then I feel my legs buckle and I lean back against the railings and steady myself. Trembling, I stare out into the middle of the empty road and the black cap lying there.

CHAPTER 29

Julie

I hold out my glass to the pretty waitress standing by the table with a bottle of white and red in each hand.

"Thank you," I struggle to pronounce the name on her badge as she pours, "Beatrycze... Beatrice? Polish?" She nods, her face lighting up with a smile. I've yet to hear an Irish accent among the staff here. I look around at the marble floors, the silver grey table linen, the burgundy and ivory flower arrangements that match the bridesmaids' dresses. It really is like something out of a magazine spread. I've just eaten the Connemara salmon, lobster bisque, and a sorbet between courses that Rita thought was dessert. She's one of the few here with a satsuma tan, which has got to be a sign of a classy wedding. The bride is perfection itself, a size eight in simple white silk. Jenny has Billy's black hair and blue eyes, whereas his other sisters are pale blondes. She's a sweet and lovely girl but I'm not sure about her groom. Proprietorial was the word Billy used about Tom. I met him a few times during the week, back-slapping older men and throwing his money around in the village. Mind you, his family do own most of it.

I think back to our wedding, the quickie ceremony at Manchester Registry Office on a windswept Saturday morning followed by a meal for twenty at the Premier Inn in Didsbury. I wore a dusty pink, low-waisted Marks and Spencer's dress and I was as sick as a dog all day because I was two months gone with Bridget. I collapsed into bed at ten while Billy, in Burton's navy pin stripes, partied on with the guests at a charity night in the

Irish Club. I was deliriously happy, though. I'd just married the sexiest man in Manchester and I was having his baby.

The jazz band starts to warm up and the saxophonist plays a few bars. I wave over at Dad but he is too busy flirting with Billy's Aunt Nancy to notice. Nancy is a great wit, elegant in silver grey, and Rita had better watch out, though she's too caught up with the band to notice, clicking her fingers and tapping a stilettoed foot, her enormous hat swaying to the beat. She's promised to sing later.

My eyes linger on Billy's cousin Ted as he gets up and goes to the bar, then I see Carmel, Billy's mum, watching me. She is sitting alone on the other side of the table. Flustered, I pick up my glass and reluctantly sit next to her.

"Billy did a great job of the speech, don't you think?" I say. "He was ever so nervous."

"He did a grand job," she sniffs.

"And all those lovely things he said about his Dad," I add, searching her face for a flicker of emotion, some acknowledgement that she felt something, but she looks away. I feel like shaking her out of her dispassionate state and loosening the poker stuck up her backside. Her face, creamy skinned and pretty if she ever allowed it to be, remains as still as stone. As I'm raising my glass to my lips we both jolt at the sound of a thunder clap outside. The buzz of conversation in the room becomes a murmur and people move over to the windows and look out at the darkening skies.

I ramble on for a while to Carmel about the kids, her grandchildren being one of the few joyful things in her life, then she excuses herself and goes to her room to freshen up. I sink back into my chair in relief. Is it any wonder Billy left home so young?

I look around for him. He's been gone for ages. I can't see Davy either.

Ted returns with his pint.

"Seen Billy?" I ask, as he pulls Carmel's chair close to mine then sits down. I flush and stiffen. He shakes his head, his eyes searching mine. "Guess I upset him about his buddy."

I look down and fiddle with the hem of my dress.

"He and Jal were very close."

"Oh, man. I really did upset him."

The expression on his face is genuinely remorseful. He's no racist, he's just been to hell and back after seeing so many of his friends die. I touch his arm lightly.

"Buy him a pint later and he'll forgive you."

He nods and looks directly at me and I hold his gaze longer than I should.

We've spent a lot of time in Ted's company this past week and for some strange reason this muscular Al Pacino type with his edgy New York accent seems to have taken a liking to me. I look at his profile as he reaches out for his drink. The nose is on the long side but it somehow fits in neatly with the strong jaw line, wide sensual mouth and dark eyes. I like watching and listening to him. He's like someone straight off the set of C.S.I., but he's a proper detective, the real deal.

I can't remember the last time I had any extra marital sexual attention, Chorlton Fred the butcher's allusions to his Cumberland sausages notwithstanding. Not that long ago I would have dismissed the possibility that someone like Ted could ever have the hots for me. That ever present voice inside me would have been incredulous, reminding me how fat, ugly and ginger I was, and telling me how I'd got all the signals all wrong. But I really don't give a toss anymore. Besides, I've heard redheads are in these days.

Ted looks around the room.

"Billy and I used to have such a ball around this town when we were teenagers. This place was a grotty little dance hall called The Vault. We were always in here chasing girls."

"So I've heard." I tilt my head to one side and run my fingers through my hair. Crikey. I'm turning into Rachel Cleaver.

"All the girls were wild for Billy. But he was so goddamn

moody. Sometimes, just when we thought we getting close to getting some action, he'd back off and go into himself."

I nod and give Ted a resigned look. "That's my Billy."

"He's still like that?"

"He certainly is." I hesitate for a moment. "I don't know if he told you but he suffers from depression, Ted."

His face creases in genuine compassion.

"Really? He never said a word. Is he getting help?"

I really don't want to get into this. Not today. I want to enjoy myself so I change the subject.

"Bet the girls in the Vault thought you were a bit of alright too, though." I squirm as soon as the words are out of my mouth. What was I thinking? Could I have given him a bigger come-on? I blush as he moves his face closer to mine.

"Say that again."

"What?"

"A bit of alright. I love the way you say 'alright'." I laugh.

"Alright," I say, giving it a bit more Manchester this time, rolling my "r" and elongating the "i" vowel sound in true Liam Gallagher style.

"Beautiful."

I laugh again. His aftershave smells of pears. "You make Billy happy," he says softly. " He's crazy about you. Where did you guys meet?"

"I pushed him downstairs in a nightclub then we rekindled our romance later in the frozen food aisle in Safeway."

It's now his turn to laugh, which he does with gusto.

"Safeway's a supermarket."

"You don't say."

Our eyes lock once again and I look away, suddenly very afraid. I am drunk and I look around for Billy. Where the fuck is he? He's been gone for nearly an hour now. He's probably plastered or stoned in someone's room or he's wandered off somewhere in a mood without a thought for me or anyone else. What's new there, then? I think back about how he's treated me these past few months and resentment and anger swell inside me like a balloon. I've had a new baby and a dad with cancer to cope with but has he really given a shit? I think of the incident in the kitchen, the pure hatred in his eyes and for a brief moment I want to lash out and scratch his eyes out. I gulp down the last of my wine then lean over the table, grab a spare glass and drink some of that too.

"Hey, steady girl," Ted grins.

"It's an Irish wedding," I reply, picking up my bag and standing up. His eyes travel the length of my body as I smooth down my dress

"Back in a minute," I say.

I make my way to the ladies where I stagger into a cubicle, put my mouth under a gold tap in the small sink and gulp down water. When I've peed and washed my hands I sit back down on the toilet seat and stare at the lovely marble floor. Two young girls outside are talking rapidly in Galway accents. They're chatting about college life in Dublin, flat sharing and a gap year in Chile. I imagine Daddy sitting at the island in a vast chrome kitchen writing out cheque after cheque for his darling girl. Billy would love to go to college more than anything. He told me one night when he stayed over recently. We were up late talking about the future and he said that one day he'd like to be a teacher. I had no idea.

"We'll have to wait for the lottery win for that, though," he said. "All I want for the moment is my family back."

I start to cry. He loves us so much. He can't help being depressed. It's an illness just like Dad's cancer. And yet a small part of me feels cheated. I didn't sign up for all of this when we married. We got together so quickly I didn't have time to notice the symptoms and then Bridget came along.

I sit for a while longer then I tidy my face, apply a little make up and deodorant and adjust my dress.

I leave the bathroom, feeling slightly woozy, but nowhere near as drunk as earlier.

In the lobby I pause at the sight of a young couple at the bottom of the colossal staircase. The scene reminds me of the film *The Great Gatsby* that Billy and I saw a while ago. A delicate blonde is sitting with her silvery evening dress spread across the stairs and her bloke, tuxedoed and floppy haired, is bending down and handing her a champagne flute. Their laughter tinkles around the room and I burn with envy for the glamorous lives they have ahead of them.

As I turn towards the function room I see Ted pacing towards me with an intense expression on his face. As he approaches he grabs me by the elbow and leads me towards a doorway into a corridor where some of the bedrooms are located. I move with him like I'm being pulled by a kite in the wind. He glances up and down the corridor then he pulls me through a nearby fire exit door. It clangs shut behind us and we are locked in a brutal metal stairway. My bag slides to the floor and I lean back against the wall, He places his hands on my hips and our bodies are almost touching but not quite.

"I know it's wrong," he says, his voice tremulous, "but you're so beautiful and funny and you don't even know it."

He cups my face with his hands and I let him kiss me for a long time. He is slow and deliberate. When we stop he pulls me roughly towards him, his mouth planting small kisses along the side of my neck, his hand sliding gently over my breasts, touching my nipples through the lace of my dress. I feel myself weaken and I tug the back of his shirt and loosen it from his trousers then slide my hand up along his back.

I suddenly stiffen at the sound of running footsteps and children's shouts outside the fire door.

"Come to my room," he urges, kissing me harder, then bends slightly and moves the hem of my dress slowly upwards. I think about fucking him on crisp white linen sheets.

Then I think of Billy.

I push him away.

"I can't. I'm sorry." I well up and my voice cracks. "I love him."

He steps backwards, crestfallen and nods.

"I'm sorry," I say again and pull down my dress. Then, before either of us can say anything else, I can hear the clack of his shoes striding up the stairwell and he has disappeared.

I close my eyes, taking in what has just happened. I start to panic. I take a tissue from my bag and scrub my mouth and check my face in my hand mirror. I rummage for my phone and look at the screen. Four missed calls from Davy. Shit. I completely forgot to take it off silent mode after the church service. His twins are babysitting the kids. Oh, Jesus Christ, the kids.

Shaking, I press the return call button and after three rings Davy answers. I listen to what he has to say then I let out a low cry and the phone slips from my hands to the floor. I slump back against the harsh stone wall. I always feared this day would come.

Minutes later, when I step out into the lobby, I can hear Rita singing Ella Fitzgerald.

CHAPTER 30

Billy

The crowd of smokers disappears inside at the onslaught of rain, Davy among them. Still numb with shock I stumble down the empty street, a silver sheet descending over the road in front of me, thunder growling at my back. I make my way out of the town and continue on the road home.

The image of the bombed man returns to me. After the London tube bombings a photograph of a middle-aged man with a bandaged head staggering down the street appeared all over the papers. He had a charred, bloody face and was fumbling through the chaos like a blind man. That man looks how I feel so much of the time. But at least he lived some kind of normal existence before his life exploded. I was ten years old when it happened to me.

I wipe my face with my shirt sleeve. I am soaked to the bone. Through the mist of rain I can just about make out the outline of Kelly's bridge in the distance, the short cut that leads over the fields back to the village. It's as good a route as any other. All I know is that for the moment I need to keep on walking away from the town because I don't know what I might do if I go back there.

Davy knows.

The way he looked at me outside the hotel. The way he's gone out of his way to help me out. It's because he pities me.

"We're a player short. Come on."

He was sitting at the desk in front of me, tipping back on the hind legs of his chair, his arm pinned across my books as I tried to gather them up.

"You know I can't, Davy." I pushed his arm away and he scratched his nose in annoyance.

"Say you're sick. Tell him you'll do the lesson another day."

"I can't." I felt uneasy, but I pushed the feelings away and thought about Luke Skywalker and Darth Vader instead. "Besides, I'm meeting Da afterwards and we're going to the match."

He jumped up from his chair and snatched his satchel.

"Fecking teacher's pet."

How many others know?

For years I searched for his name in the obituaries in the Irish papers. I didn't know what to feel the day I read he'd been charged and was out on bail. I wanted justice, closure even, but most of all I wanted to see him dead.

I would never have recognised him if Davy hadn't pointed him out: the sunken, thin face; the mottled, bald head; his bulbous frame diminished. Jesus. I could have passed him by in the town this past week. The eyes have always stayed with me, though. They were dark blue, almost violet, always on the look-out around school, searching, planning, calculating the next move. He was a snake disguised as a labrador, giving the impression he was a buffoon, a lovable, easy-going clown who filled the classroom with gusty laughter. And after years of austere Brothers and regular beatings, who wouldn't have been happy to have a teacher like that? Brian, Kenny and I were delighted to be his favourites. We were special. We were the chosen ones.

I stop walking and start to shake violently, gasping for breath. A red sports car slows down and the young shaven-headed driver sticks his head out of the window.

"Ya alright there?" he asks.

"Fine. Had a few too many, you know how it is," I shout back, moving off the road towards the wall.

"Mind how you go, now," he says and I watch him drive off.

I press my hands down hard on the wall to steady myself, not feeling anything as the stone's jagged edges scratch my palms. Then I turn and walk on slowly towards the bridge.

"You will tell no one what happened in there," Da said to me that day. "Not anyone. Not even your mother."

I never did.

But she knows. I know she does.

The two of us were in her kitchen the other day. Sunshine dropped through the window brightening the joyless room that's barely changed since I left: the row of saints over the stove, the stained table and chairs that my sisters say she won't change. She was bouncing Will on her knee at the table, singing him an old nursery rhyme she used to sing to us. She looked vaguely happy for once. The radio was on in the background and the Angelus rang out followed by the news, the headline story yet another cover-up by the church.

"Turn that thing off," she snapped, a cloud crossing her face as she put Will on the floor, reached over to the worktop and clicked the radio dial. Then she turned to me with a look of profound sadness and suddenly I knew. The boy in me wanted to go to her and tell her how sorry I was, how it was all my fault, but she moved away to the window and stared out at the fields in silence. Is that what's been eating away at her all these years? The root of her misery? That deep down she thinks she failed to protect her child? And yet she clings to the church as a form of denial, which is really just another cover up because she can't face up to the truth of what happened.

I cross the bridge, salty tears falling into my mouth, my soaking trousers and shirt weighing me down like chains. I look over at the roof tops of the houses in the town, wondering which one he lives in and how easy he'd be to find. He's facing fifteen charges of abuse on boys from this area and he's ended up back here? Surely to God it's only a matter of time before someone gets to him, Brian Meehan's family for one. He left a letter detailing the abuse. Brian had it worse than any of us.

I trudge on across the fields. Black clouds are rolling low in the sky, obscuring the tip of the mountains. I can hear the squelch of my shoes in the soft, muddy earth as the rain continues to batter down. A heron cries overhead. I pass the old bungalows that are familiar to me, the new houses that are not. I climb wearily over walls and keep on going until I can see the outline of the village and Davy's quarry, the diggers silhouetted on high mounds of earth above the cavernous holes below, some of them seventy feet deep, blown into the tranquility of the landscape.

I carry on, knowing now exactly where I am going, asking myself if I've known all along.

I pass through a rusty iron gate and walk up a sodden path by the side of a freshly painted beige house. The remains of an abandoned barbeque litter the back garden and water drips down from the side of a trampoline. I come out into one of the most sought after roads in the village, where new builds are now hunched next to each other. When I was a child there were just a couple of houses along this road, one a neat bungalow occupied by Mary Corley, a cheerful bird-like spinster who wore a red headscarf. My sisters and I would pass her most mornings and exchange a smile and a few words. I stopped after it happened. I walked with my head down and eyes lowered, filled with trepidation in case he had returned and was waiting at the front entrance when I got there.

I punch the air in rage and cry out at the thought of him out there a free man when I've been caged by these feelings for so long.

The rain is easing off now and I pass a man in a suit in his driveway getting into an Audi. He waves and calls out to me but I ignore him and hurry on down the road that twists to the right. A hundred yards or so on it appears on my left and I go up to the gate.

The old schoolhouse is now a holiday home owned by a German family who rarely visit. In my time there were no more than three classes and forty children in the whole school. Wrought iron gates and an intercom prevent me going any further now. The façade has been tastefully renovated, the small arched windows and the stained glass are perfectly intact, and

205

the grey weathered stone is gleaming, cleansed by the rain. I stare in at the empty driveway, the manicured lawns, the trimmed hedges on either side and the explosion of red and orange roses from the flower beds.

His orange shirt was streaked with blood as he dragged me down the path by my arm, squeezing, hurting.

"Let go, Da. You're hurting me." I tried to wriggle free and he loosened his grip, barely looking at me.

"You will tell no one what happened in there." His voice crumbled as he held back tears. "No one. Not even your mother."

It was a day of torrential rain. After extra Irish with Brother Mullaney I was to meet Da outside Connors supermarket at five-thirty and we were going to watch the match together. Ballinrobe were in the semis. I was so excited. In class that morning Brother Damian had made some comments about the Star War figures. I was looking forward to the lesson but I was slightly uneasy. It was only my third time and there'd been an awful lot of chat and not much work done in the other two.

The first lesson he took me to his office in the west wing of the school.

"It's much quieter here than the classrooms," he explained as I hurried to keep up with his brisk footsteps, the clickety clack of his brogues echoing on the stone floor. "We don't want to be distracted by any football practice on the playing field now, do we?"

Football practice was never on a Thursday.

I told Da I was enjoying the lessons when he asked. "You've always had the ability, son," he said. "And now you've got a good teacher, it's time to apply yourself."

Dusk was falling outside the office window when Brother Damian cupped my face in his hands and kissed me. It was dark when he unbuttoned himself, took my hand in his and placed it between his legs. He tasted of salt and he ran his fingers through my hair and called me his beautiful boy. I didn't resist when he kissed me again in the dim lamp light and touched me. I let his fingers unzip my shorts and I gave myself to him. He was my teacher, my priest and my friend, so how could any of it be wrong? When it was over and I was gathering my clothes from the floor, I could hear him crying quietly behind me. Then I heard the noise, the rattle of the window and the shouting, and when I looked up the silhouette had moved away.

Mullaney had no chance. Da was waiting for him at the front entrance as he tried to make a run for it. When he bolted from the office I pulled on my clothes and ran down the corridor, buttoning myself up, my shoes in my hands. When I got there, Da was dragging him into one of the classrooms. He slammed the door and yelled at me to go outside. I did as he said and curled up into a ball by the flower beds, manacled by fear and battered by the rain. I put my fingers over my ears, convulsing at the sound of every thud and smash coming from inside. Warm piss trickled down my legs and the crashing and shouting seemed to go on forever. Then Da appeared, his overcoat and his orange shirt smeared with blood, his eyes glazed. He pulled me up from the floor, picked up my shoes and dragged me down the path.

He was fighting back sobs as we made our way back to the lorry parked up outside Miss Corley's bungalow. Without looking at me we got in and as he turned the key into the ignition he looked straight ahead and said, "Half past four we were supposed to meet outside Connors. It was half past four. I'm sure of it."

"No, Daddy. You said half past five."

Clouds shift above the slate roof and trickles of silver light start to appear. A car passes on the road above and I can hear children shouting. Life is getting back to normal after the storm. I curl my hands around the wet bars of the tall iron gate and press my head there. I am exhausted. Every last drop of emotion has been bled from me and I've got very little left to give. I cannot cope with the thought he might get away with it again, as he has so many other times. And he might. The guarda, the church, the government, they're still in it together, watching each other's backs, no matter what anyone tells you.

I slump to the floor and sit with my back against the gate for some time. I think about the happy times I spent around the village before he stole my childhood and I weep for my loss. I look up at the changing sky, watching the light returning, unable to move or act. Then I get a rush of energy, a vigour that picks me up and leads me in the direction of the quarry.

CHAPTER 31

Julie

Six months later

White cloud, the weather forecast said this morning. Funny expression, that. They're never really white except in kids' drawings. Look carefully enough and you usually see a pocket of grey there, holding in the rain.

Bridget runs on ahead and places her carnations at the foot of the tree. Bob next door caught her leaning over the wall, tugging at the flowers in his garden this morning. He was about to tell her off, but when he found out who they were for he went back in for his clippers and she came in with a small bouquet with roses in it, too. I watched her fold them carefully in his footie scarf that she keeps in her special memory drawer in her room. I've not managed to store him away yet. He's still with me, the shadow at my shoulder, the conversation in my head.

There's a Sunday morning sleepiness around today and not a siren or a police helicopter in sight. The park is empty apart from an early morning dog walker who stops to chat to Bridget as she jumps up and tries to throw the scarf over one of the tree's lower branches. She's shot up recently. It looks like she's going to be tall and lanky like him.

"Tell her not to worry," the walker shouts as his pit bull drags him along the path, "Nobody'll nick that scarf. In fact there'll probably be a few more up there along with it when they get thrashed again today."

Cheeky bugger. Dad would have fired something witty and

withering straight back at him if he were here. I still can't believe he's gone. He would have been seventy today.

This morning, as I was slipping from sleep to consciousness, it hit me hard and jolted me awake. I slumped back onto my pillow and thought about the last time I saw him, lying in his coffin at the crematorium. He looked so different, his face was dark and waxy and his yellow fingers looked extended and bony, almost comical, folded across his chest like that. It was the stillness and the absence of spirit that got me, though. He was so animated and funny the last time I'd seen him.

It was an October Saturday morning here in this park. He was sitting on that bench by the swings, telling Bridget stories about his childhood. He didn't stay long as he wanted to get back for the match. He kissed us all before he left, something he'd taken to doing religiously since the cancer diagnosis. Well, maybe religiously isn't the right word.

When Rita rang that evening to say she'd found him, she tried her best to contain her distress but the pain in her voice found its way out and she sobbed uncontrollably down the phone. She said Radio Five Live was still on and his glasses were lying in a damp pool of tea on the floor by his chair. His heart failed him in the end, that warm generous heart that had wrapped me in layers of love all my life. He died of a massive heart attack. But I'll always be grateful he had a quick and decent death with none of the pain and loss of dignity I know he feared from the cancer. City beat Chelsea three one that day. The Arabs had just bought them for two hundred million and we did wonder if the shock of it finished him off. I like to think he lived to hear the final whistle, though.

It was a beautiful funeral. He had it all planned out and left instructions with Rita when he was going into hospital for his op. He was cremated at Southern Cemetery in Chorlton followed by a do at the social club. He'd even put money behind the bar. The service was led by John from the Manchester Humanist Society, who had a silver pony tail and rolled his own cigarettes. Keith Bradley, the local Labour M.P. and Dad's lifelong friend, made a lovely speech, as did the Chairman of the City Supporters Club. We handed out glasses of Cava on the way in and John started off the service with Dad's favourite joke.

"As you all know," he said, "our friend Tony was both an atheist and a very sociable man. Well here he lies today. All dressed up with nowhere to go."

At the end Rita somehow managed to compose herself and sang 'My Way' as everyone left the crematorium, then I stayed behind to say my final goodbye. I clutched the City flag on the coffin for as long as I was allowed, Lennon's 'Imagine' playing in the background as he'd requested. As the curtain closed I fell to my knees and cried like I'd never cried before, saying his name over and over.

He'd gone too soon. I still had so much to tell and to ask him. In the days afterwards a searing pain sliced through me when I realised I wouldn't be able to talk to him about the everyday stuff like Bridget getting Star of the Week at school or Will taking his first steps. He was dead and he would never know any of it. He had been my rock after what had happened in Ireland, the crutch I was leaning on, then suddenly he was gone and I felt bewildered and unsteady on my feet. I was officially an orphan. It felt like a piece of me had broken off and scuttled somewhere into the past. I had lost my anchor, my protector and my friend.

We park the buggy by the bench opposite the tree. It's a massive sprawling oak just behind the playground and has just come into full leaf. It seemed appropriate to scatter half of Dad's ashes in this park on the estate, as we've spent much time here over the years. It's right next to his beloved club and you can see the top of his house from here. The rest of the ashes will rest with Mum in Ireland when I'm ready. Bridget runs off to the swings and when I see how carefully she's arranged the flowers I start to cry. Then he slips his fingers through mine and I lean my head against his shoulder, feeling the surge of relief and gratitude I feel a hundred times a day. I close my eyes. For one terrible moment I imagine I am sitting here without him, there's a red United scarf

211

hanging from the branch and Bridget is laying flowers for her daddy too.

Billy was barely recognisable that first day we visited him in the Galway Clinic. Set in landscaped grounds and overlooking the bay, it was more like a plush hotel than a private hospital. Gaunt and unshaven in a blue hospital gown, he spent most of the time sitting in a chair by the large glass window staring out at the sea or looking at the white walls. He was heavily sedated and he barely recognised his own kids. He was frail and empty, like a once magnificent building that had crumbled but not quite collapsed. He hardly spoke during our visits. They were dark, dark days.

When he disappeared at the wedding, Davy went out with a search party to look for him after a friend in the village rang to say he'd spotted him near the school house behaving strangely. After an hour or so Davy eventually found him wandering dangerously close to the precipice of the quarry. He was delirious, raging and talking to himself. Davy and three of his friends managed to hold him there until the paramedics arrived from Ballinrobe. At first he was taken to the psychiatric wing of the University Hospital in Galway, but Davy said it was too frightening and chaotic and so whisked him off to the private clinic on the outskirts of the city, insisting on footing the bill, no questions asked.

Billy was being assessed when I got there. Davy and I sat in the family waiting area on high-backed leather chairs in our wedding finery. Davy's button hole was crushed and wilted and I stared down at the hole in the thigh area of my tights where Ted's hand had lain just hours ago. Bewildered and still slightly drunk, I sipped black coffee and listened to what Davy had to say.

"He saw someone outside at the wedding that may have triggered something."

"Who?"

He could barely meet my eye.

"Mullaney, our teacher in Senior Infants at school. He was a

Christian Brother, from around here, born into a good family from Ballinrobe. The rumours about him started years ago and he retired from teaching and the priesthood early."

"What rumours?"

He stared down at the pristine tiled floor. I could see he was finding it difficult.

"What rumours, Davy?"

"A few months ago Mullaney was charged with multiple accounts of abuse against minors. He's out on bail awaiting trial now. The charges date back to the seventies and the victims come from various parts of the country where he was teaching. Billy and I were in the same class as one of the victims who brought charges. Brian Meehan." He paused. "He hung himself in Dublin not long ago."

My coffee cup trembled in my hands and I leant over and put it on the glass table.

"Are you telling me you think Billy was abused, Davy?"

"I don't know for sure. But Billy was always Mullaney's favourite. He was bright, very bright, and a beautiful child. He was always making him stay behind for extra lessons, always singling him out. Then one day Mullaney disappeared from the school. Billy was never the same afterwards. He turned in on himself and became moody and unpredictable." He grabbed my hand. "I hope to God I'm wrong, but as soon as I heard the rumours, I suspected."

I knew immediately that Davy was right. The pieces of the puzzle that was Billy fitted together at last: the rages, the depression, the silence about his childhood. It all made sense to me. I felt like someone had punched a vicious blow to my stomach, but at least now I knew.

"We were only small wee boys," Davy shook his head slowly, his olive green eyes filling with tears, "just boys."

Dad and Rita went back to Manchester and I stayed on in the village, travelling to the clinic on a daily basis. Davy and his family couldn't do enough for us at that time and I will be forever indebted to them. Billy came home with us three weeks later. Or rather his ghost did. It was like he had died the day of the wedding. He lost over two stone, didn't get out of bed at all for weeks and refused to talk about what had happened. His previous bouts of depression seemed like a roller coaster ride in comparison. I had to go back to work straightaway and Dad and Rita looked after the kids at his house. I was terrified to leave Billy alone with them. I never thought for a minute he'd abuse them, not for one minute, but I was haunted by the thought that he might try something and take them with him. You read about it all the time in the papers, dads losing it, committing suicide and killing their kids. I couldn't take that risk.

Every evening after picking the kids up, I'd stop outside the front door, take a deep breath and prepare myself for what I might find. I lived with so much fear in those first few months, but I also lived with anger, a hot vat of it bubbling deep inside me. Was he really going to leave us? To abandon his kids when his baby was barely a year old?

Then one day at the end of October it happened. The turning point I'd been praying for finally arrived and Billy said he wanted to talk. I could see he was feeling better. He was on a lower dosage of antidepressant, he was actually getting out of bed and had started interacting properly with the kids. Rita and Dad came round to mind them and Billy and I drove over to Chorlton Water Park. It's a local nature reserve with a man-made lake and Dad and I used to go bird watching there when I was young. It was a bright day and unseasonably warm. The decent weather had brought out joggers, cyclists and families with toddlers.

Billy and I walked for a while then sat on a bench overlooking the lake, wrapped in the silence we'd become used to. A light breeze whispered across the water leaving ripples in its wake and a couple with a young boy of about three were throwing bread to the moorhens and geese at the water's edge.

Billy turned to me.

"I'm sorry," he said.

I waited and the rest of his words came slowly.

"I was in the darkest place imaginable. It was too much for me, losing the business, Jal's death, the problems between me and you. When I saw his face again after all those years it all came hurtling back at me."

He leant forwards and bowed his head, his hands cupped between his knees. For a horrible moment I saw him, a young boy kneeling, his hands together in prayer, the shadow of the priest behind him. He turned his head to look at me then dropped it back down.

"That's the very reason I never told you about it," he said.

"What do you mean?"

"The way you just looked at me. Like I disgust you, like you pity me."

"I do not."

"Of course you do. I'm damaged goods."

"Not to me you're not." I took his hand, not sure how convincing I sounded. "Oh Billy, why did it have to come to that?"

"I don't know. It all came crashing down on me with so much violence. It seemed like the only option."

"I asked you so many times to get help," I said gently, as a reminder not an accusation. "Why couldn't you talk to me about it?"

He let go of my hand.

"Sure, how could I? We weren't exactly in a great place at the time, were we? We weren't even sleeping in the same bed."

He stood up, picked up a handful of stones and started to skim them into the water. Some of the birds at the water's edge scattered, the couple with the boy glanced over at us and Billy turned to me, his eyes bright with anger.

"Talk about it," he said. "That's all I ever hear. Talk, talk, fucking talk. It's good to talk. Well not if you're me it's not, not if you're working class and male it's not. I'm not part of Oprah and Jeremy Kyle's big confessional society like you. You're a woman, you can talk about what happens to you. I was trained not to talk. That's what I learned from a very young age. Oh I know about silence alright."

He knew nothing of the secret I'd kept for so many years, but I would tell him in time to come.

He sat back down and put his hands in his pockets. "Oh, I've read the survivors' stories too and there are some brave bastards out there going public about what happened to them, for justice or for money or whatever reason, but you know what? For every one of them there are ten more fucked-up men and women like me, taking their secrets to the grave, self-medicating, drinking or drugging themselves along the way. And a lot of them are over here or in America. Like me, they thought they could run away to forget, but instead they brought it with them, blighting the lives of the ones who love them along the way. How many have ended up on the streets or in asylums with only their secrets for company? We are damaged goods. All of us. It doesn't go away, no matter how much you try to bury it."

He sighed long and hard.

"Talk about it? Don't make me fucking laugh. Do you actually know what happened in Ireland when kids talked back then? How families were shunned and silenced and kids were beaten black and blue by their parents for disrespecting the church?"

His gaze was fixed out on the water.

"I was lucky. It happened to me the once," he said, his voice calmer now. "If it wasn't for Da finding me that time, it would have gone on."

He went on to tell me what had happened at the school and how his father had attacked Mullaney. He continued to talk, almost as if I wasn't there. It all gushed out from him, like water from a burst pipe.

"Mullaney disappeared from the village overnight, no one ever came after Da and he never mentioned the episode to me again. That's where I learned about silence. The official line from the school was that he'd gone to England for 'further pedagogical training', but he was transferred a number of times to other schools in Cavan and Wexford, where he abused many times over."

He gripped the arm of the bench, his face creased in pain.

"I feel guilty about every one of those other boys it happened to every single day."

"But you were a child," I said. "You weren't to blame. And as you've just said, who would have believed you?"

"When I was sixteen there were rumours at school about him returning to teach at the High School in Ballinrobe, the same place where I'd have been studying if I'd stayed on. Someone in the village must have put a stop to it because he never did return. I never told Da about the rumours, but just before he died he and I fought about me going to England instead of staying on at school. I couldn't tell him why because we'd never spoken about the abuse. It was like it had never happened."

He started to cry and he finally let me hold him. We stayed there for a while, his head in the crook of my neck and I felt the fall and rise of his shoulders close to me.

He pulled his head away and looked up at me. "I'm not who you think. I'm a bad person. I've done other bad things and I don't deserve you."

We suddenly moved apart at the sound of shouting coming from the family at the water's edge. The couple with the small boy were gesturing out to the water and a passing jogger slowed down and ran over to where they were.

I jumped up as soon as I spotted it.

"Look," I said excitedly, getting up and tugging Billy by the hand. "Look, it's a kingfisher."

We moved towards the water where the flash of blue and orange was perched on a wooden post about ten feet out in the water, its long bill pointing downwards. Then a fast, low swooping movement followed, and a plunge. Nothing, then the bird smashed up through the water, beak first, with the fish, and soared, silk fans for wings, a streak of electric blue in the white canvas of the sky.

I was hopping with excitement and when I turned to Billy he was watching me with a gentle smile.

"A kingfisher," I gushed. "Wait till I tell Dad. He'll be mad jealous."

In the car on the way home, Elbow's 'One Day Like This' came on the radio and Billy turned it up and smiled for a second time, making my heart somersault. They were tiny steps in the right direction.

When we got back home Dad was at the shops then he and Rita left immediately to go to a karaoke evening. I was still taking in everything that Billy had told me and it completely slipped my mind to tell Dad about the kingfisher then, or the next day in the park. The day after that he died.

Rita and I watch Billy pushing the kids on the swings. Bridget is standing up, her dress flying and falling around her, a look of concentration on her face. In the weeks following Dad's death she didn't seem to understand what was happening, even though we explained everything in a very matter of fact way like they say you should with kids that age She kept asking when she was going to see him again, which was hard as I was expecting to see him walk in the door at any minute myself. The inevitable behavioural problems followed at school then there was a brief shoplifting phase. She took to slipping stickers, make-up and other small luxury items into her coat pocket in Morrison's and taking things home from school in her book bag. She seems to have calmed down now, though. She's much more watchful and thoughtful and is a lot kinder to her brother. Billy thinks she may have finally discovered empathy. I'm not so sure. I think she might be planning something major.

Rita gets up. She adjusts her pencil skirt and buttons up her leopard skin jacket.

"Better be off," she says, taking out a mirror from her bag and retouching her lips. I ask her if she's going anywhere special.

"Just lunch with a friend," she says coyly.

She thinks I don't know about her new man, Larry Naylor. I

218

saw her outside Wetherspoons with him last week. He's a regular at the club and everyone knows him as Larry the Limp because he lost three toes in an accident at work and bought a villa in Lloret de Mar with his compensation. I overheard her on the phone to him last week, discussing travel plans. I've got a feeling she might be going for a long time. I'll miss her. So will the kids. She's been minding Will on Mondays and Wednesdays while Billy gets back on his feet. I wish her all the best. She's been a good friend to me and as far as I know she's not breathed a word about what happened in Ireland, which can't be easy for someone with a gob the size of the Manchester Eye. Maybe it's a bit soon for her to have found someone else, but I do think she loved Dad. I really do.

I shout over to Billy that she's leaving. He pulls Will out of his swing and I watch my boy's sturdy little legs running across the asphalt towards us. He definitely has the makings of a rugby scrum half. He and Bridget wrap themselves around Rita's legs and we all kiss and thank her. Then with a click clack of a stiletto heel, she turns and goes.

Not long afterwards we prepare to head home ourselves. Bridget goes over to the tree and pulls down Dad's scarf, then she runs over to the pram and places it round Will's neck.

As we set off I glance back at the tree.

"Bye, Dad," I whisper, watching the breeze quivering through its branches. Then Billy takes my hand.

He's been deep in thought all morning. I know he misses Dad too, but he talks about him, which helps me a great deal. Billy talks a lot these days. He talks to his counsellor, he talks online with other abuse survivors in Ireland, but most of all he talks to me. It's hard whenever his black dog comes to stay, but I understand the signs now and I cope with it much better than before. I sometimes ask myself if I should have guessed about the abuse. Should I have picked up on the clues? The nightmares, the mood swings, the anger, the silence about his childhood? But who could ever imagine the horror of that? Not long ago I emailed

Alex Durkan, Mandy's partner, and told her I had forgiven Mandy. How could I not, after what I've seen Billy go through? I don't want her to live with the guilt about what she did to me in the same way Billy shouldn't feel guilty about the others Mullaney went on to abuse. Mandy and Billy were children when it happened. They are blameless.

Living through the two trials wasn't easy. I was worried Billy might suffer a major setback but he coped well. In October, Jal's killers both got eighteen years, which was a travesty really. With good behaviour they'll probably out by the time they're thirty. Then November brought the start of the drawn out proceedings against Mullaney. He was finally found guilty of twenty-six accounts of sex offences against minors and sentenced to seventeen years at Galway Crown Court. Billy followed the story online. He said there was no point in him pressing his own charges, as Mullaney suffers ill health and is in his early seventies so he'll probably die in prison. However, Billy is considering making a private case for compensation against the Catholic Church. When I asked him what he felt now that Mullaney was locked up, he said, "I feel very little. He has damaged but he has not broken me. I just don't want to think of myself as a victim anymore."

Billy's picking up jobs here and there, but there's still not much around because of the recession. He's applied to do 'A' levels at night school with a view to going to college, then going into teaching. That's where the compensation comes in. The way Billy sees it, by keeping Mullaney out there, the Church denied him an education so they can pay for it now instead. We'll have the money from the sale of Dad's house through soon as well, plus some money he'd somehow been squirreling away in a savings account. Yes. I can see Billy in a classroom in front of a whiteboard in his creased linen suit and John Lennon specs, a battered briefcase lying on his desk. Or then again, we could blow all the money on a bigger house. Rachel Cleaver's is up for sale. She and the diddy man are divorcing and she's moved to

Hale Barns in Cheshire near Mummy and Daddy with her new man. Tabatha and Tobias are at private school there. Apparently Tobias wasn't reaching his full potential at Broadoak. I've seen Rufus in Chorlton a couple of times. He looks downright heartbroken.

I can see the O'Hagans in number eleven Corkland Avenue. The vegetable patch can stay, we'll keep the original floorboards and fireplaces, but the entire three floors will need fumigating. There'll be a few plants but not loads, a massive plasma on the living room wall and a new Star Trek kitchen where I can be a proper Chorlton mum and bake my own bread while the kids do their homework and arty stuff on one of those island things. By the time we've moved in I'll have Bridget's name down for a tutor to get her ready for her eleven plus. They start them early these days. I picked up a brochure for Stretford Grammar the other day. I'm not sure I want her in Chorlton High.

THE AUTHOR

Annette Sills was born in Wigan, Lancashire to parents from County Mayo, Ireland. After studying English at Goldsmith's College, London University, she lived in Madrid, Turin, Milan and Rome for ten years where she taught English and studied Spanish and Italian. Annette returned to London to complete an MA then landed her dream job in international recruitment where she procured English teachers for schools in cities and small towns all over Europe, Russia and Poland. She travelled to many of these wonderful places and plans to write about them one day. Annette finally settled in Manchester, a city she loves and never wants to leave. She taught English at Salford University and now writes full time. She lives with her husband Nick, children Jimmy and Ciara and cats Lily and Marmalade. Annette started writing when Jimmy and Ciara were small and used to jump up and down on her laptop keyboard.She reads anything she can get her hands on, Irish and contemporary novels in particular. Her favourites include Colm Toibin, Sebastian Barry, John McGahern, Edna O'Brien, David Nicholls, Elena Ferrante and Edward St Aubyn. She loves the short stories of Colin Barrat, Alice Munro, Raymond Carver and Kevin Barry. Annette's short stories have been longlisted and shortlisted in a number of competitions including the 2103 Fish Short Story Prize and the Telegraph Short Story Club in 2012. Her first novel, The Relative Harmony of Julie O'Hagan was shortlisted for the Rethink Press New Novels Award 2014 and she was delighted to be awarded a publishing contract with them as a result. She is currently writing her second novel.

Lightning Source UK Ltd.
Milton Keynes UK
UKOW02f0814290715

256007UK00002B/28/P